the hostage game

By Mark McShane

ZEBRA BOOKS

KENSINGTON PUBLISHING CORP.

ZEBRA BOOKS
are published by
KENSINGTON PUBLISHING CORP.
21 East 40th Street
New York, N.Y. 10016

Copyright © 1979 by Mark McShane

All rights reserved. No part of this book may be reproduced in any form or by any means without the prior written consent of the Publisher, excepting brief quotes used in reviews.

First Printing: March, 1979

Printed in the United States of America

EVENING

Edgar Carlton walked briskly along a street in Limehouse. The lighting, faint and ochre, was losing a fight with the darkness. Hidden were dangers such as uneven curbstones and sidewalk cracks. But also hidden were the signs of decay, the gutter litter and the hopeless air of the stores.

Good-bye, Edgar Carlton said mentally to everything he passed. Good-bye, good-bye.

This area of east London, synonymous with dockland brawls, opium dens, sleazy pubs and the lower levels of prostitution, no longer deserved its infamy. Limehouse had been made semi-respectable by demolition and subsidized housing, by legalization of gambling, and by the Welfare State's law against poverty.

Commercial love was mostly off the streets and on the dole. If pubs were still sleazy, it was because they were kept that way to intrigue the busloads of tourists. Opium had returned to its place in the Marxian dictum.

However, a determined philosophy of sloth kept many to the old ways; foreign sailors battled with local louts, nothing had displaced petty crime as the most interesting diversion of the young, and the Salvation Army had not yet moved on to grittier fields. Limehouse was coughing, but alive.

Edgar Carlton would gladly have sent flowers to its funeral. It and the dozen other similar areas he had known over the past few years. But it was simpler and faster to say good-bye.

He said it, aloud, to a garbage can lying on its side like a rat's horn of plenty. Speaking aloud made the fact of Edgar's escape more real. A thrill of excitement coursed up through his stomach and chest and throat.

It was caused not merely by that escape itself, but also by what could make it possible—the audacious and dangerous task that lay two short hours ahead.

A moment later Edgar was calm again. He had forced himself there by the knowledge that this evening he must be in cool control of his actions.

Edgar rounded a corner, edged through a group of lounging youths, continued at the same brisk pace. The young men hardly spared him a glance. They talked on, their breath briefly white in the autumn air.

Oddly enough, Edgar Carlton did not look out of place in this setting that was alien to him and which he detested. Partly it was due to his flashy plaid topcoat with collar upturned and the black slouch hat; partly to the fact that his walk had a tough swagger.

The latter was a passing affectation. He did it unconsciously. Edgar was responding, as always, to his surroundings. It was empathy, not a taunt.

His walk and dress would have suggested to the

youths, had they thought of it, a spiv or a burglar, a pimp or a small-time dealer in stolen goods.

Ahead on the dim street, a man lurched himself erect from a pub wall. He had seen Edgar approaching. The man's clothes were fit for a fire, his hair was as matted as a cheap wig, his face had a purple sheen.

Knowing he was due for a touch, Edgar sighed. He was unaware that he began to weave slightly. But the man seemed to change his mind. He stepped back to the wall and sagged there, as if hanging one shoulder on a hook.

Edgar was relieved. It wasn't the money. The trifle that would have been begged he could well afford. It wouldn't be spent on food, however, but on surgical alcohol or the lemonade to cut it with, thus hastening the derelict's death. Edgar could never make up his mind which was the lesser of the two cruelties, to give or to refuse.

When past the man, he said, "Good-bye."

This time he had his excitement under control: he felt a mere tickle laugh its way up his body. He smiled with confidence.

After passing a fish and chip shop whose stench made his eyes tingle, Edgar turned into a yard. It was brightly lit by a stutter of orange neon that spelled out *Dockers Social Club*. Helping was a small spotlight aimed on a poster. The wording there announced this week's attraction as The Great Carlton, Impersonator Extraordinary. The poster was curled at a bottom corner, defensive.

Edgar's swagger went. His body—average height, average weight—straightened to its limits and took on an aspect of grandness, belly in, shoulders back. His chin rose slightly.

Going through a door under the orange neon, Edgar entered a vestibule. It was guarded by a huge man in a sweater so stretched that his white shirt showed through the knit. His face looked to have been rammed by an icebreaker.

"Evening, Mr. Carlton," he said with an anxious smile.

"Hi, Bill," Edgar said. His accent was still his own—American. It would need fifteen minutes before it started to take on shades of the other man's Cockney.

"Nice clear night, sir."

Edgar nodded. He was grateful not so much for the respect as for the lack of condescension, that wry smile for the fading trouper. There had been too much of that this past couple of years.

"We'll be finished 'ere tomorrer night, eh, Mr. Carlton?"

Wrong, Edgar thought, though he said, "Sure."

"And then it's over to the Wharf Club, eh?"

Edgar let him believe it. He asked, "Good house, Bill?"

The doorman lifted ham-hands to the sides of his face, a curiously childlike gesture. "Full, guv'nor. Always is when you're doing your stuff. Why, you're a genius, Mr. Carlton, a real genius."

"Thank you," Edgar said softly.

"I even sneaks in to watch meself."

Edgar winked. "In that case, I'll be extra good tonight. See you." He went through into a passage.

From one end came raucous piano music. He turned the other way.

Squeezing past stacked chairs, Edgar mused that it wasn't the people nor their mouldy areas he resented, it was the last-ditch clubs. No artist likes criticism, and these places were outright condemnation.

Stepping over a beer crate, Edgar wished he were not so proud. But that, he knew, was pointless. Performers without pride did not exist. It was their most valuable asset, and greatest enemy.

Edgar went into a cramped room. The walls were whitewashed concrete, one grey with damp. There were two cane chairs, a table, a mirror, a handbasin.

After hanging his hat and coat behind the door, Edgar stood looking at his reflection. It was the grey lounge suit and white rollneck sweater he looked at, not his face. Except when he was practicing, he never looked at his face. There was nothing to see.

Edgar Carlton, at thirty-seven, had pale skin so smooth that he could have passed for twenty-seven with ease, for twenty with effort. To pass as much older than his true age needed hardly any work at all: eyes narrowed, features compressed, head forward to scrawny the neck and cheeks, then he was an acceptable seventy.

Edgar had eyes, a nose, lips. They could not be described except as lips, a nose, eyes. His hair was medium brown, had a slight wave, and looked short at the nape when he dropped his chin, long when he put his head back.

Overall, Edgar was facially so bland that, many years before, he had formed the habit of wearing distinctive clothing. Out in the vestibule, it was less his face, more his hat and coat that had been greeted by the doorman.

Sitting in front of the mirror, Edgar brought his makeup from a pocket. This was two sticks, one black, one red. With the former he underlined his eyes and marked in his eyebrows. The red stick he used on mouth, nostrils and eye-corners.

Finished, he looked little different from before—loud bland rather than soft—but the cosmetics would prevent his face from disappearing altogether under the stage lights.

He checked his watch, lit a cigarette. He didn't think of the show but of what was to happen afterwards. One leg twitched. To counter the excitement that was growing in him, he got up and began to pace the stone floor.

Edgar had known many dressing rooms like this over the past twenty years. There were surprisingly few differences between them, whether in Europe or North America, in roadhouse or the Palladium. Edgar had seen them all.

His entertainment career had started in a Detroit school, when he discovered his ability to imitate animal noises. It was more than a knack and might have been forgotten in a week and discarded, save for one important fact. Suddenly, he was noticed.

Before that recess session when he quacked and brayed, Edgar had been friendless and an outsider. He would not have minded being bullied, made a scapegoat, or looked upon as the school clown. Instead, he was ignored. And he was too shy to force his company on others.

His imitations changed everything. He became a character. Boys sought him out. They invited him into their groups, asked him to share their secrets, wanted to show him off at home. He had created a personality for himself.

Shy now only with those who belittled his knack, Edgar was able to be at his ease by hiding behind a changed voice, being someone else, just as many stammerers can speak precisely when they impersonate or quote others.

Edgar had soon moved on from animals to humans. He realized that his popularity could stale if he didn't branch out into new directions. He worked hard, studying timbre and lilt, pitch and accent. He became expert at dialects. He practiced with his voice the way others were learning musical instruments, but in his case he had no need to be forced to the metaphorical piano stool or music stand; he couldn't wait to be alone so that he could go through the weights and scales of speaking. His knack turned into a decided talent. He was one of the school's most popular boys.

After he had done his school routine with great success in an end-of-term production, his public appearances became regular. He performed without pay at church fund-raising parties, hospitals, charity bazaars, boy scout shows, picnics arranged by various organizations. Later, personal column ads brought him paid work at private parties, though he still went on doing the charity gigs.

It was not until Edgar was on the point of leaving high school, heading for college, that he realized the value of his average-shaped, nondescript face. He began to practice altering his features. As models he chose the well-known faces from movies and television. Some were impossible. Others were fairly easy, and they became easier as his features grew more rubbery and malleable.

When he wasn't performing or practicing, Edgar was staring at the large or small screen, absorbing mannerisms, stances, gestures. The voices he already had down pat.

Now he enlarged his act to the celebrities he could mimic in sight as well as sound, at the same time giving it a grander dimension. He was more successful than ever, the paid engagements tripled, his widower father urged him to turn professional.

Edgar, not an adventurous person, was undecided. His mind was made up for him by a stranger. He was a theatrical agent who had an accident while passing through town, spent two days in the hospital, saw Edgar performing for the patients, and told him where his future lay. Most big decisions are brought about as haphazardly as that.

The stony road to show business prominence is a mile wide at the beginning, three feet at the end. Edgar made it to and around the four-furlongs mark. He had club dates locally, then nationally. He did spots on television. He was "discovered" on three separate occasions, returning afterwards to his semi-obscurity. He nearly got a date at a plush Vegas hotel, he nearly got signed up for a coast-to-coast TV show. He did do a three-month tour of Europe, he did play fourth lead at the London Palladium for two weeks, he did top the bill in a summer-long show in a

British seaside resort, and he did manage to avoid resting, that sad euphemism for being unemployed.

One problem was, as colleagues often pointed out, Edgar's routine lacked what they called zing. Less competent impressionists were much farther ahead on the road because they had flair, color, charisma, used an appealing abundance of lights, props and fanfare, and in some cases had a half-naked girl assistant. So why didn't The Great Carlton follow suit?

Edgar demurred. He looked upon his work as more artistic than commercial. He refused to jazz up his act with frills, to gild the lily. He even declined to use the facial aids that other mimics relied on; he said they were a form of trickery. He would make it to and through the three-foot gap honestly or not at all.

The years passed. Edgar's career flagged and spurted, crawled and loped. He returned to Europe and settled in England, where he was among many other American entertainers, and where he could always be sure of being top banana in summer shows. Out of season, he was reduced to playing mostly one-week dates in working men's clubs, or one-night stands for Lions, Masons and conventions. He still did every charity show that could be fitted into his schedule.

Often Edgar wondered if he should call it quits. The work was not always rewarding, fees were not keeping step with the cost of living, and constant travel was a chore. And really, all he had wanted in the first place was to be liked.

Mona was nervous. A pulse thrummed in her neck as she stopped beside the parked car. It was a recent model and large—suitable. Trying to act casually, Mona looked all around.

The Mayfair street would have been bright even without the streetlamps. Though closed, the luxury stores gave off a carnival glitter from window lighting and neon names. There were people. Some hurried to outings, some strolled as they gazed at the treasures protected by plate glass.

For the fourth time in fifteen minutes Mona saw a dog being walked by a woman. The dogs had all been small, their owners all in furs. Mona felt foolish for her annoyance.

A couple approached. They seemed to be heading for the car. Mona was glad to believe that they were. She walked on. In any case, she told herself, stealing a car was supposed to be Kale's job, not hers.

Mona had a pretty face with a clean, tomboy look. Cosmetics would have spoiled the pleasant rhythm, the flow of natural coloration. Her lips were sweet, cheeks dimpled. Her dark curly hair was cut short, like a cap of tar bubbles, not as a style, but, like her lack of makeup, both for convenience and because of a total indifference to how she looked.

Mona's eyes jarred the picture of careless, placid youth. Large and grey-green, they were full of sorrow, except on the occasions when green predominated and the look firmed to cold, steady determination. Sorrow had gone completely then, replaced by hate.

The sad eyes were framed in darkness. It was as if they had read a week's dreary, tragic, hopeless events at one sitting and then been rubbed with newsprint fingers.

Mona stopped by the door of a Rover. It was several years old but looked sound. That neck-pulse, which had softened to normal, started up again.

Looking around, Mona saw that Kale was watching from across the street. Obviously, he too considered the car to be ideal. Mona leaned forward, giving the impression that she was trying the door handle. She shook her head and walked on.

In a moment she went to the recessed doorway of a store. Kale came over and joined her. They stood side by side, looking out into the street.

"This should have been done hours ago," Mona said.

Kale smirked. "You've got a lot to learn, Smith."

"Meaning what?"

"Meaning the closer to the event, the less chance of cop interference."

Mona said, "Yes, I understand."

"See, this way there's not much time for the number and make to be circulated, so you're not likely to get some thick pig stumbling up at the wrong moment."

"I did say I understood." She spoke truthfully. What she didn't get was why they had to be doing this in a busy, bright place. It seemed pointlessly risky. Surely it would be far simpler and safer to steal a car from a parking lot.

But she didn't care.

"I have an idea," Kale said. He went on to explain, ending, "Okay?"

"If you say so."

They left the doorway, strolled to the corner and moved along another street. Kale was tall and broad-shouldered, Mona petite. Under identical brown jackets, they both wore black sweaters, black jeans and black loafers. Their tight-fitting gloves were also black. Otherwise, as in size, they were greatly different. Kale gave off an aura of confidence.

"There's a good one," he said, his voice low. "The Jag."

Following the direction of his nod, Mona saw the Jaguar ahead. Grey and the latest model, it stood badly parked in front of a restaurant with closed and draped windows. There were fewer people on this street.

"Best prospect yet," Mona said. She hoped her tone didn't give away her nervousness. She toughened it to add, "Let's go."

They went to the side of the grey car. Kale turned his back to it. He opened his arms. Unsure now of this idea, Mona moved into his embrace. It was an innocent looking picture, yes, but she didn't want to be held.

Kale put his arms around her waist. He pulled close, smiling down at her. Eyes flicking aside, he said quickly, "There's a pig coming. We'd better kiss."

He put his mouth on hers. Mona shuddered. She didn't know if it was due to sensuality or revulsion. Deciding on the latter, she gave herself up to acting a part. She pretended. This was someone else.

Mona allowed the playing lips, she allowed the probing tongue, she held still against the insinuating loins. Again she shuddered, suspected the truth, and was disgusted with herself.

Easing back, she looked around. There was no policeman in sight. Kale said, "Gone now. And it wasn't a cop after all. Bus driver or something." His smile mocked her.

Mona glared her hostility. With a curt movement she slipped an arm around him and fumbled for the door handle. She found it and pressed the button. It gave. The car was unlocked.

"Open," she said, glad of that, and glad to be able to move back from the closeness of Kale's body. She wished he could get it into his head that she didn't like him.

But she didn't really care.

Kale said, "Hold it, Smith." He kept his hands on her shoulders. "Two men coming."

Seeing that this was true, Mona smiled up at him, as if fondly. But she wondered if anyone had ever been fond of Kale, or whatever his real name was. He didn't have a soft line in his face. Heavy brows, Roman nose, dark and deep-set eyes, lips as thin as string, fair crew cut hair—nothing hinted at warmth or indulgence. He was four or five years more than her own age, twenty-six, yet he had the expression of a much older man, one who had seen it all, had done it all, and was left with only one emotion: cynicism.

Footsteps and voices faded in, faded out. Kale released Mona in a shove as he swung around to face the car. He pulled the door open and got in. Without haste he shuffled from passenger to driver's seat.

Mona's nerves were racing. The risk seemed high.

She wanted to run. The glances she sent in all directions were fast with fear. She wasn't calmed by seeing no signs of danger.

"Get in," Kale said. He was feeling under the dashboard, behind the ignition switch.

Stooping, Mona slid onto the seat. She pulled the door closed. It closed with a loud slam that made her gasp. She changed it to a cough. Inside the gloves, her palms were sweaty.

Whistling softly between his teeth, Kale pulled a bunch of wires into view. The plastic coating of each was a different color. With sharp tugs Kale broke free a yellow wire, then a red one. He put their raw ends together.

The horn blasted.

Mona jumped, gasped, shot a look toward the restaurant, involuntarily put a hand on the door handle.

Kale was still whistling. He discarded the red wire, yanked loose one sheathed in green. Mona could see that he was unmoved by the situation. She even felt that he might be enjoying himself.

He twisted the green and yellow wires together. A small red light came on in the dashboard. Mona closed her eyes briefly in relief. Kale pressed a button. The starter whined.

Ten yards ahead, a man came out of a doorway. He walked toward the Jaguar. He was holding a key-case.

The starter was still whining. The motor hadn't caught. Kale released the button and then jabbed it again. Mona clutched the door handle. She slid a little lower in the seat. Her stomach was aching with tension.

The man with the keys came to a halt near the front of the car. He looked at the pair inside, looked at the hood. His head sloped. He seemed to be listening to the retching of the starter.

The motor caught. Kale fanned it to roaring life, his leg pumping like that of a jazz fan. This he stopped when the motor was rumbling steadily.

He also stopped whistling. Turning to Mona he asked in a non-committal tone, "Is Smith your real name, Smith?"

She stared at him. "Christ," she whispered, stunned. "What a time to ask."

"And the name?"

"No, it isn't."

"Kale isn't mine either, but it has a nice ring to it."

The man with the keys, nodding at the motor's beat, turned away and walked on. Mona sagged. Kale set the gearshift and released the brake. Steering away from the curb he said, "As to timing—it was right. Nothing's more natural than a couple in a car chatting to each other."

"Well, yes."

"You have a lot to learn, Smith. Or shall I call you something else?"

"Smith's fine," Mona said, disliking him anew not so much for his professionalism, more for the fact that it showed up her naivete.

The Jaguar slid gracefully along the street. The driver sat back with an attitude that could have been interpreted as light disappointment. The passenger still sagged down in welcome relaxation. Her worry was over—for the time being.

It was at moments like this that Mona gave thanks for Kale. She would have been lost alone. He was slick all right, she thought. Even so, there were some facets of his approach to business that were puzzling. For instance, the idea of themselves and the others all dressing alike. It smacked of the melodramatic, of childishness. She had gone along with it, however, because of that very professionalism which sometimes made her feel a fool.

The Jaguar had come into heavy traffic. It crawled and gushed with the inflow of theatergoers that follows the outflow of commuters. Around and above, lights flashed and dazzled. It was brighter than day.

Mona felt as though she were sitting in a spotlight. This was increased when the Jaguar halted at a traffic light beside another car and its male driver turned to giver her a look of appraisal. She began to lift the hood of her jacket.

Kale said a sharp, "Don't do that."

"Why not?"

"In a posh, heated car it looks wrong."

Mona put the hood down again. For the rest of the time in the traffic congestion she sat with an elbow on the windowsill and her hand to the side of her face—until she remembered that it didn't matter, because she didn't care. She sat up straight.

Harold Devon Vale put on his undershirt. Next, he picked up his bulletproof vest. This looked like a regular weskit, except that it had snaps instead of buttons and its brown surface was quilted. The weight—twelve pounds—formed not a hindrance to the wearer but a continual, comforting reminder of presence.

Vest on, Harold Devon Vale donned a white shirt, buttoned it up and tucked the tails into his flannel trousers. Taking a plain blue tie from the door rack of his bedroom closet, he began to knot it into place. He did so carelessly. Apart from that vest, he was indifferent to what he wore.

Harold D. Vale had a thin face. There were deep ridges running from cheekbones to jaw. To protect his pale, weak eyes from light, he wore spectacles with lenses tinted blue. He had a flat nose with flared nostrils, as if he were holding back rage.

His brow was permanently seamed with frown marks. His hair, in a style that belonged to the thirties, was dark with oil and brushed flat to his scalp from a center parting; the crown was bald.

The face had little charm, even when it expressed pleasure. It was a face that was loved only by his followers and the less talented cartoonists.

Above average in height, Vale had a stoop, which made him look older than his forty-six years. Age generally suggesting sagacity, this he felt was helpful to his political career.

Harold Vale took a blazer from the closet. He ignored its scattering of lint. Laying it on the bed, he sat there himself and reached to the table for the bottle of tranquilizers.

He shook out two, popped them in his mouth and then had difficulty in swallowing. He was dry. Water from the bedside carafe helped. That made six pills today. Vale always got extra nervous before a big meeting.

While putting on his slip-on shoes by touch, he gazed at a breakfront drawer. In there, at the back, was a revolver in a shoulder holster. He wondered if he would wear it tonight. He pretended that he didn't go through this uncertainty every time there was a special outing, that he didn't decide yes and then no, and then didn't at the very last minute, on the point of leaving, hurry to the bedroom and put on the gun.

Under British law, the carrying of small arms was strictly illegal. Even senior police officers went armed only on rare occasions. It was even impossible to get an answer as to whether or not the Queen's personal detective carried a gun. Vale was aware of the consequences. He was afraid every time he wore the loaded holster. He was doubly afraid when he didn't.

He started nervously at a knock on the bedroom door. He croaked, "Yes?"

A woman's voice: "That programme'll be on telly in a bit, Mr. Vale."

"Ah, thank you, Mrs. Neal."

A minute later, fully dressed, Harold Devon Vale went into the living room of his Bloomsbury apartment. It was large and comfortable, with a lavish collection of books, some paintings by the near-renowned, and chain store furniture. It was a room that showed, despite its cleanliness, the lack of a woman's touch.

Closing the door to cut off the kitchen clatter being made by Mrs. Neal, the daily help, Vale sat on a couch facing the television set. An announcer, outlining the evening's programmes, was saying: ". . . in about two hours from now, at Wainford Hall, which we will be bringing to you live. Here now is a word from our political commentator, Arthur Price."

Vale sneered. Price was supposedly a middle-of-the-road man, not affiliated with any person or party, but the fact that he was anti-Vale was easy to see if one were familiar with his phrasing.

"Good evening," the man on the screen said. He was stout and middle-aged. "Later tonight we'll be witnessing another episode in the extraordinary career of Harold Devon Vale, ex-Conservative, ex-Labour, presently Independent Member of Parliament for the London borough of Caston North. He has been called an opportunist, a racist, a man of dubious motives. He has also been called a saint, one whose first consideration is the stability of his country. Whichever, he is certainly the most colorful and discussed figure on the political scene of this day and age."

Price went on to recap his subject's past: Eton, Oxford; resignation from both major parties over policy; campaigning for and winning the seat of Caston North, an area with a heavy concentration of foreign workers.

"It was a year ago," Arthur Price said, "that the Honorable Mr. Vale made his violent attack on foreigners working in this country. It was well received. He won in a landslide."

A film clip of Vale making a speech flashed onto the screen. He sneered now as he watched because he was sure that Price would use the film with the unfortunate hand gesture, one that Vale had since discarded.

As he expected, his image on the screen was making points with the right hand, forefinger and thumb extended, with his other fingers folded in. It was what a child did when he wanted to simulate a cocked pistol.

"Take the Spanish," the film Vale was saying. "There are some ten thousand British subjects working in Spain, mostly in tourism. Here, there are thirty thousand Spanish workers in London *alone*. And do you know what our unemployment figures are? Let me give you a few instances."

The clip ended. Arthur Price returned, wearing a faint supercilious smile. He said, "The Honorable M. P. for Caston North possibly forgot to mention that local hospitals would fall into chaos if the male and female Spanish nurses were suddenly to go home. But, of course, one can't get every detail into one's speeches. And there were many, all over the country—yet only in industrial areas. Mr. Vale's following grew, especially among the young. This led to the phenomenon of the Whitecoats."

Another film came on. It showed a gang of youths. They all wore windcheaters that had been bleached of color. The gang was running along a street in pursuit of a smaller group of men, with dark complexions and wearing conventional dress. The film ended when one of the Whitecoats came charging at the camera.

Back on screen, Arthur Price said, "During this past year, four foreigners have been killed. Mr. Vale has condemned the violence, denying that the gangs were inflamed by his speeches, blaming it on groups who would like to discredit his aims in, quote, ridding this wonderful nation of those with inferior intelligence and strange customs, unquote."

Harold Vale muttered, "You bastard."

"And, it must be admitted, mob violence is a peculiarity of the age. A football match without a fight is a rarity nowadays."

"Thanks for nothing, you shit."

Onto the screen came a film of Harold Vale, walking limply, being led and semi-supported through a crowd by two policemen. His face was white. Voice-over, Price said, "His following grew in June after an assassination attempt. The bullet missed and wounded a woman in the leg. The would-be assassin, an Italian, was judged insane and deported. Mr. Vale stated that he was undeterred, that nothing would stop his crusade."

The film clip ended, Price returned, saying, "That crusade has been extended. On his blacklist now are Commonwealth citizens and Americans. But he has denied responsibility for the stoning last month of the U.S. Embassy in Grosvenor Square, also the attack on Australia House. He has suggested that his enemies hire thugs who dress themselves as Whitecoats.

"It must be said, again, that Mr. Vale is on the board of governors in his constituency's orphanage, to which he gives a tithe of his stipend."

Harold Vale smiled in self-congratulation. That was one of the wisest moves he had ever made.

Arthur Price added, "It is also worth mentioning that many people think that although Mr. Vale believes in one man, one vote, that man is himself and the vote is his alone."

"Bastard," Vale said, while the professional in him was admiring Price's glibness.

"Tonight, there is the feeling that we will see an important drift in policy. Where does he go from here? And the question remains, is the Honorable Harold Devon Vale saint or sinner?"

The screen blanked, then came alive again with the original announcer, who began to talk of the play that would follow the political telecast.

Harold Vale got up and switched off the set. He was more amused than offended by what he had seen. It was all old stuff, he thought, and as usual they had left out many facts in his favor. His supporters included respectable adults as well as young people—but those adults never made news. He had allies in all three main parties, and twenty thousand people had marched peacefully through London in protest against the government's bill to censure him and it had failed by only three votes.

Adjusting his tinted spectacles, Vale sat at an open writing desk. The mention of assassination in mind, he glanced at the pigeonhole that held this week's collection of threatening letters, which, as had become customary, he would send to New Scotland Yard on Monday.

Recalling the content in most of this year's hundreds of letters, he mused: And they say my Whitecoats love violence. They should read some of these things.

However, he reminded himself that he would have

to have a word with Maxted, ask him to talk to the boys. They were strongly in need of a much more sober image. Or at least, they should be taught how to spot a reporter, and learn the tricks of TV men with cameras hidden in cars and under umbrellas.

Vale leaned forward, rereading the typed notes of tonight's speech. He wasn't entirely happy with it though he liked the theme. It was to do with the compulsory sterilization of all Negro immigrants who had had three children. But something was missing.

After reading through the speech twice, Vale realized the paucity of God. The Almighty had been mentioned hardly at all. A mistake. You should try and get God in as often as possible—without, that is, alienating the atheists, which meant avoiding an outright statement of belief. The name was enough—God knows, for God's sake, and so on.

Vale was still putting capital G's on his notes when Mrs. Neal announced that his supper was ready.

He ate in the large old-fashioned kitchen and was served soup, meat course and dessert by the daily help, who, between courses, put on her hat, scarf and coat.

Mrs. Neal was a tall, stringy woman whose firm mouth was contradicted by kindly eyes. Her usual schedule was mornings only, but when her employer had an important meeting she stayed on to give him a hot meal.

Tucking her scarf into place, she said, "There's more of the apple pie and custard if you want it, sir."

"This is enough, thank you."

"Right then, Mr. Vale. I'll get off."

He looked up with a faint smile. "Ah, Mrs. Neal?"

"Yes, sir?"

He asked, "I trust we're still keeping our little secret?"

The woman's mouth became firmer. "We are that, sir. Silent as the grave, I am."

"You've told no one but your husband where and for whom you work?" It didn't embarrass Harold Vale to be asking the same questions he had asked last week, and the week before that. He knew the difference between common sense security and paranoia. Only twenty people knew his address, and he wanted to keep it that way.

Mrs. Neal said, "Don't you worry, sir. Me friends think I do for a lady in Ealing. My man tells people the same."

"Good," Vale said, getting up. "I'll let you out, Mrs. Neal."

"Why, just to think of that madman with the gun makes me blood run cold."

"It was an uncomfortable moment."

"Police protection, that's what you need, sir."

Vale privately agreed, and all he had to do was ask. But the news media would find out and it would damage his image.

After seeing Mrs. Neal out, he closed the door, bolted it, turned the key in its lock, put on the safety chain and checked the peephole cover. He went back to the kitchen.

Over his coffee Harold Vale mused that he would

prefer Mrs. Neal to use a different term for the evening meal. Hers always made him think of the *Last Supper*.

He returned to his speech, mulling it over, speaking the set phrases aloud. An idea occurred to him in relation to his earlier thoughts on religion. The line made him smile in appreciation. He was sorry he wouldn't be able to use it. Not yet. It was a bit strong. But in a year or so? Perhaps.

He rose, tapped himself on the chest and said, "I have been called a fascist. But, since there is no suffrage in heaven, the same thing could be said of God."

Edgar Carlton moved to the arch in the Dockers Social Club. Standing there he looked around the overlarge room. The decor was whitewash. Smoke flowed gently toward extractor fans and then sped like tracer bullets over the final feet.

Every table was occupied. People stood three deep at the long bar. The noise level was high. Beneath it, faintly, could be heard jangly thumps from an upright piano. This was a Friday-night crowd in a weekend mood.

The club had a respectable ambience that would have depressed a tourist. The average age was fifty, the most popular drink was beer, the clothing was as neat and clean as when it had first come off the peg.

Caps and mufflers were worn by many of the men. Their matronly wives had on scarves to hide hair-rollers, which would be removed for the big night, Saturday, and then replaced for the following week. There wasn't a slit skirt or a razor scar to be seen.

Edgar knew from experience, however, that these people were hard to please. They couldn't be milked like a tame theater audience. If they didn't like an act, if it didn't capture them quickly, they simply drowned it with talk. Any dissenting element was liable to be given first the fist, next the boot.

Edgar caught the pianist's eyes. The man nodded and changed from thumping tune to crashing chords. Noise volume was reduced by half. Moving to the rug-sized dance floor that doubled as a stage, the pianist spread-eagled his arms and shouted, "Now the moment we've all been waiting for. Straight from his sensational engagement in the West End, the man who has appeared at the Palladium, the man who is the top impersonator in the United States and has performed at the White House on numerous occasions, the man who, ladies and gentlemen, is none other than—The Great Carlton!"

The third of the audience near the front that had actually heard the intro offered a token applause. Edgar acknowledged it with a raised arm as he wended his path to the stage.

Talk was still going on. Edgar cut it to a hiss by producing the sound of an air raid siren, while looking around as if wondering where the piercing noise was coming from. Many were fooled. There was laughter as Edgar slapped a hand to his mouth to end the racket. The audience was willing.

Edgar worked into his act by doing a series of one-liners, each in a different regional accent. He did them all except Cockney. He never aped the dialect of the region he was performing in. To all people, it was only other people who had a funny way of talking.

Next Edgar started on his impressions of the celebrated. Using a variety of headgear, he did the prime minister, actors, a murderer of recent infamy, and popular stars of television—giving each the appropriate voice, face and patter. The audience responded with enthusiasm.

Edgar's creation of W. C. Fields was typical of his method of keeping aids and props to the gaunt minimum. He would have liked to dispense with them altogether, but one thing was essential: headwear. A head covering made hair changes, impossible in a fast-moving act, unnecessary, and the amount of brow hidden made a startling difference to the shape of a face. A hat's angle also spoke volumes in terms of personality.

For W. C. Fields, Edgar wore a straw hat tipped forward, twisted his mouth sideways like a convict, and held his nose with the tips of his fingers—thus hiding the fact that it wasn't rosy and bulbous. In the famed, sonorous rasp, Edgar told of his worry that thieves would steal his nose and sell it for a beacon.

The act went on. It lasted half an hour. Usually it lasted longer. Not tonight. Edgar was keeping it short. He was surprised that he had done it so well, had not let his excitement interfere.

He closed with one of his favorite world figures, Winston S. Churchill, whom he considered to have been the greatest showman since P. T. Barnum. When he turned from putting on the high-crown derby and pulling into view a bow tie from under his sweater neck—his shoulders hunched, his cheeks blown out, the audience gasped at the likeness.

Accompanied by the pianist playing soft marching music, Edgar declaimed the Blood, Sweat, and Tears speech, which had once moved a nation and now moved these people, many of whom had heard the original. A more sophisticated group would have been embarrassed by the flag-waving sentiment. Edgar knew his audiences.

The applause was long and loud. Smiling, happy, Edgar bowed and waved his way back to the arch. He ignored calls for an encore. He also ignored a greasy-haired youth who hissed as Edgar passed, "bloody Yank."

Ten minutes later, makeup removed, hat and coat on, Edgar was saying good night to the doorman, who ushered him out saying, "See you tomorrow night, sir."

Maybe, Edgar thought. He said, "Right, Bill."

Outside, walking the dim streets, Edgar's excitement flared. He was unable to stop it—the time to act was so close. Wave after wave trilled up his body like mild electric shocks.

The feeling, he supposed, was a combination of stage fright, pleasure and physical dread. He hoped the balance would stay like that, without the last getting the upper hand.

Again, knowing he must be calm, that unsteadiness could be ruinous, Edgar forced himself to fight down the excitement. He had succeeded, was close to normal, by the time he entered a house doorway.

A window card said Mrs. Tootle's Theatrical Boardinghouse. It was a grim building. No changes had been made since Jack the Ripper killed his last victim three streets away.

Going along the deserted hallway, lit from a lamp outside, Edgar went up one flight of creaky stairs and into his room. It was chill and bleak, as inviting as jail. Suitcases and lack of clutter showed it to be a temporary home.

Except for one group, the framed pictures were of music hall performers who had reigned thirty to eighty years before. The exception, on a table, were family photographs. Those of married cousins with their children often caused Edgar pangs. It was a form of homesickness, the bachelor syndrome. However, he had a trick of turning this off by reminding himself that relatives considered his life to be larded with glamour. Pride had its uses.

While stripping to the waist, Edgar looked at a photograph of a middle-aged man. He knew parent was disappointed with son, was unfooled by ideas of glamour. He knew there was regret that the expected heights had not been reached. He knew an attitude of indifference had to be maintained in the old Detroit neighborhood, especially for those friends who asked, smiling, how The Great Carlton was doing these days.

Edgar winked at the picture.

After putting on a plain white business shirt, he again slipped on his jacket to counter the cold. He sat on the bed and removed his shoes. The pair he replaced them with had hidden elevator lifts. He tied the laces tightly. Standing, he walked about and rocked, testing how the shoes felt. They were snug. He was two inches taller.

A glance at his watch told Edgar he had several minutes in hand. He sat down, lit a cigarette, smoked it slowly. He kept his thoughts from what lay ahead by dwelling on how well the act had gone this evening.

Cigarette stubbed, Edgar put on his topcoat and slouch hat. From a suitcase he took a flat cap, which he folded and slipped into his pocket. He also pocketed a roll of white surgical tape, half an inch wide.

From another suitcase, under the bed, he got a gun. It was a black revolver with a wooden grip. He spun the barrel several times, pleased by its smoothness, before putting the gun in the inside breast pocket of his topcoat.

He patted himself, assuring readiness. Opening the door, he switched off the light and as he left the room, said to nothing in particular, and to everything, "Good-bye."

The house was still silent and deserted. Mrs. Tootle would be busy with her gin bottle, while the other half-dozen guests were out doing their stints in clubs and pubs and the one or two vaudeville theaters still extant.

Edgar went downstairs, let himself out and walked along the dreary street. He was still keeping his excitement under control. But, as he turned a corner, he did think what a strange way this was to get famous.

Mona was unnerved. She sat leaning forward in the Jaguar's passenger seat, head down, pretending to read a map she had found in the glove compartment. Despite what Kale might say, she had raised her jacket hood.

She had been unable to believe it when Kale had come sweeping in to this large brightly-lit service station. The man seemed to have no fear at all.

He was leaning jauntily on the side of the car while its tank was being filled. He had already had air put in two tires and asked the attendant to clean the windshield. All of which Mona had considered unnecessary.

Earlier, it had been different. She could see the sense in Kale stopping on a quiet street, under a lamp, and checking the Jaguar over—though he had spent an immense amount of time poking around under the hood.

From the top of her vision, Mona watched the people in other cars and the doings of service personnel. In terms of future identification, it wasn't being seen she worried about. She did however, dread being stopped at this late stage of the planning.

Attendant paid, Kale got in and started the motor. He drove out of the station, sliding into traffic. Mona sat up, lowered her hood. She asked: "Wasn't that a bit risky?"

Kale ran a hand over his blond crew cut. "Would've been more risky at some back street joint where they get little custom. That was a busy place. No one paid the slightest notice."

There was logic in that, Mona thought. And it was

a nice change that he hadn't told her she had a lot to learn. There'd been enough of that in the past two months.

The car was moving along the Embankment. Lights from the other side repeated themselves wavily in the river. Kale was whistling between his teeth. The tune was like a dirge. He sounded bored.

When the Jaguar turned onto Battersea Bridge, Mona broke the silence. She said, "I hope the other car was picked up as easily."

"Easier," Kale said. "Size and power aren't important. Any old crate'll do."

"Of course. I meant without having to break windows and so forth."

"They'll manage fine."

"I hope so."

"Don't get steamed up, Smith. Stay loose, like me. Save your gut-ache for when it's needed."

As had happened often before, the oddness of Kale's voice struck Mona. In accent, rhythm and phrasing it was vaguely Scottish, vaguely Canadian. It could even have been ironed-out West Country. Like the man, it was a mystery.

But then, Mona thought, most terrorists were mysterious figures. The cloak, as much as the dagger, had always been their stock in trade.

It was not until Mona's grief had been six months old, and losing its trenchancy, that she had come sufficiently back to life to start her search. She expected it would take at least a year. It took six weeks.

In Mona's home area, the industrial midlands, where there were thousands of foreign workers, everyone had heard of the Anti-Vale League. It had many supporters. Many more were loud in condemnation. It was a case of the haves liking, the have-nots loathing. The latter, with insecure jobs or no jobs at all, saw the group as Judas to their saviour, Harold Devon Vale.

Using the name of Smith, Mona joined the group. Predictably it was a middle-class affair, into which Mona slotted neatly. There were earnest women in tweeds, scholarly men, pale and thin youngsters who preached the liberal ethic. Violence was abhorred.

It was for that reason, Mona learned, that a recent approach from a man named Kale had been turned down. He had advised firm action and had offered his services. The group was still talking about the approach, with embarrassment. That wasn't at all what they had in mind for the downfall of Harold D. Vale.

At the first opportunity, Mona searched the files until she found Kale's letter. Cleverly worded, its hard gist was safely between the lines. She answered it in similar fashion, using the League's letterhead and signing herself as chairman. The address was in London. She said in her letter that hereafter, for security, it would be better to use the telephone instead of the mails. She gave her own telephone number.

Some days later Mona heard that odd accent for the first time. There were almost daily calls over the following fortnight. Next, a meeting was arranged. The place suggested by Kale was Oxford, because, he said, it was halfway between them. Mona didn't miss the significance of the one-upmanship—Oxford was far closer to London than to Birmingham. She didn't care.

The rendezvous was at night outside the post office. Mona waited an hour before a tall man showed up. After the arranged passwords had been exchanged, Mona said, "I suppose you've been watching me for the past hour." She was not displeased by his caution.

"Right, Smith," he said. "And I was here watching for a stakeout three hours before that."

"I'm impressed."

"Fine. Now let's walk and talk."

That was two months ago. Luckily, Kale never asked for proof of Mona's backing by her organization. All he wanted was a per diem fee of thirty pounds sterling, to start from their second meeting a week later.

Mona had been staggered by the amount. But she knew that this was the only way to get what she wanted; that she could never manage alone, and that she had been unusually lucky in getting a lead to someone like Kale in the first place.

Mona's time between further meetings was spent raising cash: selling valuables, borrowing, getting a loan on the house. She never for a moment swerved from her determination to go on to the end.

A plan was evolved. It would need three men in addition to himself, Kale said. Two men, Mona said, for she intended to take part in it herself. The argument over that lasted for several days. Kale said repeatedly, "This is no caper for a woman." He gave in when Mona stated that unless she were personally involved, the deal was off, she was backing out.

She moved to London and took a room in a small hotel. Kale found the two men, one of whom would supply weapons and ammunition. Arrangements went ahead without hitch to the night of action, which was now.

The car sped along a gaunt, broad road south of the river, one of many similar roads that bisect the clog of narrow streets, tenements, small shopping districts and drab factories. Only the pubs had flair.

Mona saw a couple necking in a doorway. She turned to Kale, saying, "When you kissed me."

"When I kissed you what?"

"I didn't like it."

"That's funny," Kale said, glancing at her. "Seemed to me just the opposite."

"I was putting on a performance for the supposed pig. I didn't like it. You're not my type. I want that made plain."

"Smith," he said lightly, smiling at one corner of his mouth, "I really don't give a fuck."

"Good," Mona said. She turned curtly away. She believed him. She thought that he probably didn't give a fuck about anything in the world. So what was his drive?

Kale turned the Jaguar into another grim, dead-straight road. On either side were factories. All had lights, ranging from token, to the full illumination that showed a night shift was in progress.

One factory was completely dark. Kale steered onto its forecourt by passing through a gateway; the wooden gates themselves were open and drooping in ruin.

Kale drove around the building. It was a bleak shell of crumbled brickwork and broken windows. There was plenty of evidence to show that the place now served as a children's unofficial playground.

At the rear of the building, by a doorless doorway, stood a car. It was a Ford, six or seven years old. The Jaguar's lights picked out no shine on its dull paintwork. Drawing to a stop beside the Ford, Kale asked:

"Can you handle that model?"

"Easily."

Switching off motor and lights, Kale got out. Mona followed. They went into the building. In the center of a large room that was scattered with rusting machinery stood a box on which burned three stubby candles.

Waiting by the box was a man. He asked, "Okay?"

"Yes," Kale said. "How did you get on, Extra?"

They began to talk about the cars they had stolen, Kale casually, the other man with a youthful eagerness, though there was deference in his manner and he never interrupted Kale.

The man who called himself Extra was dressed in black, including gloves, plus a jacket for warmth. Of average build, he had a smooth face that was almost pretty. His lashes were long. Also long was his brown wavy hair. He looked like he was in his early twenties. His large blue eyes were flickering with excitement. He might have been a choirboy sneaking into the vestry for a smoke.

In the short time that she had known him, Mona had come to the opinion that Extra was an overgrown kid. He reveled in his role and in his foolish name. He was a romantic, a gamester, a war-lover. He was as much acting a part as she was.

Mostly, Extra made Mona uneasy with his posing, his tension and his quick movements. But there were times when she felt sorry for him.

Kale asked, "Did you check the fuel?"

Extra nodded. "Tank's nearly full."

"I hope the tires are okay."

"They're great, Kale, just great. But think, there it was sitting with the key in it."

"Nice break."

That appeared to exhaust the subject. Kale yawned. Extra stood shifting his feet and putting his hands in and out of his pockets.

Mona asked, "Isn't our friend here yet?"

"He'll be here in time," Extra said, looking at her. His eyes, as always, showed his admiration, even awe. But this was doubled as he looked back at Kale. That look seemed to remind him of his role.

Turning again to Mona he said toughly, "Yes, he'll be here in time. You know damn well he won't be late."

A solemn place, Bloomsbury. It has no sense of humor. The Victorian-Edwardian property, the color of mud, stands bulked shoulder to shoulder as if trying to edge closer to its ultra-respectable core, the British Museum.

Edgar Carlton walked along a narrow street. It

was choked with parked cars. Converted to apartments and offices from private homes, the buildings rose steeply and belligerently like bullies with big chests. That, plus dimness, caused Edgar to feel intimidated. The desertion of the area, however, that was to his liking.

He firmed his step to a steady pace. He tugged down the brim of his slouch hat, touched the side of his coat behind which lay the revolver.

Edgar turned the final corner with care. Around it he stopped. Across the street, in the middle of an unbroken row, rose a bay-windowed house with lights showing on each of its five floors.

Again, a trill of excitement ran up through Edgar's stomach and chest, finishing with a catch in his throat. He shivered, flickered a smile.

Recovered, he told himself, no more of that. It was the last time. From here on he had to be calm and totally businesslike. It was a peformance, like any other. There was no need for doubt or nerves. Confidence would turn the trick.

The street was deserted. Edgar looked at his watch, squared his shoulders and stepped between parked cars. Going between two more he reached the opposite sidewalk.

He didn't hesitate on coming to the house. He went up three broad steps and pushed open the door—a high, old, heavy slab of oak that nonetheless moved with ease and in silence.

He was in a lobby. It was carpeted and softly lit. Ahead was an old-fashioned cage elevator beside a staircase. Edgar went forward.

"Good evening, sir."

At the sound of the unexpected voice, Edgar jerked to a halt. Both hands moved in the direction of his right topcoat pocket. He swung his head.

Rising from a desk in a corner was a man. He rose lazily. Tossing down a newspaper he came across the lobby. He was wearing a sport shirt and slacks. Draped around the chair he had been sitting on was a windcheater. It was almost white from bleaching.

Edgar straightened from the semi-crouch of his fast halt. His heart was running at speed. He told himself he had been a fool to think that Harold Devon Vale wouldn't have some sort of protection.

The man stopped beside him. He was aged twenty-five or so, with a camel-ish face of disdain and the body of a heavyweight boxer. The way his arms hung at his sides seemed unnatural.

He said, "May I ask who it is you're here to see, sir?" It was a phrasing he had obviously been taught. Repetition had made it a slippery drone.

A smile coming and going, Edgar said nervously, "Um—a lady. One of the residents." He was thinking that it was all over, finished. The planning and waiting and daring had been for nothing. It was over before it had started.

The man said, "And may I ask who that would be, sir?"

"A friend. She lives on the—um—" Edgar paused, unable to remember the difference between American and British systems of counting. For the top floor should he say fifth or fourth?

"And the lady's name, sir?" the Whitecoat asked. His dangled arms were swinging gently.

Edgar collected himself. He managed to produce a

hint of haughtiness to say, "That is hardly any of your business, young man."

"You an American?"

"I am. Over on vacation."

The Whitecoat asked, "Would it be Mrs. Wren you came to see?" There was a clench of amusement under his eyes.

Edgar felt there was hope. He glanced around as if furtively. "The lady's name is immaterial," he said. He added a stern, "Why are you asking me all these questions?"

"I'm the porter, sir." His arms had stopped swinging. "It's me job to keep out people what shouldn't be here. You get thieves and all kinds if you're not careful."

"I, young man, am not a thief."

"Yes, sir."

"Now, if you will please excuse me. I'm late already."

The Whitecoat stepped back and produced another parrot phrase. "I am sorry to have troubled you, sir."

Edgar nodded. He turned and walked on. His heartbeat was still not back to normal. He wondered, hadn't capitulation come a little too easily? Would the young man telephone the woman he had mentioned and make enquiries?

Edgar reached the elevator. Its cage was above. He glanced around. The man, standing watching, said, "Ring the bell, sir."

Edgar couldn't bear to drag the situation out any longer. Making a gesture to signify that it didn't matter, he moved to the stairs and started up. His progress was noiseless on the thick carpet. Around the first corner he stopped. He listened.

For a moment there was nothing from below. Then came the creak of a chair and the rustle of newsprint. That continued for the rest of the full minute that Edgar listened. He went up.

His nerves had settled by the time he came to a door on the third floor. He was pleased to note that the hall had one low light. It made things easier.

He took off his slouch hat and stuffed it into a pocket. From another he took the flat cap. He put it on. The collar of his coat he turned up; the topcoat itself would be acceptable, if noticed.

Bringing out a handkerchief, Edgar held it to the lower part of his face. He positioned himself squarely in front of the peephole. Last, he pressed the button.

Now, he thought, it all hinged on whether or not there was a code ring, or a combination of that and a knock, or some other kind of signal altogether.

In the middle of the peephole a dot of light appeared. Edgar coughed. A voice asked, "That you, Maxted?"

With only his eyes showing between handkerchief and cap, Edgar said, "Yes. Something's come up, Harold. Damn bloody nuisance." He was mimicking the voice of Vale's second-in-command.

"Something serious?"

Edgar coughed again. "Got an awful cold. No, not too serious. We'll settle it quick enough."

Harold Devon Vale said, "You could've telephoned."

Edgar shook his head. "Time's too short." He went into a bout of coughing.

The peephole light died. After some seconds of aching suspense for Edgar, he heard the rattle of metal. The door swung open.

Harold Vale was turning away. He said, "Lock up properly."

"Of course, Harold."

Vale moved along a hallway. "Ah, I'd better not get too close to you. It would be really jolly if I caught a cold just now."

Edgar came inside. He swiftly swung the door closed and shot a bolt. He turned. Harold Vale had stopped by a doorway. He said, "Don't forget the safety chain. It's a . . . ." He faded off, staring.

Edgar had stuffed the handkerchief into his top pocket and pushed up the peak of his cap.

Vale stared on. He began to raise a pointing finger. It was unsteady. He said, "You . . . What . . . ?"

Edgar brought out his gun. He held it before him as he went forward. Mouth and eyes hard, he grated, "Don't make a false move."

Harold Vale backed off. He bumped against the doorframe in going through. He moved in a strange crouch, his arms half lifted at either side. In a high voice he stammered, "What is it? Who are you? What d'you want?"

Edgar followed into a living room. He closed the gap until there was a yard of space between Vale and himself. With proximity and stronger light, Edgar saw clearly enough to be shocked.

The politician's face was a yellowy white, like spoiled milk. His open mouth was trembling. The mid-air hands shook. His knees sagged. Behind the tinted lenses, his eyes were wide with fear, and fixed on the gun.

Edgar was worried, more so than if he had met with resistance. He hadn't expected a reaction like this, not from a man who had experienced danger.

Vale moved back. He came to a stop against a couch. Not looking away from the gun he whispered, "Anything. I'll give . . . I'll give you . . . ."

His eyes slowly closed. His head and arms drooped. His body began to sag. He fell with a crash to the floor.

Quickly Edgar moved forward and knelt down. He rolled the man over. His hand went to the chest. He could feel no heartbeat.

Edgar gasped, "Oh, my God!"

Then his hand told him there was some sort of obstruction, a heavy undergarment that could be muffling the heart. At the same time he noticed a pulse throbbing in the neck, and he heard the heavy breathing.

Harold Devon Vale had fainted.

Edgar let out a long sigh of relief.

His mother was shouting at him to hurry, hurry. He could hear her voice clearly, despite the clamor being made by the other parents. Knowing how angry she would be if he failed to win the race, he ran as hard as he could. But he was slowed by not having the use of his arms. Somehow they were being held behind his back. And now he could hear the thud of running feet—the other boys were gaining. His mother's voice rose to a shriek. He could imagine the expression that would be on her face; and he knew what to expect, if he lost, when she got him home. It would end with him being put in that pitch-black airless closet under the stairs. He cried out in fear as he struggled on.

Harold Vale's dream disintegrated. Gasping, he came to the surface of consciousness. Slowly he lifted his head. His neck was sore. He realized that for some reason he had been asleep sitting up.

Still drowsy he looked around and down. He found that he was on a straight-backed chair. It was the one that usually stood by the writing desk. Now it was in the center of the room.

Vale next realized that he was tied, a prisoner. He couldn't move. His body tensed and he forgot the nightmare. He recalled the man who had pretended to be Maxted, the man with the gun who had threatened him. "Christ," Vale whispered.

Each ankle was fastened to a front leg of the chair. Behind him his hands were bound together as well as to a part of the chair.

He could hear nothing. On the couch lay a topcoat, a suit jacket and the phony Maxted cap. Lying there also was the gun.

Vale took hope and courage from the silence. He thought that perhaps the man had been a burglar, had made his search and then been panicked into a fast exit, leaving some of his things behind. Or he may have replaced his old clothes with better stuff.

Vale said a tentative, "Is anyone here?" When there was no response he called out, "Hello there!"

He tensed again. From beyond the open door had

come sounds. They grew louder. It was someone approaching. Vale gritted his teeth to prevent himself from moaning or whimpering or whatever it was that his fear wanted him to do.

In the doorway appeared a man, the same bland-faced one as before. He was hatless and in his shirtsleeves. Weirdly, under the circumstances, he wore a friendly smile.

He was holding a safety razor. Gesturing with it he said, "I hope you don't mind me using this. I'm shaving."

Vale quavered, "What's going on? What is this?"

"You look a bit better now."

"What happened to me?"

The man said, "You fainted, Mr. Vale. I guess the faint turned into sleep since no one tried to bring you out of it. That happens."

Harold Vale fumbled for a moment before muttering, "But I'm tied up."

"Sure. I did it."

"Why, for Christ's sake?"

The question was ignored. "I tied but didn't gag you," the man said. "I will, though, if you try shouting for help."

Shouts would be a waste of time, Vale knew. The walls were soundproofed, the window was double-glazed as well as heavily curtained.

He asked again, "What's going on?"

"I'll explain in a minute," the man said. "By the way, allow me to introduce myself. My name's Edgar Carlton. You might have heard of me."

"No. Never. I don't know you."

"Relax, Mr. Vale. I'll be back when I've finished

shaving." He turned to leave. Insanely, there was soap foam on the crown of his head.

Vale, alone gaped about him stupidly. He was frightened but able to hold on because of two factors—the lack of menace in the man's behavior, his use of Mr. Vale.

Vale turned over the name of the stranger in his mind. Edgar Carlton had no significance for him. Nor did the North American accent mean anything. And the face was one that would be easy to forget. Was he an old enemy in the political game, a common burglar, a liquidator imported from the States?

Harold Vale quickly turned his thoughts from the last. He considered the situation. Perhaps it wasn't as hopeless as it seemed.

He tried to move his hands. There was hardly any give. The same below with his ankles. He looked down, craning his neck. The tying material, he saw, was surgical adhesive tape. It had a terrible appearance of permanence. Vale went back to being frightened.

Presently the man returned. His manner was brisk. Turning around, he pointed to the back of his head and asked, "How's that?"

Where the foam had been was now clean, and clear of hair. It looked like a larger version of a priest's tonsure. The edges were sharp.

The man who called himself Edgar Carlton said, "It should pass for natural baldness, I think. At least without a close examination. In any case, the size and position are right."

"What're you talking about?" Vale fretted, torn between fear and exasperation. "Untie me at once."

The man turned. "Can't do that," he said apologetically. "Not just yet. You'll have to be patient." He sat down on the arm of the couch.

With a chill added to his fear, Harold Vale began to wonder if this Edgar Carlton was sane. His manner was suspiciously mild. He could, in fact, be a dangerous psychotic.

"Mr. Vale," Carlton said. "You asked for an explanation."

Vale nodded. That seemed the safest.

The stranger went on, "What I am doing is possibly immoral, decidedly criminal. I'm prepared to take the consequences. They should, I believe, be moderate."

"Moderate?" Vale was stung into saying. "For all this. Why would you believe that?"

"My gain will be no one's loss, after all."

"What about my freedom? You're depriving me of that."

"It's only for an hour or so. I don't like doing this. I mean you no harm."

Bravely, Vale said, "You mean me no harm. Oh, no. Of course not. You merely burst into my home, armed with a lethal weapon, tie me hand and foot, and have me at your mercy. But you mean me no harm."

Carlton pointed to the revolver. "That's not real. It's a stage gun, shoots only blanks. A noisemaker. I've used it in my act."

Vale sagged. "Christ, I wish I knew what you were talking about."

Edgar Carlton folded his arms. He said, "Mr. Vale, I am an entertainer. I'm in show business.

I work in theaters and clubs. I'm performing presently at a club in Limehouse and my digs are at a Mrs. Tootle's. Both, like me, are quite respectable."

"You're an actor?"

"A mimic, Mr. Vale. An impressionist. My name is not unknown to the public—I've worked in this country for years—though I can't make any claim to being famous. However, famous I am going to be. Tonight, as a matter of fact, if all goes well."

"How will you do that?" Vale asked. He was telling himself it was best to humor this man, be he a simple crank or an outright maniac.

From a pocket of the topcoat on the couch, Edgar Carlton took a soft black hat. He straightened it out with care as he spoke. "I am going to take your place at that meeting tonight, Mr. Vale. I shall impersonate you. I will be seen not only by the audience of several thousand, but also by perhaps five million television viewers. I shall fool them all. After I've given a speech in your voice and style, I will end the impersonation and tell them who I am." He smiled. "Thus instant fame."

Vale forgot about humoring. He burst out, "That's the craziest thing I ever heard in my life."

The stranger put the hat down neatly on his coat. "Why? Personally, I think it's brilliant."

"Why?" Vale repeated, looking around. "Why? Well, because it is, that's why. It simply won't work. You don't look the least bit like me, even with that bald spot you've made."

"It'll work, Mr. Vale. I'm good at my trade, though I do say so myself. You should see my act."

"Crazy. It's absolutely crazy. We're so different."

"Well, what are going to be a great help, I'll admit, are the tinted lenses of your spectacles. Eyes can't be changed, even with different-colored contact lenses. It's the whole surrounding area, not just the eye itself. Your glasses were what made me decide on you over the others."

"What others?"

"After I'd come up with this idea of instant fame," Carlton said, speaking easily, "I narrowed the possibilities down to four. The other three are television personalities. I could have mimicked them like twin brothers, except for the eyes. That wouldn't have mattered as far as the camera was concerned, but to get that far I would've had people to deal with face to face, people close to the genuine article."

Vale said, "I think you're—confused."

"Not at all. It's been thought over with great care. The glasses will help me fool those who know you intimately on my way between here and the podium. The rest—a piece of cake."

Shaking his head wearily, Vale said, "But you're not anything like me, except for build."

"And that, the height, comes courtesy of built-up heels."

"I'm a good ten years older than you are."

Edgar Carlton said, "Age can be fixed."

"My voice is different."

"That's the easiest of all. I fooled you with Maxted's, didn't I?"

Harold Vale went on shaking his head. "It won't

work. You're wrong. You should call the whole thing off."

"No, thanks."

"Look, Carlton. Listen. I'll tell you what. You let me go, forget this wild idea, and I promise I won't say a word about it to the police."

The mimic shook his head. "Sorry."

"God damn it!" Vale snapped, jerking forward. "This is an important speech I'm due to make. I won't have it ruined by you."

"I'm not going to make your speech. You can give it some other time."

"I won't stand for this!"

"I'm afraid you have no choice," Carlton said, again apologetically. He looked at his watch and rose. "If you'll excuse me, I'd better finish getting ready."

But instead of going away, he came forward.

"What d'you want?" Vale gasped, fear rushing in anew. "Don't touch me!"

Carlton came close. With a swift movement he removed the tinted spectacles. "Thank you," he said. "I'll see you in about fifteen minutes."

Harold Vale blinked at the brightness. "You bastard!"

"Please, Mr. Vale. Try and look at it this way. A week from now, you and I might be having dinner together and laughing about this."

"Madman!" Vale shouted, jerking at his bonds. "Lunatic!"

In front of the bathroom mirror, Edgar picked up the razor, dry, moved close to his reflection and drew the blade carefully over one eyebrow.

A curious fact in the aging process is that as hair appears in previously hairless regions—inside and on the nose and ears—it decreases in its lifelong locations of jaw, eyebrow and head.

Edgar thinned his eyebrows to the sparsity of a man many years his senior.

Next he attended to the sideburns, a detail he had noticed only minutes ago, when near Harold Vale. Their front corners were lower than the rear.

That done, he went out and headed for the bedroom. On the way he called out to his prisoner, whom he could hear muttering to himself, "Take it easy, Mr. Vale!"

Edgar was worried about the politician. That white-faced, trembling response to the armed intrusion had been unnerving. The man had looked as if he were on the point of having a heart attack.

Edgar, in fact, was more concerned about Vale than about the outcome of the impersonation. He was confident now. He had found the calmness he had hoped for once the affair was underway. Having gotten this far, he felt sure that the rest of it was a foregone conclusion.

This stage had seemed an improbable goal during the weeks of planning. Edgar had often smiled with disbelief even while following Vale in an effort to discover his address. He had mocked himself even while talking to the man who supplied the chauffeured limousines that took Vale to meetings and on lecture tours. He had mused that he was wasting his time even while watching the Bloomsbury house to note the comings and goings of various people; and when standing near Maxted in a pub to listen to his voice; and when perfecting his mimicry of Harold Devon Vale. But now he knew it was going to work.

Edgar did have one doubt. It had nothing to do with his talent, his ability to bring off a successful impersonation. On that score he was sure. What nagged was his knowledge that he was not a brave man.

During his life Edgar had been in dangerous situations. He had come through them with something less than glory. If he were challenged tonight, would he have the courage to bluff it out?

That, Edgar decided, was a non-question. He would not be challenged. His talent would carry him through. He would be Harold Devon Vale to a T. After all, he knew everything about the man—except, perhaps, his professional ethos.

Edgar had been non-political in the States, was even more so in Britain, a country not his own. He did know that no one was indifferent to Vale. He was loved or hated. That, his fame or infamy, was good enough for Edgar.

In the bedroom he moved to the vanity table. He was putting a ring of plastic into one nostril. It was a piece that he had sliced off ordinary domestic piping, a half-inch in diameter. When a second ring had been inserted in the other nostril, Edgar's nose had taken on a new character.

The rings, slightly ellipsoid, pushed the wings sideways, at the same time pulling in the tip. It was the flared, flat Vale nose exactly.

The discomfort of the plastic rings would wear off

after a while, as Edgar knew. Twice he had worn them all day, and once had slept with them in place.

With a soft-lead pencil he drew lines in his natural crow's-feet and in the ridges he created for himself by frowning. He put light shadows on his cheeks, temples and under the corners of his mouth. All this he had done so often lately that there was no hesitation.

Using one of Vale's own bottles, Edgar shook thick dressing onto his hair. He saturated it, rendering it lifeless and several shades darker. Carefully he formed a middle parting and combed the hair flat.

He went to the clothes closet. There were flannels on hangers, but he had already decided that the trousers of his grey suit would pass well enough. He took a plain tie and put it on, making sure the knot was slightly off-center.

Turning to the bed Edgar picked up the blazer. He had taken it off Vale before tying him to the chair. The blue garment was liberally scattered with lint. Obviously, Edgar thought, this had been collected when the politician had been lying on the floor.

Edgar was meticulous about picking every bit of lint off the blazer.

Back in front of the mirrored vanity table, Edgar donned the jacket and put on the tinted spectacles. After rounding his shoulders, he set his agile facial muscles into play.

He frowned. He lengthened his top lip, flattened the lower. He forced his jaw forward and down, thereby drawing deep depressions in the cheeks.

The result was so good, with the aid of the

original's own clothes and glasses, that Edgar was impressed himself. After letting the Vale face go long enough to grin, he assumed it again.

He would be making brief rests like that whenever he had the opportunity. Should he fail to do so, the ache in his muscles that would come in time could unthinkingly cause him to let them relax.

Using the Vale walk, and with the Vale habit of hands in blazer pockets with the thumbs out, Edgar left the bedroom and went into the living room. In the Vale voice he said, "Ah, good evening, good evening."

The politician stared, eyes narrowed against the light. His upper body, which had been in a slump, slowly craned upright. His thin-lipped mouth sagged open. At this moment, he looked less like Harold Devon Vale than Edgar did.

"Good God," he mumbled.

Continuing his mimicry, Edgar asked, "Still think it won't work?"

Vale had nothing else to say. He stared on, his eyes searching Edgar's face and form. The response was as good a compliment as the impersonator could have asked for.

He decided to stay in the role from now on. Going to a TV set he switched it on and noted that it was dialled to the channel that would be broadcasting the speech. "Ah, there you are," he said. "Now you can watch the meeting, see how well you do."

Vale was still staring. Edgar went out and along the hall. By the main door was a squawk-box. He pressed its button. Through the ensuing crackle came a voice: "Porter."

"Vale here. Has the car arrived yet?"

The Whitecoat sounded surprised. "Why no, sir. It always comes to the exact second. Ten minutes to go yet."

"I see," Edgar said, with a mild feeling of alarm at his mistake. An excuse was given to him from the box:

"Maybe your watch is fast, sir."

"That must be it, yes."

"I'll let you know as soon as it's here."

"Never mind," Edgar said, deciding to give his role a thorough test with the porter. "I'll come down and wait."

"Yes, sir."

Edgar released the button, went back to the living room. His attention was immediately captured by Vale's searching, bewildered, astonished eyes. He said, "I suppose I'd better gag you."

Harold Vale murmured absently, as if unaware of speaking, "The place is soundproof, walls and windows."

"Thank you," Edgar said, accepting. But to make sure he checked behind the heavy drapes. Back by the doorway, he said, "In that case, I'll be running along. I should be here again in, ah, under two hours. Until then, old chap."

Vale stared on. He might have been an amateur musician seeing the ghost of Chopin.

Edgar gave a long, gracious nod, turned and left the room. He let himself out of the apartment, went to the elevator. The cage was there. Inside, descending, he twitched his lips, the way he had seen his model do on his last television appearance.

When the elevator stopped below, Edgar walked out to find the porter-Whitecoat waiting nearby. The young man was standing almost at attention, and the gesture he made with his right arm was almost a salute.

"Good evening, sir," he said smartly.

"Ah, good evening, good evening. What's the weather up to?"

"Bit chilly, sir. Maybe you shoulda worn yer coat."

"One tries not to be too soft," Edgar said. "Even in one's extreme old age."

The Whitecoat laughed politely and with restraint. He hadn't unbent from his stance.

Shoulders rounded, hands caught by their thumbs in his pockets, Edgar began to pace back and forth across the lobby. His confidence was thriving.

He asked, "Did I ever tell you about the time I was stranded in a snowstorm in Scotland?"

"No, sir."

The anecdote that Edgar went on to relate, using all the Vale verbal mannerisms, was one he had read of in a biography of the politician. It was well known. It was also well known that Harold D. Vale told the same anecdotes year after year. They all had charm and were lightly against himself.

The Whitecoat gave no sign that he had heard the story before. He listened with a quiet smile that Edgar recognized was born of pride.

It startled him to realize that the young man was greatly boosted merely by being addressed directly by Harold Devon Vale. He was like a soldier hanging on the words of a well-loved general, and hoping he would be asked to volunteer for a risky mission.

Edgar was still talking, embellishing, when the car arrived. He had not dared a silence. The man might have talked of domestic arrangements, asked questions to which Edgar had no answers.

From outside came a horn blast. The Whitecoat said, "Excuse me, sir." He hurried to the door, opened it, went outside and looked both ways.

Making the same scrutiny of the street was another young man. He had gotten out of a limousine that was standing between the curb-lined cars. He wore a bleached windcheater.

The porter looked back. "All clear, sir."

Edgar walked outside and past him. "Thank you. Good night."

"Night, sir."

The other Whitecoat had opened the car's rear door, was posed there rigidly. As Edgar got nearer he snapped a wave. A salute it would have been if the elbow had pointed to the side instead of forward, and if the hand had been flat instead of nearly closed.

He said, "Good evening, sir." The greeting was echoed by a man at the steering wheel. He wore a chauffeur's uniform.

"Good evening, gentlemen," Edgar said as he settled himself on the broad seat. He hoped he was not overdoing the good manners that Vale was reputed to have in private as well as in public.

Whitecoat back in the passenger seat, the car glided smoothly away. To forestall the possibility of answerless questions, Edgar won the silence of the pair in front by murmuring, "Now I must, ah, think over that middle part of my speech."

He shuffled to the side. There, out of range of the rearview mirror, he let his features relax. He smiled. He felt marvelous. He was so sure of himself that he was even able to enjoy riding in a luxurious car.

The limousine was in traffic, moving along a broad road. They stopped at two sets of lights. At the third they stopped near a movie house from which people were streaming. A crowd was waiting for the pedestrian signal.

A voice called, "Hey, there's Harold Vale!"

Then all the people were moving forward, jostling for a look into the back of the car. Some waved. One woman started to clap. Two giggling teenage girls blew kisses. Another girl sneered.

Edgar, having resumed the Vale face, smiled and bowed.

As the car moved on, a man pushed through to the front. He made a humorous remark. At least, Edgar took it for humor, which is why he thought it odd that the man should be scowling, and why the Whitecoat should look back with a fist raised.

"What's the next step, Vale?" the man called. "Concentration camps for left-handed people?"

The room of the derelict factory glowed with candlelight and there was silence except for soft, metallic clicks.

Mona stood apart. She smoked a cigarette while watching the three men. They were loading the automatic pistols, handling the weapons with more love than care, like children with new toys.

The guns had been brought in a paper parcel by Steve. He was a man of early middle-age. Though short, his body had a breadth that spoke of strength, not mere bulk. His face was crumpled and faded, with puckers and pouches and a mass of fine lines. He had thinning white hair and a white moustache. He wore black clothes like the others, gloves, and a soiled trenchcoat.

It was typical of the man, thought Mona when he arrived, that he would assert his individuality by not wearing a jacket to match the other members. He was a born rebel.

Mona liked Steve the least of her three partners. His manner was hard; his eyes had sly movements like those of a small, dangerous animal. He seemed to take pleasure out of exaggerating his Irish aceent, as if in some way this was a put down of the listener.

All Mona knew of the man's background was that he had recently been in the Irish Republican Army. He had tried to start a radical, super hard-line splinter group under his own command, failed, and had been severed from the organization. Before leaving, he had raided one of the armories.

The three men finished loading. They stuck guns in their belts, put spare shells in the pockets of their jeans. Kale came over to Mona.

Dropping her cigarette, she accepted the proferred automatic and a handful of bullets. "Thanks."

Kale asked, "Know this kind of gun, Smith?"

She put it under her sweater, beneath her belt.

"Yes," she said, lying. She had never in her life handled a gun of any type.

Glancing at his wristwatch, Kale, the leader of the group, said, "Coats."

Mona slipped the shells into her hip pocket before taking off her jacket. She collected Kale's and those of the others, went out into the darkness and to the rear of the Jaguar. She put the garments in the open luggage compartment. Kale had forced it open with an iron bar. A box of bullets was already in there.

Back at the doorway she said, "I'll wait in the Ford."

Steve grinned. He had a crooked slant of the mouth. "There's an eager colleen for you, be Jasus."

"Nothing wrong with that," the youngest gang member said, looking at the speaker with uncertainty. Extra always acted as if unsure how he should take the Irishman.

Kale said laconically, "We have five minutes yet, Smith."

Mona nodded. "I know. I just want to get the feel of the car." She turned away and went to the Ford.

Inside, Mona let her gloved hands stray over the gear shift and instruments. She felt nervous, alien. It was strange to be at the wheel of a car again after so long.

When her grief had been new, Mona drove the family car for only a week. During that time she found her steering erratic, but was unconcerned about its oddness. Then one day she realized she had the urge to crash, to tear off course and into whatever would be the most destructive. She was aghast. She sat petrified while veering close to the traffic in the approaching lane. With a wrench, she made herself go into the side and stop. She left the car there and walked home, sending a friend to bring it back. She didn't drive again. When she needed money, the first thing to go was the car.

Mona told herself that the quirk was over, a thing of the past, a suicidal part of grieving. It had gone, along with the sharpest of the pains. She would drive perfectly.

Mona stiffened as the faint glow in the building's doorway flickered out. Next, the three men appeared. The time was now.

Kale and Steve walked to the Jaguar in a businesslike manner and got in without fuss, Kale behind the wheel. Extra emerged like a movie gangster. He looked in all directions, flipped away a cigarette, patted the gun in his belt, and swaggered as he walked to the Jaguar.

Mona sighed. But she didn't care.

The other car moved off. Mona started the Ford and followed. They left the factory grounds. Soon they were traveling along quiet residential streets. Traffic was thin. Mona was relieved to find herself calm—and driving normally. She loved the feel of the gun against her stomach.

Although not staying directly behind, she kept the Jaguar in sight. It was moving at a fraction under the legal speed limit of thirty miles an hour. Mona was pleased that Kale seemed to have toned down his recklessness.

From time to time, Extra's juvenile face appeared in the rear window as he gave a lazy-seeming look behind. Mona knew he was happy.

The cars went back across the river. They passed the old Scotland Yard building and then the Houses of Parliament, both apropos under the circumstances.

Over to her right, above the silhouetted buildings, Mona could see a shiny grey mass. It was the roof of Wainford Hall. The name was synonymous with conventions, title fights, exhibitions and religious revivals.

To Mona it meant the circus she had seen there one Christmas when she was a girl, on a visit to London with her parents. She could remember the vastness of the place. She could remember her rapture.

Sadness came over her like moving into shadow from sun. That she balked by touching the gun in her belt.

The Jaguar led the way through narrow streets. It turned into a road lined with lock-up garages. At the end was an open gate. A sign identified it as the service entrance to Wainford Hall.

Through the gateway, the two cars went down a long ramp. Off it, they were in an open space. It was brightly lit by high lamps. At one side rose the building, a mammoth in concrete. The wall was windowless, but broken at ground level by a row of double doors without handles.

Parked in the open space were half a dozen vehicles. All were empty. One was a police car, the others belonged to television companies or catering firms.

The Jaguar made a smooth turn and stopped by

one of the doors. Mona, after making the same turn, went on a little way before also halting. She switched off the motor, got out, walked to join the others.

They exchanged looks but not words. While Extra and Steve stayed by the Jaguar, Mona and Kale went to the end of the concrete wall. Around its corner they came to a window. It was at shoulder level and small, not much more than a foot square.

Kale brought out a screwdriver from the leg pocket of his jeans. He set to work prying the window open. The inside catch was frail. He had loosened it himself two nights earlier when at Wainford Hall during a table tennis championship.

Whispering, though there was no one around, Mona asked, "What if it doesn't give?"

"We break the glass."

"That's risky."

"Everything we're doing's risky," he said, his voice tight with effort. He was pressing hard, levering with the screwdriver.

Mona suggested, "Maybe if we got a tire-iron."

"Shut the fuck up, woman," Kale snapped. And, as he spoke, he won the struggle.

With a whine of wood parting from metal, the window came away from its frame. Kale pushed it wide open, saying, "You worry too much."

"Okay, I worry too much."

With the screwdriver point, Kale began to scratch on the wood beneath the glass. Finished, he had made the initials K.E.S.S.

Mona said, "I thought we'd agreed on V.A.L.E."

"This just occurred to me. It's as cute as hell."

"And it means?"

"It's our initials," Kale said. "Mine, Extra's, yours and Steve's."

"Sure. As cute as could be."

He gave her a hard look before tossing the screwdriver aside and moving to touch the wall. He stooped, bending horizontally from the hips. "Up you go."

Mona got onto his back. Upright from the knees, she eased her head and one arm through the small space. Light coming from under a door inside showed a dim room full of cleaning equipment.

Directly beneath the window, conveniently, was a table.

Mona got her other arm through. Pushing them both backwards, she winced as her breasts scraped over the sill. The gun clanked as her waist came next. Her hips reached the space and filled it firmly.

She stretched down to the table with one hand, using the other to push on the wall. Her hips seemed to be making no progress. She strained, jutting her jaw, breathing heavily. She panicked at the idea that everything would be ruined because of this one foolish little detail.

Kale's hands came to rest on her buttocks. But they were not helping, pressing. They began to shift in small, caressing motions.

Mona hissed in anger. She whipped up her supporting hand and slapped it with the other against the wall, making an immediate and violent shove. Her hips came through—fast.

She fell. Gasping, she landed on one shoulder on

the table. From there she crashed to the floor. To break her fall she rolled. She rolled into a stack of buckets and mops.

The noise was deafening. It yammered and clanged, bouncing from wall to wall. Even so, above the racket she could hear Kale laughing.

Silence came. Mona leapt up and went to the door. She was trembling. With the side of her face to the wood, she listened. She could hear nothing, no sound of approach.

From outside, through the window, came Kale's, "All right?"

"Yes," Mona said, her voice sounding high and palsied. "I'm on my way."

'Take your time. We're running a couple of minutes ahead. See you." The window was pushed back into position.

Without knowing why, Mona began setting the mops and their buckets upright and neat. By the time this was done, her trembling had stopped. She was even able to see the accident as farcical. But she didn't smile.

Cautiously Mona opened the door. She looked out into a passage. It dead-ended to her right, turned a corner the other way. She went to the bend after closing the door behind her.

Ahead stretched a bleak corridor. Some three yards wide and two hundred yards long, it was lit by naked bulbs. On one side were double doors at regular intervals, those same doors that Mona had seen outside.

Opposite was nothing but blankness, save for the

stone staircase that rose beside Mona. Under the stairs, hidden from the corridor, Kale and Extra would wait.

A tapping sounded from the nearest door. Mona went to it and pressed down on its handle. The door opened. She left it ajar after slipping outside.

The three men were bunched together nearby, the youngest twitching with eagerness, the other two as calm as if they were waiting for a bus. Kale asked, "Okay?"

"Yes, fine," Mona said.

"No one around?"

"Not a soul."

"Good," Kale said. "Now the masks."

Each of the four produced a black mylon stocking. Starting to slip the hose over his head, Extra said quietly, "Listen. It might be neat to disable these other cars."

"What for?" Steve asked. He was arranging his stocking like a skullcap, the leg tucked in, the top in a roll that circled above his ears and eyebrows. In an instant it could be pulled down to cover his face.

"So they couldn't chase us, that's why."

Kale said, "The plan has been settled. That's that."

"All we need do is shoot out the tires," Extra persisted.

The Irishman said, "Listen to the broth of a boy, would ye."

"What d'you mean?"

"Laddie, the shots would be heard for miles."

"Yeah, maybe."

Steve added, "Even if it wasn't for them coppers."

"Eh? What coppers?"

"Them two watching us from over there."

Extra whirled. He looked around wildly, then sagged and turned slowly back again. Like someone who had just heard a monk blaspheme, his face wore the smoothness of bewilderment as he looked at each of the others.

Steve was chuckling softly. Mona, like Kale, was unmoved. She had grown used to the Irishman's dark-stained and ill-timed sense of humor.

Mona had fixed her stocking like Steve's and for the same reason: it might not be needed as a mask. She said, "About the cars. We could take out the rotor-arms."

In glancing at Kale, she was startled by the change in his appearance. The black nylon was down over his face. He looked evil and grotesque.

The bottom part of the stocking moved sinuously as he spoke. "If someone should come out here and find he couldn't start his car, we could be in trouble. Even if he didn't get suspicious, he'd be here, in the way."

Mona thought the risk of a chase was greater; but, not caring, she held back from saying so.

Extra nodded. He had recovered from the assault on his sensibilities. He was young. "Yes, you're right, Kale," he said. "I hadn't seen it that way." He pulled his mask into position over his face.

Mona looked away from the two men who were now darkly covered from head to toe. She hoped she wouldn't have to use her own mask. She would hate her appearance to match the way she felt.

"Okay," Kale said. "That's it. You know the rest of it, Smith."

"I do. Backwards."

"And, Steve, you keep your motor running."

"Sure and I will."

"So long."

He and Extra moved away. They passed through the door and drew it closed behind them. Steve went to the Jaguar and got in. Mona heard him starting the engine as she walked to the Ford.

She got behind the wheel. Glancing at herself in the rearview mirror, she thought that, from a reasonable distance, the stocking looked like an ordinary beret.

She started the car and moved on. Going onto the ramp that led to the street, she glanced again in the mirror, looking behind her. Vapor was floating lazily from the waiting Jaguar's exhaust.

Cold and calm, Mona changed gear and put on speed. She headed for the place where she would run interference.

Edgar Carlton was no longer relaxed.

The limousine moved grandly along a broad thoroughfare. The stores, though closed, were all gaily lit, as were theaters, hotels and clubs. There were many strollers. It was a cheerful scene.

Edgar was too tense to be cheered. Although not much of a drinker, he wished he had a double brandy. He was wound up tight. Everything had gone so smoothly that he felt the next step just had to be a stumble. It was a law of averages in which he suddenly believed. His previous confidence was faint. It had slackened in proportion to the distance left to cover before reaching Wainford Hall.

In a corner of the rear seat, Edgar again had his features in their natural form. He held a hand in front of his face, fingers to brow, in case the Whitecoat should unexpectedly turn around. Edgar wanted to give his muscles a final, long rest before the work ahead.

With more ache than tingle, more nausea than pleasure, that familiar trill chased up his body. It had been caused by him seeing an increase in the brightness on the road ahead.

"There we are, sir," the Whitecoat said.

Assuming the Vale face, Edgar sat up straight. In the Vale voice he said, "Rather an impressive place. I do hope, ah, that we have a full house."

"You always do, sir. Always." The young man spoke with casual pride, as if he had invented Harold Devon Vale in his spare time.

The driver cleared his throat, turned his head. "Excuse me. Are we going the back way or the front?"

Edgar didn't know the answer to that one. Luckily, the Whitecoat did. He said, "Front, mate. Mr. Maxted told me as there was no trouble expected."

"Trouble?" Edgar asked. Then he realized that he would be supposed to know what was meant. He added, "No, of course there won't be trouble. Not tonight."

The car was slowing. They were getting near to the start of a long, long marquee that blazed with light. Hundreds of people were stretched out beneath it and bunched at the center, with equally as many lined up on the opposite side of the street.

In evidence were dozens of uniformed policemen. They mingled with the noisy crowd and patrolled the curbs to keep the roadway clear. There were two officers on horseback. They stood impressively one at either end of a people-free space by the entrance.

Into that space glided the limousine. At once the noise of the crowd swelled. It was as if the volume knob on a radio had been twirled. Edgar took deep, settling breaths.

The car stopped. The Whitecoat, who had opened his door in readiness, jumped out smartly. Other young men dressed like him bustled forward, the crowd surging at their backs. A police constable, skilled in these maneuvers, reached the car's back door first and drew it open.

Loudly, Edgar said, "Thank you, driver."

"Welcome, sir. Good night."

Edgar got out and straightened. He next thanked the policeman, who saluted, an act which was required of him in dealing with a Member of Parliament. His face was curiously expressionless.

The crowd was loud and active. People waved, called out, clapped. There were pro-Vale banners. Flashbulbs popped like baby lightning. Whitecoats and constables were pushing people back.

Edgar was unnerved. He became more so when a struggle broke out near the rear of the car. From the scuffle a hoarse voice shouted, "Bloody shit!"

Hands took hold of Edgar's arms and he was propelled forward. He went through an alley of people. Most were smiling and applauding. One woman tossed a flower.

The next moment he was in the comparative peace of a lobby. He began to calm. However, he thought it odd that, though the center of attention, he should be standing alone there while the encircling, hundred-strong crowd made no move to come forward.

Most of those present wore identity labels on their lapels. Many had small banners. All, without exception, were smiling.

A man moved briskly out of the crowd. On recognizing Clifford Maxted, Edgar tensed. He wished it weren't so bright here. He wished, fleetingly, that he had never started on this insane scheme.

Maxted was tall, strongly-made and in the early fifties. The baldness that he hid with a cap whenever possible was compensated for by a goatee. The beard suited his long, curved, inquisition nose and dark eyes. He was impeccably dressed.

His walk as he came forward had a swagger. It suggested smugness, as if he were aware of being envied by the crowd.

Edgar had his right hand semi-raised. He didn't know if a shake was the usual thing. Also, he realized as Maxted stopped in front of him, he didn't know how he was supposed to address the other man.

Clifford Maxted put his hands behind his back. He smiled, showing his bottom teeth. "Good evening, Harold."

"Ah, good evening, good evening," Edgar said.

Continuing to raise his hand, he patted his tie. "You're looking in the pink."

Maxted twisted his smile. "I am? This morning you told me I needed more exercise."

All Edgar could think of was to give the Vale laugh. While doing so he swept his eyes around. Everyone was still watching. A yard to his rear stood two Whitecoats. Behind them was the constable who had opened the car door.

Looking back at Harold Vale's second-in-command, Edgar said, "Well, obviously, you've done quite a bit of running around since this morning." He laughed again.

Then he noticed a change in Maxted. The man had stopped showing his teeth and had eased back. His eyes roved over Edgar's face, moved down.

He nodded, asking, "When did you buy the new blazer?"

"Ah," Edgar said slowly. "New blazer?"

"Yes. That can't be your old one, surely."

"Why can't it?" Edgar said, stating nothing.

"It's clean, Harold. Neat as a pin." He raised his eyes again.

Edgar poured discipline into his facial muscles. Recalling the lint, he said, "Dear Mrs. Neal insisted on giving it a brush. She likes to mother me."

Maxted shrugged. He looked at his watch. "We have a few minutes left. Any questions?"

"Not a one."

"Speech all right?"

Edgar gave one of the politician's catch-phrases: "As right as it will ever be in this vale of cheers."

Maxted edged closer. "Tell me, Harold," he said

in a low tone. "Have you thought over that matter we discussed this morning?"

"Really, you know, what with working on my speech, I haven't had a thought to spare."

"The money would be extremely useful. We have to consider that. Take Capetown alone." The bearded man went on talking. Edgar gathered that the matter was a proposed lecture tour of South Africa.

He asked, padding time, "How many appearances would it be altogether?"

"Between eight and twelve," Maxted said. "It's not been finalized yet." He looked at his watch. "I'll shift now and let the fans have their turn. Smile pretty, Harold." He moved away.

This, Edgar understood at last, was the ritual. First Clifford Maxted did the greeting, then Vale's chief supporters paid their respects. Now the crowd swarmed forward.

Surrounded, Edgar became busy shaking hands, chatting, closing his eyes briefly by way of thanks to praise, nodding at the oft-repeated encouragement to give 'em hell tonight.

Twice Edgar created the opportunity for relaxing his features, this while bending to pick up a handkerchief he had dropped. Once he gave an autograph—"For my little girl, Mr. Vale, who adores you"—and, since he hadn't the vaguest idea what the politician's signature looked like, he hoped the scrawl wouldn't be examined until later.

Press photographers appeared to angle and flash whenever Edgar greeted a celebrity. These were not only political. There was a recently knighted actor, an Australian opera singer, three world-class football players, the country's most popular television comedy team, and a retired general whose pro-war novel was the best seller of the year.

Edgar got a jolt on coming face-to-face with one man, a politico whom he had often impersonated in his act. Seeing him was weird. Edgar had the feeling that he was playing two parts at the same time.

But on the whole he was managing well, he told himself. And if some of the people seemed to look at him a little too searchingly—that was probably imagination. Even so, he had a continual ache in his stomach.

Edgar was still shaking hands when Maxted returned, his bottom teeth on show to those who had not yet had a turn at greeting. The bearded man took Edgar's arm and steered him aside.

"Surprise for you, Harold," he said.

"What's that?"

"Someone's here to see you. She's in the bar. We have enough time, if you keep it short."

"Who is it?"

Maxted said, "Your sister."

Edgar nodded slowly, resettled his glasses, pocketed his hands with thumbs outside. All this gave him time to think, which made him draw the hidden fingers into fists.

Meeting Vale's sister was out, he mused. It had to be avoided. He felt he couldn't survive a test that strong. He wasn't even sure he had survived the one with Maxted.

"Come on, Harold. It's this way."

Edgar resisted the pull on his arm. "My sister, did you say?"

"That's right. She drove in from Surrey to surprise you. Or is it Sussex?"

"Listen," Edgar said. "Wait. Hold on."

"Mm?"

"Let me tell you about my sister."

Teeth no longer showing, Maxted frowned. "What d'you mean?"

"I must have mentioned this before to you. Yes, I'm sure I have."

"No. What?"

"My sister," Edgar said. "She makes me nervous."

Maxted put his head on one side. "You look nervous already."

"You see? That's the effect she has on me. So I certainly do not, repeat not, wish to see her immediately before an important speech."

Maxted's frown faded, leaving his face void of expression. He said nothing.

Edgar turned away. 'Excuse me. I must finish saying hello to these people."

A woman whose eyes were sincere to the point of desperation, she held beside her face a box of soap powder, stroked it and crooned its miracle properties.

Harold Devon Vale sighed. Being a prisoner was bad enough, he thought, but being one who was forced to watch the inanities of television, that was too much. It was a form of modern torture.

Since he had been left alone, some twenty minutes ago, Harold Vale had made no attempt to free himself. He felt it wasn't worth risking damage to his wrists; he might even cut off the supply of blood to his hands. He had sat in a slump, staring moodily at the TV set.

Vale was no longer afraid. He was despondent. He knew the mimic meant him no harm and that when he returned this confinement would be over. But the evening was ruined, the speech stillborn.

And the impersonation, Vale thought, that could have a disastrous effect. Whether or not it worked for Edgar Carlton was beside the point. It could put the original—the mimic's model—in a foolish light. There was nothing more destructive than laughter.

Vale slumped still further at the idea of what a field day his enemies would have if Carlton got as far as the podium. And there was every chance of him doing so. Seeing him come into the living room in his disguise had been like walking toward a mirror.

Vale sighed again, shuffled. He was not as yet uncomfortable on the chair, but he was beginning to feel hot inside his bulletproof vest.

Cartoon germs had taken over the TV screen. They were being chased around a kitchen by a can of antiseptic spray. They were cornered. They fought. They lost.

Harold Vale sneered. He gave his body a convulsive, peevish jerk. By doing so he shifted the front of the chair sideways. He was about to make another move, turn himself out of sight of the television set, when the screen cut to an announcer. He said, "And now for our live transmission of tonight's speech by the Honorable Member for Caston North, Mr. Harold Devon Vale. Over to our political commentator, Arthur Price, who is waiting for us at Wainford Hall."

The screen flicked. On came the interior of an auditorium. The camera ranged over the packed seats while the voice of Price welcomed viewers with smooth patter.

"That bastard," Vale muttered. "It would have to be him." He pouted as he thought of all the twists the commentator would give to the impersonation.

The camera zoomed slowly to a podium, where sat half a dozen people. They were each named by Arthur Price, who added, "And Lady Wardwell will make the formal introduction, in—let me see—in about two and a half minutes from now. Mr. Vale has arrived, I know, so there should be no delay."

Onscreen came Price, sideview. He was looking at a monitor. The way he turned to face the camera had a casualness so professional that it seemed as if he were forgiving the viewers for being in the wrong place.

"Turd," Harold Vale said, with loathing and respect.

"I believe," Arthur Price said, "that there was a slight incident outside, minutes ago, when Mr. Vale got out of his car. Nothing too outrageous. A man tried to get close to the M.P. in order to hand him a letter of protest. He was beaten back by some of Mr. Vale's—er—assistants, and after being questioned by police was taken to a doctor."

Harold Vale smiled. "Hope the radical, wog-loving sod caught it nicely."

Arthur Price glanced aside. In a brisker tone he said, "It's almost time. I see Lady Wardwell is collecting her notes. Let's take the camera to . . . ."

Bottom lip lowered to expose his teeth, Maxted was easing his way though the people in the center of the Wainford Hall lobby. "Excuse me. Thank you. Sorry to have to break it up. Pardon me."

He reached Edgar and announced to those around him, "Sorry, friends. I have to take Mr. Vale away. You know how it is."

The actor who had just shaken hands with Edgar said, "Time and telly wait for no man." The crowd laughed.

Edgar agitated his shoulders in the Vale chuckle. It was not all pretend. He was feeling nervously relieved. Much of his confidence had come back. He was fairly certain he had fooled Maxted, had definitely fooled the chief supporters, and had neatly gotten out of having to face the sister.

Edgar had thought later that she might not exist. It could have been a trap set by a suspicious Maxted. But from comments by one of the supporters, Edgar had learned that Vale's sister was indeed having a drink in the bar.

Cementing his role by showing a touch of the politician's vaunted wit, Edgar winked at the actor and quipped, "If I said that about time, *Newsweek* would abuse me roundly."

The laughter that followed was out of proportion, too lavish a payment for what had been received. Even the upstaged actor managed a snicker.

Clifford Maxted neither laughed nor smiled as he turned away.

An arm raised in farewell, Edgar followed on through the sycophantic beams and went toward a doorway. It was in a corner of the lobby.

Waiting there were the two Whitecoats and the police constable. They tailed behind when Edgar and Maxted passed through. No one else followed.

Ahead stretched a passage, broad and long, lighted starkly by naked bulbs. There were doors at one side, a flight of stairs at the far end.

As if continuing a conversation, Maxted said, "Abuse you? *Newsweek?* You must be kidding, Harold."

Edgar asked warily, "Which means?"

"They couldn't abuse you much more than they have already. That recent essay they did on you, for instance. What was the author's name?"

The footfalls of the five men clattered and echoed in the corridor. It sounded like derisive applause. It reminded Edgar that there were still hurdles to go, that he shouldn't let his returning confidence lull him into carelessness.

He said, "I refuse, ah, to remember the names of my enemies."

"Enemy is right. The only hot air in a chill British summer, that was one of his gems. The mildest."

"Charming."

"Then he went back on that by saying you were as innocuous as leprosy."

Edgar looked at his companion while going through the pretence of adjusting his spectacles. Maxted wore his odd smile. He appeared to be enjoying himself, as if proud to be associated with a man who had received such strong attention.

Or perhaps, Edgar thought, Vale's second-in-command was joking. Surely that kind of abuse was too violent to be thrown at a prominent political figure.

"Powerful stuff," Edgar murmured.

Clifford Maxted nodded happily like an epicene masochist in a chain store. "And his last line was a real stinker. 'They ask is he sinner or saint, but I ask if he sick or Satan?' "

Edgar said an involuntary, "Good Christ!" It made him stop walking. He had been startled into speaking in his own voice.

Maxted went on two strides before coming to a halt and turning. The three other men bunched up behind. Maxted's face was smooth and expressionless, as had happened earlier.

He asked, "You'd forgotten?"

Edgar coughed into his hand, assumed the Vale tones. "No, just hoping I had. Let us change the subject."

"Of course, Harold."

Edgar stepped forward, the group moved on. He asked, "How much further?" And he knew at once that he could have made a mistake; Vale might have been here before. He added, "I always get confused in these places."

"At the top of those steps," Clifford Maxted said, pointing. "We should be in perfect time for the end of Lady Whorewell's introduction."

"Lady . . . ?"

"Wardwell. Sorry, the other name's yours. I shouldn't poach."

Edgar laughed. "It is not, I agree, polite to steal."

Abruptly, the bearded man asked, "How's the cat?"

Edgar became wary. It was partly the casual lilt in Maxted's voice, partly because as far as he knew Harold Vale had no cat. This had the smell of a trap about it.

But Edgar could think of no way to answer. He kept walking. He could feel Maxted giving him a searching look finally saying, "The cat, Harold. I asked about the cat."

Again Edgar brought the group to a stop. He turned to face Vale's second-in-command. "Look here," he said. "You keep chattering on about this and that, and all the time I'm waiting for you to say something."

The bearded man appeared to be startled. "Eh? What's that?"

Edgar put his hands on his hips. "Don't tell me you haven't noticed. You're usually quite observant."

"I—I don't understand."

Edgar took two steps backward, as if to set himself on view. "For God's sake, man, don't I look any different?" He pretended to sound irked.

Maxted nodded, his bald head catching the light. He was eager, on the defensive—and sounded relieved. "Yes, Harold, you do, you certainly do. I noticed it tonight as soon as you came in."

"And?"

Maxted floundered. "Well, I can't put my finger on it exactly, Harold. You just look, well, different, that's all."

"A little younger, would you say?"

More eager nods. "Yes, you do. That's it. Younger, fresher. You look fine, Harold, fine."

"A little plumper in the face?"

"That too, yes."

Edgar smiled, both as part of the act and because he knew he had won conviction. He said, "Good. It's a special treatment I've been having. Had another session today. I'll tell you all about it later."

"It's done wonders, Harold. Honestly. And I did notice."

"Come on," Edgar said. Stepping forward he tapped Maxted's shoulder. They began to walk again.

The stone staircase was close. Edgar felt like running up to it, and onto the podium. There could be no more danger. In ten minutes, the whole caper would be over.

They reached the foot of the stairs. "About your sister," Maxted began as they started up. He didn't finish. He, like Edgar, like the three men following, came to a fast, surprised halt when the voice rang out.

It boomed, "Hold it!"

The sound was still chasing along the corridor when a man appeared beside the stairs. He was covered entirely in dark clothes. The head covering was a stocking mask.

He held a gun.

Maxted again left a sentence unfinished. He produced a limp, "If this is a game—"

Edgar was stunned. He thought not of a game but a dream. As he stared at the gun he told himself this was all fantasy. He would wake up in a minute, after one of his dressing room naps, and find that he had dreamt the whole scheme of impersonating Harold Vale.

To make things more absurd, another man appeared. Except for build, he was a darkly-clad replica of the other, who now ordered, "Put your hands at the back of your neck. Everybody."

No one moved.

"Now!" the man snarled.

With a rush, Edgar and the others obeyed, shooting up their arms in unison. Edgar still didn't believe that any of this was actually happening.

The police constable said, his voice surprisingly steady, "Careful with those guns."

The taller of the masked pair, the obvious leader, grated, "Shut your trap, sonny. I'll do the talking." The bottom of the black stocking moved strangely when he spoke.

His accent had automatically been placed by Edgar despite his stunned condition. It was basically lowlands Scottish with overtones acquired in a Spanish-speaking country, though not Mexico.

"Yeah, we'll do the talking," the smaller man said.

Looking at him, Edgar began to accept that he wasn't dreaming. Unlike his calm, firm partner, the man was darting his head about, nosing the automatic from side to side, shuffling his feet. He was real, in a state of high stimulation—very dangerous.

Maxted mumbled, "Look. Listen a minute. Let's talk about this."

"Shut up," the leader said, moving forward. "Back down, off the steps. All of you."

His partner snapped, "And no funny business."

Edgar, arms up, moved backwards down the stairs. He had no thoughts to spare in regret for the glory he had been on the verge of winning. He was too full of fear.

Now believing the truth of this situation, he couldn't take his eyes off the nearest gun. He was able to fleetingly sympathize with Harold Vale's reaction to the armed intruder. Facing a weapon that could deliver instant death was a terrifying experience.

In a fluttery voice, Maxted asked the constable, "Why don't you do something?"

The policeman asked evenly, "Why don't you?"

"Keep those hands in place," the leader said. "And keep moving slowly backwards. All except Vale."

Edgar, off the steps, continued walking in reverse, even when the order was repeated, "All except Vale."

The smaller man came to him swiftly, grabbed his lapel and jerked him to a stop. "Are you fucking deaf?"

Edgar said a stupid, shaky, "No."

He drew in his breath as the man's gun came up and rested at the side of his neck. The shudder that ran through him was not from the coldness of the metal.

"Then do as you're told, Vale."

The leader was saying, "That's it, you others. Keep on going."

From behind him Edgar could hear the shuffling feet of Maxted and the escort. That his features were no longer pulled into a resemblance of Harold Devon Vale was of no interest to him; he was not fully aware of the fact.

The smaller man, still holding the lapel, said, "This way, you. Nice and easy. You can put your arms down."

His superior said, "No, he can't. Not yet."

Edgar kept his hands clasped at the nape of his neck. He would have made them scratch each other had he been so ordered. The gun was nuzzling his throat. Meekly he allowed himself to be drawn along toward the closest exit.

The leader said, "You four are doing fine. Be good and you'll live. Go on moving back."

Maxted asked, faintly, "But what's it all about?"

"We're taking the Honorable Vale for a little drive. Show him the sights."

"I don't know what you mean."

"That's what I call real sad," the leader said. "Now belt up and listen. We'll be leaving you in a couple of seconds. I want you to know that the first one to come after us gets a bullet in the belly."

Reversing, the smaller man came to the doors, which he opened with a push on the handle. He drew Edgar outside by the lapel. There was a smell of exhaust fumes in a bright parking area.

Shifting so that they were side by side, and moving the gun from neck to spine, the man said, "That way, Vale boy. And play it cool or I'll blast you."

Edgar was taken to a large grey car. Its rear door stood open. Obeying the gun's urging, he got in. There was a man at the wheel who didn't look around. He wore a skullcap.

The smaller man said, "Down, Vale. Let go your neck and crouch on the floor. Easy does it."

Edgar squeezed between front and back seats on his hands and knees. He sank as low as he could get, resting his sweaty brow on the carpet. By sound and pressure he knew that his captor had climbed onto the rear seat.

Before closing the door, the man called out, "Let's go!"

There was a thud from the building, running footsteps, the front passenger door opening and closing, the leader's voice saying an urgent, "Move!"

The car lurched away with a squeal of rubber.

It was a street of row houses. Each had an identical wedge of squashed features, ugly as drought, and old as the Industrial Revoltuion. No window had light. The homes had long since been turned into offices. The street lighting was meager, token.

On one side, at the midway point, the row was broken by a space. Some ten feet wide, it was the mouth of a lane that ran rigidly straight for five hundred yards, ending where it opened onto a main traffic artery. The mouth had a sign saying No Entry—One Way Street.

Twenty feet from there, across the way, stood the aging Ford. It was the only car in sight. At the wheel, holding it tightly, sat Mona.

She was pleased to be surrounded by closed offices, in this place that was traffic-busy only in business hours. Residents would have found her lone, waiting presence odd and memorable.

But then, Mona thought, that was one reason why this spot had been chosen. The other, that was because of the useful situation of the one-way lane. It saved the local wise a roundabout trip of over a mile.

Mona released the steering wheel, clenched her fists. Her body was stiff with the tension of waiting. She felt cramped all over, even though she had gotten out of the car a dozen times since parking here.

The uncertainty was another factor that was holding her emotions in a knot. If only she knew for sure that the others were on their way, the prize caught.

There was a third nagging problem—though Mona kept telling herself it was nothing of the kind, due probably to imagination and nerves. Even so, it was the reason for those dozen exits from the car.

The nagging feeling came again. She tried to ignore it, failed, hissed with impatience and opened the door. Out on the roadway she stared at the front tire.

Well yes, she thought, it did look a bit lower than the last time, a bit more bulbous at the bottom. There could be a slow leak. But even if there was, it wouldn't matter if the Jaguar came soon.

Which took Mona back to the worry of whether or not the others were on their way. She got back in the car—and suddenly noticed a dashboard radio. Her gloved hands flew to it.

After half a minute of twirling knobs and pressing buttons, she realized with disgust that the radio was broken.

A planning mistake had been made in that area, Mona thought. She should have been equiped with a transistor. The news of the abduction would have been given as a flash within minutes of the event. She could have worked out arrival time from that.

What if they'd been caught? What if the Jag had been in an accident? What if that front tire went down?

Mona couldn't sit in suspenseful inaction any longer. Snapping the ignition key on, she started the motor. She drove forward a few yards and stopped opposite the lane's mouth. In the distance she could see cars passing on the artery.

But suspense had merely been shifted from a near corner to a far one. Also she was in the way here. Mona reversed to the original position, and ignored a pull to one side in the steering.

She switched off, got out, began to pace. Repeatedly she touched the gun at her waist. She was successful in her decision not to look at the suspect tire.

Mona hadn't meant to stride as far as the lane, but she did, drawn like a bystander to an accident that might be unbearable to see. As soon as she reached the corner, the far end burst into light as a car came into view. Mona's heart jerked. It jerked again when she saw that the car was not a Jaguar.

Running, she went to the Ford and stayed behind it until the other car had come out of the lane and gone on its way.

She went to the front. She looked directly at the tire. She was shocked to see how far the bottom fatness had increased. No longer could she blame it on nerves or imagination. The tire was going down, and rapidly.

Though there was nothing to be done, Mona squatted. From this position she could hear a faint hissing. She licked her finger, put saliva on the tire's valve. That was the fault. The saliva bubbled.

Thinking there might, after all, be something to be done, Mona stood up and looked around, while absently patting her pockets. If she could find something to block the valve. . . .

There sounded a distant horn-blast. It had the right tinny sound, that distinctive and curiously frail tone that was so odd in a large, expensive car.

Mona ran to the corner. Headlights were coming up the lane at speed. The lights dipped. Mona saw that the car was a Jaguar and that its color was grey. Next, she recognized the driver. It was Steve.

Mona raced back to the Ford. She slammed inside and pressed the starter. It whined. The motor failed to catch. The starter went on with its lonely whining.

Mona gasped. She pressed the button viciously, her body jerking back and forth in fast, pleading swoops. She bared her teeth.

The horn-blast came again from the lane.

The Ford's starter whined, coughed, whined. Then the motor caught. Mona revved like a pilot at takeoff. The noise made her blink. She saw but didn't hear the Jaguar as it burst into view. It rolled into a turn, heading the other way. It began to slow.

Mona sent the Ford forward. Fleetingly it occurred to her that if there was a pursuit car right here and now, she would be hit.

Almost at the lane, Mona braked and swung the steering wheel. The car went into a sharp swerve. It turned. It was nearly in the reverse position when it crashed to a stop against one side of the lane's mouth. The other side was three feet away.

Mona looked back as she jumped out. There was no vehicle giving chase. But there could be one seconds away. She ran for the Jaguar, which was stopping fifty yards off. Mona had covered ten of those yards before remembering the key. She swung around and hurried back, got the ignition key and threw it from her as she turned.

The Jaguar was waiting, a rear door open. In the front were Steve and Kale. The latter had taken off his hood, as had Extra, in the back. But where was Vale?

Running, Mona reached the car. She halted—and her spirits soared. Beneath her, crouched on the floor, was a man with a bald spot on the back of his head.

Twisting around in his seat, Kale said, "Yes, Smith, that's our boy."

Steve snapped, "Get in, get in!"

Kale, manner lazy, told him, "Keep your shirt on.

There's no one hot behind us."

"We don't know that for sure."

"We'll be home and dry before the alarm gets full circulation."

Steve said, "Get *in,* Smith, for the love of Jasus."

Mona climbed onto the seat and slammed the door, and then was thrown back as the car hurtled away. Recovered, she knelt and turned her back to Extra, who asked, "Any problems? Anyone see you?"

Mona was looking down at the balding man. She couldn't trust herself to speak. She shook her head. She felt like crying.

"With us it was a piece of candy," Extra said, his tone breathless and excited. "They didn't even see the car. And we really made 'em crawl."

"Shut up," Steve said tersely. "You've done nothing but gab ever since we left."

"So what? We did a clean job, man. Right, Kale?"

"Sure."

Extra said, "Smith, you can take the stocking off. Kale says we don't need 'em anymore. Steve don't agree." He sounded amused by the last statement.

The Irishman glanced around. "Bloody right. Vale could finger us afterwards. I'm going to pull mine down as soon as we get there." He swung the car into a fast corner.

Kale said, "Please yourself."

Mona didn't care. Languidly she pulled off the stocking cap and stuffed it into a pocket of her jeans. She was still looking down at the lowered head. For the first time in months, she was happy.

Slowly, gently, Mona placed her hand on the prisoner's shoulder. She closed her eyes.

Harold Devon Vale stared at the television set. He was completely taken out of himself, as fascinated as a child at the monkey house. He had been this way for some time, starting from the moment the commentator had interrupted himself to say a sharp, "Hold on. Something's happened."

Since then there had been confusion and uncertainty, with the camera flitting to and fro fretfully between Arthur Price and various parts of the auditorium.

On the podium there had been urgent consultations. People had run on and off. A crowd clustered there and called up for information. A slow hand-clap had died for want of support. At one stage, a section of the audience had begun to rush the nearest exit following a rumor of fire.

Now the camera was panning across the crowd. Everyone was standing, some on seats. The podium had only three people, one a man waiting nervously by the lecturn. Arthur Price, voice over, was saying, "Still nothing definite, ladies and gentlemen. I keep getting contradictory reports as to what's been going on behind the scenes here. The aisles are blocked. It's almost impossible to get in or out. People are ignoring the request to sit and be calm. Er, what's that?"

The camera flipped back to the commentator. He was listening to a man who was whispering in his ear, listening while holding a forefinger toward the camera as if commanding it not to move.

Harold Vale stared on. He didn't even blink. His eyes, without the protection of tinted glass, were growing sore from the television glare, but he didn't notice.

On screen, the whispering messenger straightened and left. Arthur Price faced the camera. He said, "It may be just another rumor. I don't know. Anyway, here it is. Mr. Harold D. Vale, who was to have addressed the meeting here at Wainford Hall, is said to have been wounded in an attempt at assassination."

Vale's mouth sagged open. He was staggered. What he had been expecting to hear was that Edgar Carlton had been arrested, his impersonation a failure. That forgotten now, there was a bubble of emotion under Vale's astonishment, but he didn't know whether it was pleasure or terror.

"Another version of the story," Price said, "is that the Member of Parliament has actually been killed. Nothing, however, is anywhere near sure. Oh, I see that Lady Wardwell is coming back to the podium."

The screen blanked. Vale tensed. Next he groaned as a film of children dancing around a giant candy bar and chanting its name repeatedly came on. "Idiots," the politician growled. "Bloody morons."

The commercial finished. Another started, but snapped off after two seconds. The screen was filled with a long-shot of Wainford Hall's interior, where a woman on the podium was waving for silence and tapping the microphone.

Arthur Price said, "One doubts if her ladyship will get fast order from this crowd, or any order at all. There's a semi-panic going on here. There's a mood of ugliness, of violence."

Above the noise of the crowd, Harold Vale could hear a voice droning unintelligibly through loudspeakers. He clenched his tied hands with impatience and leaned forward in the chair.

"That stupid Whorewell," he said. "If she were only poor, I could tell her to piss off."

The screen switched to a close-shot of Arthur Price. He was reading a piece of paper and had one finger raised. Looking up with an expression of importance, he said, "Ladies and gentlemen, here is a police statement, no doubt the same one that Lady Wardwell is trying to give to the audience. Here it is."

Price nodded gravely. "Harold Devon Vale, M.P., has been taken prisoner, abducted."

Vale went back to the mouth sag.

"The Member of Parliament," Price said, "was separated from his escort by two armed and hooded men. They drove away from the rear of the building in a grey car, believed to be a Daimler or a Jaguar. It was seen leaving by a security guard on the roof.

"That is official, ladies and gentlemen. Harold D. Vale has been kidnaped. Police ask the public to be on the lookout for a grey. . . ."

Harold Vale smiled. He chuckled, shoulders shaking. He began to laugh. He strained forward from his bound wrists, head nodding, and let the laugh grow. He laughed until the tears ran thickly from his reddened eyes. He choked and whooped and yipped.

The laughter was beginning to run out, sigh off, when in a spate of his own silence Vale heard from the television, ". . . repeat, Harold Devon Vale has been abducted by two armed . . ." and he swept back into fierce laughing. It was not without a measure of hysteria.

At length Vale calmed. He sat weakly, smiling at the screen. The live telecast from Wainford Hall had ended. Showing now was a situation comedy.

That sweet old bitch Fate, Vale thought, shaking his head in amused appreciation. Fate had never played a better trick. She lets that Carlton fool get along just so far with his game, and then turns the tables on him beautifully. Now he was in the hands of a gang of terrorists or lunatics or whatever. An armed, dangerous gang. It was justice. It would serve the fool right if they killed him.

Vale spent some minutes wondering about the abductors, who they really were and what they aimed to do. He came up with no sound possibilities.

He went back to Edgar Carlton, amused anew at how shattered the mimic must be at this development. Next, Vale realized that the situation would have a short life, for surely the man's true identity would soon come out.

On that realization, all trace of amusement left Vale's face. He creaked up to a taut erectness on the chair. Rapidly he told himself that the gang would quickly get at the fact of their mistake, would learn that the one they wanted was alone and helpless, would come here and easily force their way in past a door which had been left unbolted and unchained, would have him at their mercy.

Vale began to struggle violently.

Edgar braced himself as the car cornered at speed. Twice already he had hit his head against the door when thrown forward. It was a fast, rough ride, and being unable to see the way, made it more unnerving. Edgar hoped it wouldn't get any worse.

As if in answer to that, a voice from the front said, "Go careful along this stretch. No sense in drawing attention to ourselves."

Edgar recognized the voice as belonging to the tall man, the leader. He was answered by the driver, the one who had complained about the unmasking: "For all we know, they could have the number by now. Let's get to where we're going."

Quietly: "Careful here, Steve. Careful."

The car slowed. Edgar relaxed his taut muscles and let his hands lie flat instead of digging his fingers into the pile of the carpet.

Since being first put into the Jaguar, Edgar had recovered much of his presence of mind. He was unharmed, for one thing, and had the impression that murder was not the gang's game. For another thing, he was no longer staring into the mouth of a gun. For a third, he had a safety card up his sleeve: he was the wrong man.

And, Edgar thought, maybe it would be best to let them know about that as soon as possible. If he left it too long, if he let them build up their hopes, they could turn vicious out of frustration.

Cautiously, Edgar raised his head. When it reached seat level he turned it to the side. He was startled. He found himself staring into the face of a girl.

Looking down, she returned his gaze steadily. The last gang member to get in the car, the one who had been addressed as Smith, she was dark and pretty and had short hair.

What kept Edgar staring, instead of revealing his identity, was the expression on her smooth face. Its only changes were external, caused by lights flashing by. Her features were perfectly still. It was a Mona Lisa face of quiet triumph, or satisfaction, or something else he was unable to fathom.

Edgar felt unsettled. He looked down again.

Before he could think about the girl, her presence here, the way she had looked at him, the silence in the car was broken abruptly by the driver.

He said, "A cop!"

"What?" the leader snapped.

"There's a copper."

"Where?"

"End of the street. Waving a flashlight."

The atmosphere in the Jaguar became tense. The leader said, "It's some kid."

"A cop, I tell you."

The smaller man in the back said, "Yeah, a pig. On foot."

The driver: "Hell and Christ."

"Run the bastard down."

From the girl called Smith came a jerked, "No!"

"All get down out of sight," the leader ordered. "Steve, get past him any way you like."

The car shot forward. Edgar braced himself. He felt the girl crouch partly on his shoulders. A hand, gloved, touched him, as had happened earlier. This time is rested on the back of his neck. In the touch there was a feel of possession.

The motor roared. The Jaguar swerved. There was an outside shout, a clatter as something hit the car, and then the three men were laughing.

The one in the back crowed, "You missed, Steve mate."

The driver said, "Stupid sod threw his nightstick. That's a great way to stop a car, so it is."

"Hope he lands heavy," the leader said. He laughed again. The sound was unpleasant.

The car held to its speed. As the girl eased up from him, Edgar decided not to delay any longer. He was frightened by the callous way the men had reacted to the policeman.

The two in the front were discussing whether or not the authorities had the Jaguar's number, or if it was merely that an order had gone out to stop all cars, which would mean roadblocks on the main arteries.

Edgar lifted his head. Not waiting for the talk to stop, he said, "Listen. I have something to tell you."

The man in the back leaned across and down. Edgar saw his face. It was babyish. He looked to be no more than twenty, which was even younger than the girl.

This increased Edgar's worry. He wondered if he

had been captured by a gang of reckless juvenile delinquents.

The man said, "Belt up, mate. Oh sorry, I *do* apologize. I mean the Honorable Mr. Vale."

"That's it," Edgar said. "That's what I want to tell you."

"Belt up. Shut your beer hole. When we want you to make a speech, we'll send you a formal request, engraved and everything."

"Please listen."

The driver said, "Sounds different in person, doesn't he? Sounds like a fucking Yank."

"If he doesn't behave, Extra," the other man in front said, "give him a tap on the head."

"Damn right I will."

Edgar looked at Smith. Her face was the same as before as she looked back at him. He had the feeling that he had been under her gaze without a break ever since she had gotten in the car.

He said, "You're making a mistake about me."

The boy named Extra thrust his gun down. "One more word, you. Just one more word."

Edgar lowered his head, giving up for the time being. He thought it better to wait until they could see his face clearly, and with the tinted glasses off. They would discover the error for themselves, see he wasn't Vale.

Which led Edgar to consider what would happen then—quite apart from how the gang would react. He realized that he would have to tell how he came to be at Wainford Hall in disguise, tell what he had planned, and where and how he had left the politician. He would be forced to tell. He didn't believe for a moment that he could stand up to pressure, torture.

Edgar thought about it with care as the car went on its way. He wasn't distracted by the men's talk, the bursts of hurtling speed between sedate stretches, nor by the sounds of other traffic.

Edgar came to the conclusion that he was morally obliged to protect Harold Vale; that, in fact, he would have to carry on with the impersonation—at least until someone went to the Bloomsbury apartment and found the politician. At the outside that meant waiting for the morning, till the maid went there at eight o'clock. News of the mistake would be broadcast.

It's the least I can do, Edgar thought. I put him in that helpless spot. And maybe he's already been found. And the gang's reaction, well, they couldn't say I didn't try to tell them.

For the next five minutes there was silence in the car, apart from the motor's growl of speed, the squeal of tires on bends, and the click of smooth gear-changes. Sounds of other traffic had ended. No longer were lights flashing by.

The leader said, "Good. That's that."

Oddly, although there was a downward trend in his voice, as if he were disappointed, there was a palpable easing of the tension in the atmosphere.

Extra said brightly, "Yeah, if they were putting up roadblocks, they were too late. We're in the clear."

Steve, the man with the vaudeville Irish accent, said, "That's what comes of having a brilliant driver, me boyos."

The other two men jeered. There was light banter back and forth. Edgar found assurance in the fact that the voices of the pair in front sounded older, more mature. He also recalled that the girl—who took no part in the joking—had made a quick protest when it looked as though the policeman would be run down.

"There it is, Steve," Extra said. "The For Sale sign."

"Sure and it is. You got eyes like a hawk. We're home."

"Great. I need a big fat drink."

In his quiet, firm way the leader said, "Small and thin."

That was another bit of comfort for Edgar, though the younger man grumbled, "Aw, come on, Kale."

"This isn't a picnic."

"No, I know. But we've pulled it off, this caper. Matter of fact we should've had a bottle of champers waiting."

"We'll celebrate when it's really over," Steve said. "The caper's young, still at the nipple."

"I know, I know. I was only—"

"See to that gate," the leader ordered.

"Sure, Kale. Yes."

The car was slowing. When it came to a halt, the back door opened and Edgar heard the younger man getting out and walking forward.

"That there sign," the driver said. "I think we should take it down."

"Why?"

"Someone passing might take a notion to come in

103

and have a look at the farm."

Kale said, "No one has in months, so I've been told. The place has been on the market two years."

"Even so. It could happen."

"What's more likely, if we took down the sign, is that someone might think that funny and decide to investigate."

Steve said, "I guess you got something there, Kale."

"I have. Drive on. And anyway, we won't be here long enough for that to be a worry."

The car moved forward, stopped, moved on again when Extra had climbed in and slammed the door. He said, "Dark as a bastard out here."

"What you expect?" the driver snorted. "Piccadilly Circus?"

The Jaguar swayed and bucked over roughness. After a distance that Edgar guessed at about a thousand yards, the tires began a gentle thudding: cobblestones. The car came to a final stop, the motor died, the lights were switched off.

They all got out. Edgar was last, under Extra's guard. Looking around, he saw silhouetted against the night sky a long rooftop and trees. There was not a sound to be heard.

The Irishman had a flashlight and he led the way over to the house. Edgar was prodded forward by Extra. They stood outside while the others opened the door and went in.

"Don't try anything," the younger man droned.

Edgar said, "I shouldn't dream of it." He used the voice of Harold Devon Vale.

The open doorway and a widow showed a warm

glow. Candles, Edgar thought. He was urged forward by the gun. Entering the house, he saw a large living room. It was bare except for a saggy couch, an armchair and two wooden boxes. The candles were spaced along a mantelshelf.

"TV first," the leader said briskly. "We should be just right for the news."

Steve was already lifting a portable television set from behind the chair. He put it on one of the boxes, clicked a switch. His head, Edgar now noticed, was covered with a stocking mask. Like the others, he was darkly clothed.

Extra jabbed with the gun. "Over there, you." He gestured toward an inner door that was standing ajar.

"He can watch this," Kale said. "I'm sure he'll find it fascinating."

They all stood in a half circle, looking at the television. Its screen bloomed to black-and-white life with a film of an expanse of water. Floating in it were dead cattle, furniture and general flotsam. A voice was describing the devestation in India's latest flood.

Covertly, Edgar glanced aside at the leader of the gang. Kale was in his last twenties, blond, crew cut, hard of face. His present expression was one of light, almost bored amusement, as if he were watching a comedy show for children.

Edgar sensed that he himself was being stared at. He turned his head. The watcher was Smith. He looked at her. She stared on. After a moment Edgar gave his attention back to the screen.

It was showing the President of the United States. He stood among a crowd at a country barbeque, eating a piece of chicken with his hands. Everyone was smiling except the Secret Service men.

Edgar was thinking that such protection was not, as he had formerly believed, exaggerated, when a barked, "Stop that!" made his nerves jump.

The speaker was Kale. He was looking at Extra, who had one glove halfway off, and who asked a startled, "Eh?"

"*On*. All the gloves stay *on*."

The younger man's blush was apparent even in the poor light. He said, "Sure. I know. Of course. I wasn't taking 'em off, Kale. Straight. I only wanted to get a bit of air in, see. My hands're sweaty."

Shrugging, Kale turned away.

Strange that he should be careless about masks, Edgar mused, but particular about leaving fingerprints. The inconsistency was out of keeping with the appearance and style of the man.

"And now back to the domestic scene," an announcer said. "We end tonight's session with more on this evening's sensational news from Wainford Hall. Harold Devon Vale is undoubtedly the man of the moment, and for once it was none of his own doing."

"Brilliant deduction," Steve said.

Announcer: "First a word from Chief Inspector Raymond Atkinson, of New Scotland Yard, the man in charge of the Vale abduction."

The screen wiped to an outdoor shot, a close-up of a middle-aged man with a heavy face, pouch-hooded eyes and brindle hair. Disembodied hands held microphones under his chin. He said, as if disgrunted, "All I am prepared to say at the moment is this. Mr. Vale is believed to be unhurt. We expect to hear tonight or tomorrow from his abductors. There are two, possibly three, men involved. They used a grey Jaguar with, perhaps, the number ending in six, four, two."

Chief Inspector Atkinson paused to frown at the hands, which were jostling for position, and went on, "Mr. Vale and his kidnapers might be in the northeast part of Greater London. And they might not. Anyone who has, or comes across information, is asked to telephone his local police station rather than the Yard. That's all." He turned away from the pushing microphones.

Steve said, "That copper on the road, he got a bit of the number."

Extra laughed. "Fat lot of good it'll do 'em."

"That's why they have northeast in mind," Kale said. "Bit of luck for us. We headed west after that."

The television screen was showing a diagram of Wainford Hall. A hand appeared and began to draw chalk marks along a channel at one side.

"All right," Kale said, "Let's get him settled, our undoubted man of the moment."

As if to make up for his previous near-gaffe, Extra acted the swaggering tough guy to the edge of caricature as he herded the prisoner away.

Edgar was reminded of his own youthful impersonations of actor Jimmy Cagney. But he didn't find this laughable. He reflected that Extra could be the most dangerous of the four.

The back room was totally empty. It lacked even a

fireplace. The one window had been boarded up with planks; the nails, judged by the size of their heads, were at least six inches long.

Steve had followed with a lighted candle. This he set down on the bare boards in a corner. A stocky man, his movements gave away that he was no longer young.

He left and Extra said, "Turn around, lean on the wall, put your feet together."

Edgar obeyed. Looking down, he saw a pair of handcuffs snapped into place around his ankles. He was surprised when the youngster did nothing about his hands, when he simply left the room and closed the door.

Shuffling, Edgar turned. He leaned on the wall and slid down to a squat. His face was his own. While in the other room he had worn only a vague likeness to his model, and that intermittently. He looked around and sighed.

In a moment the fantasy of the situation wore off. Next, Edgar passed through despondency, then he began to feel restrainedly cheerful. He thought: The abduction of Harold Devon Vale was the hottest news of the week, maybe the month, perhaps the year. Certainly the attention drawn was fifty times greater than would have been given to his speech. The denouement, the unveiling of the captive as professional mimic Edgar Carlton, not Vale, would be done in the center of spotlights and fanfare and the crashing of cymbals. The scheme had to end in an undreamt-of triumph.

Edgar smiled dazedly.

Mona was trembling.

It was the emotional, aftermath reaction she had expected. It had come upon her as soon as Harold Vale had gone in the back room, out of her sight. Mona began steadying as she thought of the next step. She took deep breaths. Her trembling started to fade.

She looked around the farm living room, its door closed, the window curtained. Kale was switching channels on the television set. From a passage came rattling sounds and talk: Extra and Steve, in the kitchen, seeing to the refreshments that had been left here earlier.

Mona took the last of her deep breaths. Her trembling had stopped. She was reasonably calm as she told herself that now was the time. Her stomach muscles tight, she crossed the room and went to the closed interior door.

As she reached it, Kale asked, "Where you going, Smith?"

She turned to look at him. Her face performed with nonchalance. It was not an easy thing to do. She said, "To stand guard, of course."

Kale left the TV, came over. "Right now, our friend in there is too shaken to try anything. He's chicken anyway."

"That right?"

"Also, you have another job to do."

Tense, Mona asked, "What's that?"

His smile was superior. "You can't have forgotten the phone call, Smith."

"No. I thought it might be best to leave it till later."

"No time like the present, to coin a phrase. And the telly's just told us who is the right man to contact. Convenient, eh?"

Mona said, "It might save all of ten seconds."

Kale's smile curled away. His voice took on a different tone, his body a different stance. "Just make sure you get the message right, that's all."

Mona saw hope here. She asked, "Wouldn't it be safer if you did it yourself, Kale?"

"Why?"

"Then you wouldn't have to worry."

He shook his head. "All that's been settled. There'll be no changing of plans. You make the call."

She tried another tack. "Perhaps I should talk to Vale first. Get him to give me a word to pass on. You know, to prove that we've got him."

Exasperated, Kale said, "They know we've got him. Why're you stalling? Maybe the phone call's a big problem for you."

She shrugged. "No. I'll manage."

"Scared to go out alone in the dark?"

"Don't be sarcastic."

"Okay. Forget it. I suppose you've got enough change."

Mona tapped a pocket. "Plenty."

"Right. So listen."

Looking down at her sternly, like a teacher with a backward pupil, Kale went over what he wanted her to say at a slow pace. Mona nodded from time to time, even while thinking she had never heard anything so absurd in her life.

Finished, Kale, asked, "Got that quite straight, Smith?"

"I'll be word perfect."

"A reasonable demand, I think."

"Perfectly reasonable," she lied.

"One last thing," Kale said. He was casual again now and looking at her mouth in a way that seemed obscene.

"What is it?"

"Keep it short."

"I know," she said. "So they can't trace the call."

"That's only in the movies. Tracing's a long and complicated affair. They couldn't do it under half an hour. But then, females do tend to lose track of time on the blower. So careful, eh?"

Without another word or sign, Mona turned away. She went to the front door and outside, where she paused to hiss her way free of her rage at Kale. It was more from his interference than his offensiveness.

Patience, Mona thought.

She moved on. A flashlight would have helped, but she would rather have fallen, than go back in the house again. The car loomed up. She touched her way around to the back, lifted the lid and got out her jacket.

She put it on as she went back. At the side of the house she came to a motor-assisted bicycle. Steve had stolen it that morning, choosing the same make that Mona had rented recently in order to practice.

First she switched on the lamp. Pushing off, she

swung into the saddle and started pedaling. The feeble engine came to put-put life and took over the work.

Mona steered around to the rear of the house. There, she glanced toward the window that was boarded up on the outside as well as in. She told herself she would be back soon, that she had to play this necessary part.

Ahead was a field which had been allowed to lie fallow. Mona bumped her way across it, went through a gap in the hedge and continued on over two more uncultivated fields.

Beyond a locked gate, over which she had to lift the bicycle, there was a mud lane. She turned left. She went for only a hundred yards before stopping, alighting, and leaning her bike against the hedge. She left the motor running.

Mona brought the gun from under her belt. She held it under the headlight. There was, as she just realized, a safety catch on the side of the automatic. Half an inch long, as thick as a kitchen match, it lay pointing toward the embossed word On.

Mona moved it to Off, which took considerable pressure. She practiced moving the lever back and forth. It became easier. Satisfied, she returned the gun to its place and went on her way.

After a quarter mile, the lane joined a secondary road. Now there were lights in the distance. Mona headed for them and held her jacket hood in place with one hand.

The lights were from houses in a new development. Mona went through it and saw no one. There was no traffic. After another mile she came to a village—church, pub, cluster of cottages. The pub was closed, the homes were dark. The sole light came from a public call box on a corner of the village green.

Mona kept straight on. Not until the settlement was well behind did she turn and head back, with her engine now switched off. In silence she pedaled to the triangle of grass.

Dismounting, she leaned her bicycle against the red telephone booth and went in. It was difficult getting coins from her pocket with a gloved hand; but she managed. She lay them on the shelf. There was less trouble getting out the black stocking.

Mona doubted if anyone would be watching. Still, to be sure, she kept her head lowered and put the receiver inside the hood, and had the balled stocking hidden in her hand as she held it over the mouthpiece.

She fed the coin slot, dialed Whitehall one-two one-two, heard almost at once a male voice say, "New Scotland Yard. May I help you?"

"I want to speak with Chief Inspector Atkinson."

"Name and address, please."

"Look," Mona said in a gruff, masculine tone. "I want Atkinson. It's to do with the abduction of Vale. Now don't keep me waiting or I'll ring off."

"You have information on the case, sir?"

Mona said, "No, we have Vale."

After a pause came, "Oh."

"Now get me Atkinson."

There was another slight pause before the man said, "The Chief Inspector's very busy. You might be genuine, you might be another crank—the fiftieth so far tonight."

Mona asked, "Has it been broadcast yet how we got into Wainford Hall?"

"Not so far as I know."

"Right. Then I'll tell you. We had prepared a loose catch on the window in the storeroom of cleaning equipment. We forced it from outside and climbed in."

"Yes," the man said, "but I dare say a lot of people know about that by now. Isn't there something else?"

"There is," Mona said. "A word. We scratched it on the windowframe with the screwdriver—which, by the way, we left there."

"Right. The word, please."

"Kess. *K.E.S.S.*"

"Right again. What does it mean?"

"Look," Mona snapped. "Don't waste my time. Put me through to the boss at once or I disconnect."

There was a click, and a voice said, "Atkinson here."

Using the same male gruffness, Mona said, "Listen carefully and ask no questions. We have Harold Devon Vale. We will release him at twelve o'clock noon tomorrow if the following demands are met. Are you listening?"

"I am."

"One, we want one million pounds in used notes. Two, we want the release and safe conduct out of the country of the three Japanese jailed last month. Three, we want an assurance that the House of Commons will ask for a vote of censure against Harold Devon Vale. Four, we want the money delivered by the prime minister in person."

Chief Inspector Raymond Atkinson asked, "Is that all? Sure there isn't a little something you've left out, like us promising nicely to blow up the House of Lords?"

"Those are our four demands. Understand?"

"Not quite," the senior officer said. "I'd like to know what organization you represent."

"That's none of your business."

"You must have left that word on the windowframe for a reason. It must have significance."

"Only as identification," Mona said. "It's meaningless. And that brings us to the end of this chat."

"Wait," Atkinson said sharply. "I'd like you to go over those demands again."

"No need. You heard all right, and, if you've forgotten, just play back the tape you no doubt are making of this call."

"No tape. How many Japanese terrorists did you want released?"

"You heard," Mona said. "That's all. I'll call again tomorrow for your answer. If the demands are not met, I imagine you can figure out the consequences."

"No. Tell me."

"We destroy Harold Devon Vale. At noon tomorrow. Good night, Chief Inspector."

"Wait a minute—"

Mona chopped the receiver back in its cradle. While pocketing her stocking and the unused coins she shook her head for everything that had just been said.

Pushing back against the door she went outside.

She stood looking around. The night was clear. As before, the village was still and dark, silent and deserted. The black silhouettes of the cottages made Mona think of gravestones. She liked the analogy of a cemetery. It appealed to her. She held to it as she wheeled her bicycle quietly across the grass.

Edgar looked up as the door opened. He had been on the point of dozing off, lulled by happy thoughts of how this development was going to turn out.

The man called Steve came in. He was carrying a packet of sandwiches and a mug that gave off steam. He kicked the door closed behind him.

The Irishman's stocking-flattened features were made more grotesque by the low, waving candlelight. Edgar thought he had never seen anything more sinister. But he refused to be pulled down by that. He told himself it was probable that Steve's uncovered face would be open and friendly.

Edgar put his own features into a slight semblance of Vale's, the total being unnecessary in the dim light. His muscles, however, were at ease after their half-hour rest.

Edgar knew now that keeping up the impersonation was going to be fairly simple, since his captivity had to be of short duration—that eight A.M. arrival of the maid, if nothing happened before.

"Here's a spot of supper, honorable you."

"That's thoughtful. Thanks."

The Irishman came to where Edgar sat against the wall, manacled legs straight out in front. "Don't thank me, Vale. It wasn't my idea at all, at all."

"Thanks to the others, then."

"They're out of their minds."

Edgar took his supper. First he sipped from the mug. It held coffee that had a distant, metallic hint of thermos flask. After grateful gulps he opened the packet and asked, "Why are the others out of their minds?"

Steve had retreated and was leaning beside the door. He said, "You're bloody cheerful for a man in your position." There was grudging respect in his tone.

"I always, ah, try to make the best of things."

"That's smart."

"And my question?"

Steve nodded. "They're out of their minds because here they are handing out royal treatment to someone they hate."

Edgar tapped his chained feet together and glanced around the room. "Hardly royal, in my view. But is it true they hate me?"

"It is. I swear it on me mother's grave and me father's liver."

"Why's that?" He bit into a sandwich. It was beef. Discovering to his surprise that he was ravenous, he took huge bites.

"Don't ask stupid questions, there's a good dear man."

"Mmm?"

The Irishman folded his arms. "All the miseries you've caused in this country, and you have the nerve to ask why people hate you."

Edgar swallowed food. "I can't be as bad as that."

"Worse. Rotten to the core. A thoroughly polished shit. A genuine purveyor of fear. A real pro."

"And so, believing that, you all hate me."

Steve said, "Not me, lad."

"Oh, not you?"

"No, sir. Me, I love you."

Mouth full, Edgar slanted his head to express surprise and to ask the obvious question. He wondered if this man were what he jokingly claimed the others to be—not quite sane.

"Love you and envy you, Vale. You're one in a million. I'd give anything to have your hard professionalism, that cleverness in taking things slow and careful. Me, I've always been one to rush straight in, bang bang. It's green with envy I am."

Edgar finished his sandwich. "And love?"

"You're so gorgeously typical of the English," Steve said. "You keep my faith alive. At times I meet decent folk over here, and I think I might've been wrong all along. But then there's always the ones like you to straighten me out."

"I see."

"The English are scum that'll have to be exterminated. Yes, Vale, I love you. Many thanks."

Edgar, working his way through the second sandwich, was surprised to realize that the man seemed to be speaking the truth. At least, no air of menace or animosity was coming from him, and a twist in the stocking showed that he was smiling.

When Edgar had finished eating and had drained the coffee mug, he asked, "Are you all Irish? I.R.A.?"

Steve shook his head. "We're just a bunch of friendly people."

"You must belong to an organization."

"Me, I don't belong to nothing. I'm me own man."

"Extra, that boy, what's he in this for?"

"The lad's a dreamer. When he grows up he wants to be dead."

Edgar began, "He wants . . . ?"

Steve said, "With a gun in his hand and a brave smile on his lips. He wants that scene to be the rest of his life. The lamb."

"Kale and Smith, what's their aim? Why are they in this?"

"You ask too many questions, me man, you do indeed."

Edgar said, "You might as well tell me what it's all about. Surely I have a right to know." What he wanted more than information was a cigarette. He wished Harold Vale was a smoker.

Steve lifted his head, listening. Edgar did the same. Faintly, he heard the putter of a small gasoline engine. It was the same sound that had come from outside earlier.

He asked, "What's that?"

"Questions, questions."

"All right, but the kidnaping. I have a right to be told. What're you doing it for?"

"Me, honorable sir, I'm doing it for the money."

The engine sound outside had faded away. Edgar asked, "Ransom?"

"There's a swift brain for you. He worked it out all by his own little self."

"I hope you're going to ask plenty for me."

"Enough. My bit'll be very pretty. I've always wanted to know what it's like to stink of dough."

"Where's it going to come from?"

"Search me, Vale. Maybe the government. Maybe your millions of fans, by popular subscription. Maybe the enemies of Britain who think you're lovely. It doesn't matter who actually pops."

Playing the politician heavily, Edgar said, "Ah, I suppose that Maxted will be able to arrange something."

"He's a good arranger, that one. An all-round type. Hard. Almost in your class. My envy runneth over. Oh, but I can stand it. I'm strong."

"And that's all you're asking for—money?"

"My good man," the Irishman said, "what else is there?"

Edgar looked at him carefully. "I see. So you people are criminals. This has nothing to do with politics." He felt more secure knowing that he was a golden goose, not a pawn.

About to answer, Steve held off and pushed himself erect as the door opened. He said, "Well, well, look who's here."

The girl called Smith came in. Her face was flushed as if from a brisk wall in a wind. Her eyes went straight to Edgar. She didn't return Steve's greeting, and merely nodded when he asked if everything had gone all right.

Edgar spread his hands. "As you can see, young lady, I have been fed."

"He's one very chirpy lad, isn't he, Smith?"

The girl said a cold, "If he's finished, you can fasten his wrists again."

"Again, me darling? They wasn't fastened before. Kale says it's not essential. And Kale knows everything, right?"

Smith gave a one-shoulder shrug. Her eyes were still on Edgar. She continued with them that way as she moved forward, stooped, lifted the empty mug and went back again.

As before, Edgar was mystified by the girl's expression. She seemed devoid of feeling and at the same time a turmoil of jangling, seething but contained emotions. One way or the other, due to nerves or feelings, she seemed tense to the snapping point.

Smith held the coffee mug toward the Irishman. "Here. You can go now. I'll take over the watch."

Steve made no move to reach for the mug. His voice a low croon, his black nylon lips smiling, he asked, "You wouldn't be after giving us the orders, would you now, me darling?"

The girl turned to look at him, the first time she had done so since coming into the room. Her eyes were bitter. Steve's manner projected amused ease, but it was patent that this was acted. Edgar was uncomfortably aware of the strain, and of the gun poking from each belt.

"Not orders," the girl said. "A request." She let her arm sink.

"No, luv," Steve said. "I'll tell you what. You take that mug to the kitchen yourself. There'll be things for a lass to do there, I've no doubt."

Smith tightened her lips. For a moment it looked

as if she would react violently, if only in speech. Then, settling, she took a long breath.

The man went on, "I don't mind laboring away here for a while longer, sweetheart. A devil for punishment, that's me."

The girl turned away. She snapped the door open and after passing through pulled it closed with a careful firmness that told of restraint achieved with difficulty.

Steve shook his head. "The ladies, bless 'em. They will get these silly notions of equality."

Edgar said, "Nothing wrong with that."

There was a shift of features underneath the stocking. "Don't tell me you've changed your mind, honorable sir."

"I don't know what you mean."

"In a speech you made a couple of months back," the Irishman said. "You claimed that most women were happy with the truth, which was that they were second-class citizens. Don't tell me you've forgotten that."

"I make so many speeches. That one sounds like political suicide. He—I must have lost a million female followers."

"Aye, boyo, and gained two million of the other sex. Clever, you are."

"I'm happy you think so."

"It was sheer brilliance, another time, when you talked all around compulsory euthanasia without actually saying what you meant."

Edgar stared. "Compulsory what?"

Panting, his weak eyes brimming, Harold Devon Vale looked with tired loathing at the television set. On it, a toothy master of ceremonies was conducting a panel game.

Vale was exhausted. He had been struggling for over an hour. His ankles and wrists were raw. His hair was mussed, his face white and drawn. The head renowned for its noble uprightness drooped on a weary neck. His white shirt and flannels, recently so immaculate, were creased as well as being covered with dirt and carpet fluff.

Once in his struggles Vale had toppled over, his brow thudding against the floor. The feeling of helplessness had tripled. Using head and knees, it had taken him fifteen minutes to inch over to the couch; using toes and shoulders, he had spent another quarter hour getting his chaired self back erect.

Resting from that ordeal, in a daze of sweaty depletion, Vale had whimpered for help. He thought of his mother for the first time in months. He was ashamed at being remiss. It was she who had always aided him, made sacrifices, pushed him on his way. His father had been amiable but weak.

Vale had recalled, with a poignant smile, his first experience of his mother's protection. He had been sent from from prep school, accused of cheating on an exam. She asked, "Is it true?" Although dreading her anger, and that cupboard under the stairs, he nodded. Instead of a slap, he got a pat on the shoulder, along with: "The means are justified by the end, Harold. The aim is to get to the top, no matter how. Always remember that."

The same day he had been taken by his mother

back to school, where he was reinstated. It was accepted, the story that the crib sheets had been slipped into his pocket by a class rival—whom he gallantly declined to identify.

Now, Harold Devon Vale moaned. Never in his life had he been more wretched, worn-out and frightened. Several times he had veered close to tears. All that had kept him from weeping was the thought of being seen by a rescuer bursting in.

The TV master of ceremonies offered another of his inane grins—and at last Vale gave way. He dropped chin to chest and began to sob.

It was a relief. It was grand. He bathed voluptuously in the self-pity. He twitched his hands and feet to feel the hurt, intensify his gentle orgy. He rocked his head, licked at the slow fat tears and whimpered thoroughly. He wallowed.

Vale was drying up, feeling mellow and sensuous, by the time the panel game ended in grins and applause. He gave the television his attention when a woman announcer said:

"Tonight, in place of *Weekly Press Review,* we are presenting a programme devoted to this evening's kidnaping of Caston North's Member of Parliament, Harold Devon Vale. Here is Arthur Price, our political commentator."

Price came on, his face suitably grave. He said, "First, let me tell you it is understood that the kidnapers have made contact with the authorities. There is no official confirmation as yet, but we're hoping there will be soon. Meanwhile, let's go back."

Arthur Price started to talk about the abduction

itself at Wainford Hall. He showed filmed interviews with one of the Whitecoats who had been present, the security guard who had glimpsed the car from the roof, and a man who claimed to have seen two masked men carrying a hamper along a Soho street.

"The question which everyone is asking," Price said, "is who are the abductors? In various parts of the country there are some fifteen organizations devoted to opposing Mr. Vale, his aims and ideals. Most of the groups have already been contacted. Not one claims responsibility—the reverse. Of a liberal persuasion, they reacted with dismay to the suggestion that they might be involved. So, who are these people?"

Vale had asked himself the same question, with no result. Despite his dislike of Price, and still feeling mellow from his weep, he became absorbed in the screen.

"These are the seizing seventies," the commentator said with a rhetorical sway. "These are the days of hijack, skyjack, kidnap. Planes, buildings, ships and towns are grabbed and lives put in jeopardy. By whom? More often than not, by individuals, people with no affiliations. They are terrorists without a conscience. They are the modern version of the mercenary, that soldier for hire who hardly exists anymore—at any rate, in that form.

"Nowadays, if one of the pocket nations needs military assistance, it doesn't call on the dogs of war, a tricky and expensive procedure. It invites *advisers* from whichever giant to east or west is the most sympathetic. Thus the tragic U.S. involvement in Vietnam, to mention a single instance among many.

"The mercenary is out of a job that had at least the trappings of respectability. But he is still on call, covertly—as a terrorist, to countries too big to ask for the giants' help. Also, there are multinational companies that are not above arranging destruction where, for instance, one of their firms seems in danger of being nationalized. More assassinations are perpetrated for commercial than political reasons.

"Also, of course, the terrorist might be acting without sponsors when he blows up an airport, fires a building or takes a hostage. He is doing it for gain, or to advertise his skill and availability, or out of the inbred perversion of his being. The terrorist is a phenomenon of our time. He will murder for anything, or nothing."

The screen burst into action with a film of running crowds. Vale saw it only vaguely. His mellowness had gone. He was thinking of murderers and the infirm condition of the door to his apartment.

Every burst of gunfire that came from the TV made Vale's body twitch. Imagination gave him his own film, one of masked men running up the stairs and breaking down his door with a single disdainful kick.

When Vale next gave his full attention to the screen, it was to see it filled with the face of his associate, agent, second-in-command and friend, Clifford Maxted. The bearded man said, "I am talking to you, Harold. I feel sure you'll be watching this with your captors, who will want to know how we are all taking this and what moves we are making.

I have no information for them on that. I just want to say this to you, Harold."

Vale smiled wanly. He felt a fondness for the other man which he had never experienced before. He felt passingly safe.

Maxted went on, "It has been said by foolish people, and by the more irresponsible segments of the press, that you, Harold Devon Vale, are a physical coward. What rubbish. What nonsense. We who are close to you know the truth. We know that you are brave, that you will be strong in this time of peril, that you will prove superior to this new attack on your person and ideals, that once again you will survive a martyrdom in your long, arduous struggle to help the people of the country you love." Maxted lifted his chin. "Harold, you are a man of great courage."

He faded, the commentator came back, and Vale sank into helpless, frightened giggles.

Kale, whistling tonelessly through his teeth, was breaking up a box to feed the small fire he had made in the hearth. The flames helped the candles give visual warmth to the bleak room.

Extra leaned on a wall. He had been wearing his tough expression—slitted eyes, downcurved lips—while watching on the portable TV a programme about the abduction. Now the screen was showing an old Bugs Bunny cartoon. Extra's mouth had sagged. He was entranced.

Looks sixteen at the most, Mona thought. She was

lifted out of herself and the situation by the young man's avid face. For a moment, she was without tension.

Mona had taken off her jacket. Holding a glass of whisky and water that she didn't want, that had been put into her hand by Kale, she was standing in the middle of the room. She came back to herself abruptly as the inner door behind her gave a click. She swung around. The drink slopped over and spattered to the floor.

"Aren't you the jumpy one," Steve said, appearing from the other room. He closed the door behind him. "But there it is, girls will be girls."

Mona said, "You—you startled me."

"Smith me darling, you look as sick as old pal Vale."

Kale glanced around from his fire. "It's catching up with him, is it? I thought he was taking it all a bit too lightly."

"Chirpy as a wee bird he was—until I told him about the deal we're making."

"I don't suppose he cares for that."

Steve pulled the stocking off his head, then used it to wipe his face. "He insisted on knowing, the dear man. The demand he thought crazy. The alternative, that threw him for a Cork jig. He's not chirpy now."

"Good," Kale said. He broke another piece of wood in two and tossed the halves on the fire. "Very good."

Mona, tense, put her glass down. She said, "I'll take my guard turn now."

Blinking himself alert, Extra pushed off from the wall. "I'll do it, if you like."

Mona blurted, "No!"

The three men looked at her; Kale with amusement, the Irishman with a frown, Extra with dopey surprise. Steve asked, "What's up with you, Smith?"

In a normal tone, Mona said, "I'm getting tired of the female put down, especially from you. I have a quarter part in this deal. I insist on doing my share."

Kale shrugged. "Okay. Go ahead. Take another candle with you."

Trying to act casually, but feeling wooden and artificial, Mona got a candle from a pile lying on the floor. Going to the interior door she pushed it open. She went in. The light from the room's one flame showed Edgar sitting as before, legs out, back to the wall. Mona closed the door.

Briefly, the prisoner looked quite different, which, Mona knew, had to be a trick of the poor illumination and which was proved right a moment later as the well-known Vale features took form. He stared at her.

She stepped sideways to the corner, sank down, lit her candle from the other and stuck it upright on the floorboards. Rising, she moved closer to the sitting man.

Mona felt empty. That, she mused, was unfair. It was disappointing and even sad. There should be something. Something grand and white and wonderful.

Adjusting his tinted glasses with a nervous gesture, Edgar spoke. His voice was almost a whisper. He asked, "It's not true, is it?"

"What?"

"That if the demand isn't met I'll be killed. At twelve o'clock tomorrow."

Voice equally low, Mona said, "That isn't true, no."

"But he told me so. The Irishman. He told me a few minutes ago."

"He doesn't know."

Edgar Carton said, "I see."

There was no sound to be heard other than their own soft voices. The candleglow was kindly. That, the peace and the light, Mona found suitable. It made up for her traitorous feelings.

Vale was looking up at her more intently now. He asked, "What is it?"

Mona said, "It isn't true that you'll be killed tomorrow, at twelve or at any other time."

"I see."

She sighed. "No. You're going to be killed now." There, from the statement she did at least derive a little emotion.

Edgar slowly rested his head back against the wall. He drew up his knees in front of him and clasped them together with a hand on either side. He whispered, "What's that?"

Mona nodded. She drew the gun from her waist. After putting off the safety catch by touch, she let the automatic hang down at her side.

She said, "I am going to kill you."

"*You* are?"

"I am. Here. Now."

"You can't mean it."

"I can. I do."

"I don't believe you," Edgar said after a pause,

though it was obvious that believe he did. His face blanked so much with fear or shock that he became unrecognizable.

"It's true," Mona said quietly. "I want you to accept it. I want you to know that it's going to happen. I need it that way."

He struggled for words. "The—the demand. The ransom."

"That's nothing to do with me. I want nothing. Except for you to be dead. That's my prize."

Again he paused before speaking, "I don't understand."

"I know. That's why I'm going to tell you about it. You must see this for what it is—justice."

"Justice," he repeated stupidly.

Mona's nod was firm. In a tone that pleased her with its calmness, she went on, "Until a few months ago I was happy. I had a delightful home, a handsome and charming husband. We loved one another. We had everything going for us. In another year or so we would have started having children."

The words were not good enough, Mona realized. Their triteness couldn't convey everything her life had been—the joy of waking every morning, the pleasure in serving, the magic in each mundane detail of her existence.

Mona tried again. She said, "He was everything to me, my husband. I lived for him. I prayed that our sons would be him in miniature. I loved him even when we argued. I couldn't get enough of the feel of his hands and lips on my body. The hours I spent alone were long and useless."

It was no good, she thought. The words sounded

like something from a penny romance. It couldn't be helped. You had to be a poet to make love sound real.

Taking the caress out of her voice, Mona said, "My husband was a chemist with a big company up north. They thought highly of him, not without reason. He was brilliant at his work. His future was bright. At his age there wasn't a technician in the country to touch him. He was twenty-eight."

The sitting man whispered, "I still don't."

"Listen," Mona said. "Just listen."

Edgar clasped his hands together and put them to his mouth. His eyes moved constantly back and forth between the passive gun and her face.

She said, "One night we left a restaurant, my husband and I and some friends. It was in a district like Soho, lots of exotic restaurants—Greek, Chinese, Italian. We heard a commotion along the street and went in that direction, to see what was going on. It was a mob, mostly young men, but with some older ones and a few girls. Many of them wore bleached jackets."

Edgar's legs twitched. Mona asked, "Are you with me now?" He gave no answer. She said, "I'm sure you are, and I'm sure you know the rest of it. Though I did forget to mention my husband's nationality. He was French."

The sitting man whispered, "What happened?"

"The mob had just come from a hall where you had been speaking. They were out for trouble. Already they'd smashed windows and turned over two cars, a Fiat and a Volkswagen. My husband and our friends were talking in French. The mob heard. They attacked. I won't say murder was intended, but it turned out that way. Others were beaten up too but my husband was the only one who died. He died in hospital two days later."

Mona was breathing heavily. Her chest hurt and her throat felt raw. It was a sensation she had lived with for months and which had faded only recently. There was a hint of perverse pleasure in having the familiar back again. She continued: "You, Vale, had created that mob. It was your weapon. I hold you responsible for my husband's murder. Therefore I am going to kill you in the name of justice."

Through Mona's mind passed the thought that she was not being fair to the other gang members. She would be cheating them of all they had risked and worked for. But she found it easy to dismiss the idea.

Slowly she raised the gun. She held it at waist level and aimed for the left side of the man's chest. He unclasped his hands, crossed his forearms. He stared at the automatic, mouth in a gape.

It disturbed Mona slightly that he bore no resemblance to the man she hated, just as she disliked the fact that he wasn't snarling defiance or begging for mercy. Yet she knew it would be foolish to expect the reality to match the way she had pictured the scene a thousand times. It was that scene, that daydream, which had set her on the road to here and now.

She asked softly, "Have you anything to say?"

He mumbled, "Mistake . . . not Vale . . . mimic . . . you can't. . . ."

He wasn't making sense, Mona thought. And she had wasted enough time. Sentence had long since been pronounced. Now it had to be carried out.

Mona moved a step closer. She straightened her arm. From the nose of the gun to its target was no more than four feet. To miss would be impossible.

The sitting man was making sounds but not words. His head, pressed back against the wall, rocked gently from side to side. His eyes were unblinking behind the tinted lenses.

Mona tightened her finger on the trigger. She tensed her arm. Of its own accord her jaw thrust out with determination and belligerence.

But she was unable to shoot.

She would come back later.

Turning away, Mona put the gun under her sweater and beneath her belt. She felt hollow, drained. She went to the door. Leaning on it she had to stop. She was shaking.

NIGHT

The uncertain division between evening and night was well behind, to the relief of people who worried about things like that. Night had taken a firm grip.

There was little overt activity in the vastness of Greater London. Streets were mostly deserted. In purely residential areas the sole movement was a shadow play on drawn drapes. Pubs, movie houses and theaters had closed. Still open were clubs and dance halls. gambling establishments and restaurants in the luxury class, plus hole-in-the-wall coffee shops frequented by cabbies, thieves and pimps. Hospitals were quiet. Busy were police stations and newspaper offices.

New Scotland Yard was bustling. The one hundred detectives placed under Chief Inspector Raymond Atkinson to handle the Vale Affair were hurryingly active, spurred on by the time limit—the twelve or so hours left to the deadline.

Atkinson sat in his modern office. He pondered, smoked, issued directives, drank the tea that was brought in at regular intervals by his sergeant. A believer in law and order, the Chief Inspector was working himself and his men hard to break the case, despite the fact that he considered Harold Devon Vale to be contemptible.

Raymond Atkinson had come up from the beat. He was not, as the cant phrase had it, a bent copper. He had never taken graft. On the other hand, he had never informed on those few colleagues whom he knew for sure to be getting their palms greased. Atkinson had his own standards.

Some of his men were going over files. Some, armed, went off in cars to get people from their beds and bring them in for other men to question. Some were searching slimy districts for paid informers. Some, visiting prisons, were interviewing inmates and offering vague promises of remission in exchange for information, or hints, or guesses.

Each of these detectives was doing the work of two men, for another hundred officers had had to be sent on a heroin swoop. It had been planned for weeks. It couldn't be called off now because the lives of the undercover men were in danger.

Two detectives from the Yard's stolen car detail had gone across the city. They were in the offices of the Vehicle Registration Bureau, which had been reopened for them by a disgruntled, sleepy official. He sat watching while the files were gone through carefully by the two men, who wished he would go so they could nip from the bottle of wine they had brought along to relieve the search tedium.

In a council flat in Kentish Town, Mrs. Neal sat before the electric fire. Harold Vale's daily woman was in her robe and drinking her fourth pot of tea so far tonight. Unable to sleep, she had been shuttling between kitchen and living room, tiptoeing so as not to awaken her husband.

Mrs. Neal was highly stimulated. She felt herself to be at the core of a drama, a great event, an affair of international proportions. She pitied everyone she knew; but most of all she pitied herself, because she wouldn't be able to boast of her position at the core.

Throughout London, local police stations had men on overtime. They were checking all garages, both private and commercial. They were calling on known political radicals, as well as their anti-Vale people. In addition, they were busy handling the usual crop of business. This, before the night was over, would include: one hundred and seventeen burglaries, two murders, eight muggings, a smash-and-grab raid, one rape, two child molestations, two reports of sexual exposure, one armed robbery of a strip joint, a nail-file fight between two prostitutes, eight arrests for loitering with intent to commit a felony, forty-two arrests for public drunkenness, a dozen wife beatings, one case of the battered-baby syndrome, one non-fatal stabbing, one suicide.

There was gloom in a suburban villa. It was the home of the constable who had been present when Harold Devon Vale was kidnaped at Wainford Hall. The policeman's wife had locked him out of the bedroom. She no longer saw three stripes in his future. He lay on the couch, thinking of all the rotten things he would say to her in the morning.

The two Whitecoats who had been present at the same time were lying in an alley. One was unconscious, the other nearly so. They were covered with blood. After spending hours avoiding fights with their friends, they had finally, viciously, fought with each other.

The Ford, its tire flat, had long since been towed away from where it blocked the one-way lane. It was in a police compound. Assumed merely to be one of the fifteen or twenty low-value cars that were stolen and then abandoned every day, mainly by teenagers, the Ford was not then or at any time in the future connected with the Vale Affair.

Its theft was reported at eleven-thirty by a Mrs. Greel. Two plainclothesmen went to see her. She was young and pretty. She said she had not missed the car until a few minutes before, when going out to post a letter. Her husband would not be back until later, she said. She said he was a waiter, which made the detectives smile.

In Fleet Street, night editors cursed their reporters, who complained to their police connections, who sulked because no one upstairs was saying what demands had been made by the kidnapers for the safe return of their prisoner. Newspapers were going to have to be put to bed without new developments.

Mrs Neal made her sixth pot of tea. Although excited, she was also worried. Her employer must be suffering. No doubt he was chained and gagged in the criminals' lair. Of Mr. Vale she was very fond— in the abstract. In person he didn't come over quite so well. She liked him best when she was at home.

At different times during the night, in widely spread parts of the city, a score of young men wrapped up warm and set out into the darkness. Eager for adventure or headlines or whatever rewards might be in the offing, they were going to try to find Harold Devon Vale by themselves. Most of them had deserted houses in mind.

Police traffic patrols were busier than usual. Besides chasing speeders, arresting seven drivers who failed the breathalizer test, dealing with fourteen accidents—two fatal—and giving ninety-four tickets for sundry motoring offences, they were stopping all vehicles which had enclosed bodies, ranging from small van to large panel truck. This was on the orders of Chief Inspector Raymond Atkinson. He believed it possible, because of the time element, that the abductors could be using a hideout on wheels.

At midnight, the Bloomsbury apartment house porter put on his bleached windcheater. It was time to go off duty. He didn't know why he hadn't left before, since there was no Harold D. Vale to guard. He made this observation to the replacement Whitecoat. They left together.

Clifford Maxted telephoned New Scotland Yard for the tenth time. The receptionist, as before, was cool and uncooperative, and declined to connect Maxted with the Chief Inspector. He did, however, offer the information that the gang would be making contact again in the morning. Maxted asked politely, "Would you pass a message to your superior for me, please?" The officer answered affirmatively. Maxted said, "Tell Chief Inspector Raymond Atkinson to go fuck himself." He lowered the receiver into its cradle. He felt partially satisfied.

At the farmhouse all was peaceful. Kale dozed in

the armchair he had placed against the interior door. The Irishman read a suspense novel by candlelight in the kitchen.

Extra prowled the farmhouse outside and in. It was the greatest night of his life and he wasn't about to waste a moment of it in sleep. Once, made bold by the various visions of himself, he knelt by the couch, where the girl he knew as Smith lay staring at the ceiling. Stroking her shoulder, he asked was she lonely? Her answer consisted of two words, the first of which was what he'd had in mind, but which was abnegated by being paired with the second. Unruffled, back to visions, Extra prowled on.

Before sleeping at long last, Mona spent the time wondering how she could get Kale away from that door, and what she would do if she succeeded.

At two A.M., Mr. Greel the putative waiter came home. The detectives, who had been waiting in a car nearby, placed him under arrest. This was not because of his police record or the burglary tools found on his person, but for his having stolen the Ford three months before.

Mrs. Neal was drinking tea. She had worked out the reason why she liked her employer. Harold Devon Vale had given her something to hold to; almost, you could say, a religion. Before his climb in the public eye Mrs. Neal had been in the habit of blaming the ills of her life on the weather, the government, the last war, too much education, or the poor quality of this here younger generation. Now she knew what was wrong with the country. It had too many foreigners. Having the answer was nice, solid. It was like being a child again and going to Sunday School.

Mrs. Neal was a decent, kind, innocent person. She was an average person.

By three A.M. the false calls to police stations had started to peter out. All claiming either to have seen or to be holding Harold Vale, they had averaged, at their peak, one every seventy seconds.

In Shepherds Bush, road patrol stopped a furniture removal van. While the officers were looking in the back, the driver and his mate made a fast exit down a side street. The van was full of stolen cigarettes.

At four in the morning a detective from the Yard went to an all-night truck stop. There, by arrangement, he met a reporter acquaintance. They had done business before. In exchange for twenty pounds, the officer told the reporter what the abductors were demanding and the time of the deadline. The reporter called his office and found the paper had gone to bed. Thereupon, he went to the hotel where were gathered some sixty foreign journalists, both local stringers and new arrivals. He sold his information for eighty pounds plus two bottles of brandy to a man from a German daily.

Mrs. Greel was sitting at her vanity table. She wore her best clothes. Still numb from the knowledge that her husband of one year was a criminal, she watched her expressionless face in the mirror while swallowing pill after pill. When all forty-two had been ingested she lay on the bed. She went to sleep. She never woke up. She was the night's one suicide.

The heroin swoop was over by five o'clock. It had been a failure. Dully, the officers joined the force of Chief Inspector Atkinson, but tended to cut corners rather than work in a fever. This was made up for by fresh men coming on duty, and by the assistance of twenty agents from the Special Branch.

These undercover men believed they should have been handling the case in the first place. They made their own file searches, their own arrests, sought out their own contacts, and had they found anything, it was doubtful if they would have turned it over to Chief Inspector Raymond Atkinson, whom they considered pleasant but thick.

At six o'clock it was stated officially by the Home Office that there would be no deals with the kidnapers.

The telephone woke up TV commentator Arthur Price at six-fifteen. A friend was calling to tell him the time of the deadline and what was being demanded for the return, alive, of Harold Devon Vale. Friend had received the news fifth-hand. It came from a man whose cousin had a girl friend who worked in the canteen of the international telephone exchange. She had gotten it from a male admirer who handled the Northern Europe lines, and who had heard the talk in German between a journalist and his Berlin editor. The girl had promised not to tell a living soul, and she hadn't, except her boy friend, who had this cousin, who knew. . . .

At about that same time, Harold Vale awoke from a nightmare. Despite knowing his apartment was soundproof, he began to scream for help. He screamed for fifteen minutes, until his voice gave out. He remembered that at eight o'clock, if he could stay safe that long, his char would come and set him free. He cried himself back to sleep.

With smudges of light in the eastern sky, New Scotland Yard was still working. New people were being brought in for questioning, others were being released. Chief Inspector Atkinson was pressing his men to find an additional twenty possibilities turned up by informers and constant file-combing. One of the men was known variously as Ajax, Kaplan, and Kale. The agents from the Special Branch exchanged looks of amusement because they knew the Vale Affair was a Russian caper, and that most of the possibilities were abroad. Ajax, Kaplan, Kale—he was in an Israeli prison.

In the living room of the farmhouse, Mona slept deeply. There was a smile on her lips and tears on her cheeks.

At seven o'clock Mrs. Neal began to get ready to go to work. She made her eleventh pot of tea and fried two eggs. Not until she was topcoated and about to leave did she realize there would be no point in going to the Bloomsbury flat today. Mr. Vale wouldn't be there, waiting for his breakfast, and the place would be overrun with policemen looking for clues and things. With no regret, yawning, Mrs. Neal went to bed.

MORNING

Edgar semi-awoke to the pain of an awkward position. He saw, eyes slowly opening and closing, a grey wall with a door that was lying horizontal. Coming fully awake, he remembered where he was and realized that during sleep he had slipped down sideways. Groaning, he pushed himself up. He gazed drearily around his prison.

The candle had burned itself out. Artificial light, however, was no longer vital—though it would have been welcome as a taste of color. Through the boards over the window seeped a greyness that formed a perfect match for Edgar's spirits. He was low.

He was also thoroughly chilled. Briskly, he began an alternate rubbing of arms and legs. When he felt warmer he dealt with his stiffness. He swayed his head and massaged his neck while repeatedly huffing his shoulders. The muscular aches went. He felt much better physically, which meant there was nothing to distract his emotions. He was low, low.

Getting up, Edgar shuffled to the window, a yard away. There were cracks between boards, and one had a knothole an inch in diameter. Even so, there was nothing to be seen except other pieces of wood.

Leaning there, Edgar recalled last night's visit by the girl named Smith. She had said she was going to kill him. She had aimed the gun. All around her there had been an aura of death.

Mouth open, Edgar experienced again that terrible sensation that had stabbed into him. There was nothing he could liken it to. He supposed it was the ultimate in fear. Now he could believe that it was possible to die of fright.

When the long minutes had ended, Smith gone, he had been taken by a bout of shivering which had scared him all over again with its intensity.

Edgar wondered why Smith had held back from pulling the trigger. He believed the story of her dead husband; it had the sad ring of truth. She had been in quiet, cold earnest when she had pronounced the death sentence.

What, Edgar mused, had kept her from shooting? Did she want to play cat-and-mouse? Was it her intention to savor the act that she had planned for so long?

Edgar snatched a look at his watch. He was relieved to see that it was after eight o'clock. By this time, he knew, Vale's maid would have arrived at work. Freed, the politician would have contacted the police. Perhaps the news of the masquerade would already be out. Safety could be a matter of mere minutes away.

Shuffling, a hand on the wall for support, Edgar began to move around the room, driven by nervous excitement. To keep himself calm he turned his mind from the expected freedom. He thought of Vale, the public man and his philosophy. He also thought, once, that the girl was not being too extreme when she talked of having justice on her side.

Presently the door opened. In came the leader of the gang, Kale. He was carrying a mug and a packet of sandwiches. Opening the door with his shoulder, he said, "Glad someone else is awake in this house."

Assuming the Vale voice and face (probably for the last time, he thought), Edgar asked, "Any news?"

"What kind of news?"

Edgar fumbled, "Well, you know, developments."

"Have the cops got the place surrounded, you mean?" Kale said mockingly. "Are the Marines going to be sent in? Has the cavalry arrived? Is rescue at hand?"

"I didn't mean anything in particular."

"The answer is no. Sit down."

Edgar lowered himself against the wall. Kale came over and handed down the breakfast, then stood nearby, thumbs in his belt, watching while Edgar got on with the meal. The hot coffee was especially welcome.

"And as to real news," Kale said. "We forgot to bring a radio. We only have the telly, and that gets up later than radio does. We'll have to wait a while."

"What time's the first programme?"

"Dare say you're real keen to see what kind of a splash all this is making, eh, Vale?"

"Nothing wrong with that."

"The station opens with a news roundup at nine. We'll let you watch. We're a decent lot."

Edgar chewed, swallowed. Making talk, he asked,

"And if the demand isn't met?"

Kale said, "You know. You've been told." He spoke as mildly as if he were discussing the weather.

It came to Edgar that the gang leader, obviously, did not know of Smith's intentions, which would seem to be personal and private. How she and Kale happened to be together in this was another matter, a mystery, for everything pointed to Smith being an amateur. Kale, he was a pro. In that there was a certain amount of safety. The immediate danger, should the situation be drawn out, came from the girl.

Edgar finished his breakfast. He said, "About Smith."

Kale grinned. "Nice looking chick. Cute ass. But maybe you didn't notice."

"She's pretty, yes."

"Don't fret, there'll be plenty like her in hell."

Edgar asked, "What, ah, is she hoping to get out of the kidnaping?"

"None of your business, Vale," Kale said lightly. "Like all politicians, you talk too fucking much, ask too many questions."

Whether or not he should tell about Smith, that was settled for Edgar by Kale's attitude. It appeared to suggest that he knew all that was going on, had no doubts in any direction.

Which, Edgar thought, could mean that Kale had been a party to the death-threat scene last night—which could mean in turn that the gang wanted to keep him in a state of fear and high tension, ready to do anything, say anything, write anything.

But it wasn't important, Edgar assured himself.

As far as his own part in this was concerned, it would soon be over.

He asked to use the bathroom. Kale said, "You mean you have body functions just the same as us poor mortals?"

Edgar put on a Vale expression of disapproval. "The unnecessary answer to that is yes."

"Okay. Come on."

Edgar got up. In his old man shuffle he was led out to the other room—Smith asleep there on the couch—and along a hall to a doorway.

"In here," Kale said.

"Thank you."

"Don't be too long about it. And if you feel like shouting through the window, why, go right ahead."

Edgar went in the bathroom and closed the door. Its bolt, he saw, had been ripped off. The window, though open, was too small to allow passage to anything except a child.

When Edgar came out again, Kale took him back to the living room. The Irishman was now present, kneeling near the television set, which gave out music while showing a test pattern.

Steve glanced around. He was not wearing his stocking mask. White-haired and with a moustache to match, he had a saggy, baggy, lined face. He was by far the oldest of the gang—up in the forties, Edgar judged.

Probably because of the prisoner's attention, Steve abruptly realized that he was maskless. He shot a hand to his face, then threw the hand aside with a grunt.

He said, "So have a good look, dear man. I'm handsome enough."

Kale laughed. After standing Edgar by the wall he asked, "Where's Extra?"

The Irishman replied, "Like sexy Smith over there, he's asleep. He's chosen the kitchen table. The wee lambkin, he's worn out from playing Humphrey Bogart all night."

The test pattern was replaced by a clock. It showed the time as almost nine. The second hand worked its way up. As it reached the top, trumpet music blared out and the screen switched to showing flashed scenes of the TV studios.

Kale shouted, "Smith!"

The girl's body jerked. She twisted around and slammed up into a sitting position. Quickly she looked all about. Her eyes were red, her face was taut.

"Wakey-wakey, sleeping beauty," Steve said. "They're about to play our song."

The girl's eyes settled on Edgar. He flinched at their projection of loathing. He felt glad that the others were here; and he wondered all over again about the genuineness of Smith's threat. He consoled himself with the thought that she was simply playing her part to the hilt.

An announcer came on the TV screen. Preliminaries over, he read the news headlines. Smith watched stolidly. The three men fidgeted, Edgar more so than the other two. He was eager for Vale's discovery to be announced, but at the same time he worried about how the gang would react when it was.

"Now to the big news story of the moment," the man onscreen said. "Here is our expert on the political scene, Arthur Price."

The commentator appeared, relaxed and confident-looking. He went over details of the abduction. There were film clips. Some had already been shown last night. New ones were brief interviews; Lady Wardwell expressing her dismay, a grim Clifford Maxted complaining about the lack of police cooperation. There was a still of a car, the same model as that of the kidnap Jaguar, which had been traced. Its number was given.

Edgar couldn't understand why all this had to be gone through before they came to the point. He perked when Arthur Price said, "Last, two new and important items. The first is an official statement from the Home Office. Quote, Under no circumstances will we give in to the terrorists' demands for the return of Harold Devon Vale, unquote. The second item relates to those demands, and is an exclusive of this station."

"No deals," Steve said. "They're kidding."

Kale shrugged. "Listen."

"As you all know," Arthur Price said, "the demands made by the gang have been kept under close wraps by New Scotland Yard. However, through my various contacts—highly-placed sources which I am not at liberty to name—I have been able to find out what those demands are."

Steve sneered, "Aren't you the clever one though."

"The gang wants one million pounds in cash. They want the money to be handed over by the prime minister himself. They want the release of the three Japanese terrorists who were recently sentenced here to life imprisonment. They want the House of Commons to vote on the censure of Mr Vale."

The commentator paused. He leaned forward to add slowly, "And if those demands are not met, Harold Devon Vale will be killed today at twelve o'clock. Twelve noon."

He leaned away, nodded, went on, "It's a clever move to try and get the prime. . . ."

The rest was drowned out by raucous laughter. It came from Steve. He had sat back on his rump and was rocking as he laughed. "Highly-placed sources," he gasped. "The man's a clown. My various contacts. Oh Jasus and Mary. It's rich. It's lovely."

Smith said, "What's the joke?"

Grinning, the Irishman shared his glance between her and Kale. "Release of prisoners. Vote of censure. The prime bloody minister. Now where on earth did he get that crap from?"

There was a moment of silence. The girl said, "But it's true."

Steve stared at her. His smile went. He asked, "What's that?"

"It's true. Those are the things I asked for on the phone yesterday."

"You're not serious."

"Of course I am."

The Irishman got swiftly to his feet. "Now wait a minute," he snapped, his face darkening.

"Hold it," Kale said. He turned to Edgar and jerked a thumb. "In there, you."

Edgar was taken into the back room. Before

closing the door, Kale pushed. Edgar went stumbling forward. By reaching ahead to the wall he stopped himself from falling, but then lowered himself to the boards anyway. He lay limply.

Edgar was stunned. He had no thoughts for the demands, which sounded totally insane. He was beginning to realize that, the daily woman delayed or ill or having a day off, Harold Devon Vale might not be discovered until much later. Until, in fact, after twelve o'clock.

The man on the television screen was saying, "A spokesman at New Scotland Yard, queried only minutes ago about the gang's terms for an exchange, replied that he was in no position to comment. That, in my opinion based on experience, means—"

Steve switched the set off with a hard twist of his hand. His body leaning forward, he turned again to face Mona. He went on looking at her fixedly while he spoke, although Mona knew that he was really addressing Kale.

"All right, me girl. Let's have it. Why did you say all them stupid things to Atkinson?"

"Because I was told to," Mona said indifferently. "It was what you all wanted."

"I must be hearing things," the Irishman said. "Going deaf in me old age. That's what *I* wanted?"

"Well, wasn't it? Isn't it? Those must have been the terms you had in mind all along."

Steve said, "Girly, I don't know any bloody Japs. I don't give a cuntful of cold water about Vale being censured. Me, I'm playing this little game for the lolly, the cash, the bread."

Mona rose from the couch. "I think you're forgetting that little matter of one million pounds."

"And a load of rubbish that no one would say yes to. You heard the man. No deals, says the Home Office. Money by itself they would've played along with. That other crazy stuff—not on your life."

Kale took over. He strolled across to the other man while saying in a placating tone, "Steve, Steve, take it easy. You have to try to understand these things. You need to see them in a different light."

Not until Kale stopped nearby did the Irishman look at him, and not pleasantly. He asked, "I'm a bit stupid, you reckon? Slow?"

"Not in the slightest."

"Listen. I want to know what you and this girl are playing at. You're leaving me out of things."

"I know what I'm doing, Steve," Kale said, speaking easily. His right hand was resting on his waist, near the gun.

"Good. So explain."

"No deals, they said. They always do say that to begin with. And we say we'll accept nothing less. It's a marketplace situation of buyer and seller. Next, the haggling starts."

The tension flowing back and forth between the two men was so strong that it caused Mona to step away. She left the couch and went to stand by the window. She could still feel the tension.

Kale said, "We ask high and come down. They start at nothing and come up. It's the usual thing. At which midpoint it'll finish I don't know. But we won't be losers."

"I should hope not."

"If we only get a quarter of the cash we asked for, you won't complain, will you?"

Steve was easing down from his physical tautness. He folded his arms, rested on one hip, looked away. "You make it all sound easy, a piece of pie."

"It is. I've been through this before. And the prime minister, no, of course he won't make the delivery. So we take a lesser person, but still someone up high, a VIP. You know why?"

"I will when you tell me."

"It's so the law won't try any tricks or traps that could hurt the precious VIP. It'll be a clean, safe delivery."

The Irishman said nothing, but it was patent by his face and stance that he was accepting what still sounded absurd to Mona. Not that she cared. She was wishing they would both leave so that she could go into the back room. Sleep had made her miss an opportunity last night. Now she was ready.

Kale said, "In a little while, Smith here will make a call to Atkinson again. We'll see what develops. Believe me, we hold all the cards. Okay?"

Steve nodded. "I should've been told, that's what it comes down to. People don't like to be left in the dark."

"I thought I had told you. Sorry about that. I had quite a few things on my mind."

Abruptly, the Irishman laughed. He flapped his arms against his sides and shook his head. He said,

"Oh well, it'll be the same in a hundred years, be Jasus. Look on the bright side, that's me motto."

"Good man."

"What do you say to a wee dram to drive the cold away?"

"That's the stuff," Kale said, moving toward the passage. "You coming, Smith?"

"I'd better stay here," Mona said. "Keep guard."

The two men went off toward the kitchen. Her tension growing, Mona waited until she heard them there, and safely occupied, before crossing the room.

She listened by the interior door. Beyond, all was silent. She hoped, hoped fervently, that the politician had gone back to sleep. After all, she thought, he must have had a poor night, lying without a cover on bare boards.

"Hello."

Mona swung around at the voice. It belonged to Extra. Yawning, the young man was coming into the room from the kitchen. He whined, "They woke me up."

Mona pointed to a door beside the hearth. "There's another bedroom in there. Use it."

He gave his head a heavy shake. "I'd best stay awake now." He began to amble around the room, his sleep-creased face petulant. He looked young enough to spank.

"Look," Mona said, controlling her impatience. "You won't be worth a damn to anyone if you're half asleep."

He mumbled while turned the other way. It sounded like, "I don't want to miss anything."

"Then stay here. Lie on the couch."

"Well, yeah, I suppose I could do that."

"And sleep. We'll wake you if anything happens."

"Should stay awake."

Mona said, a threat, "Kale won't like it if you're not sharp and on the ball."

Extra looked at the couch. "What did they say on the news?"

It was another ten minutes before he settled on the couch, five more before he closed his eyes and stopped talking. There was no sound from the kitchen.

Mona softly opened the door and slipped into the back room.

Harold Devon Vale was not asleep. He was on his feet. And, oddly, he was standing with his upper body pressed to the boards that covered the window. It seemed as though he were trying to push through with his hands and the side of his face.

He was unaware of Mona's presence.

She brought the gun from her waist. Her tension was high. She felt as if she were reaching for a crescendo which had to be explosive, a shot.

After snicking off the safety catch, she held the gun out at arm's length. She aimed for the middle of the man's back, telling herself with beautiful calmness to pull the trigger.

Instead, she was shattered to hear herself shout, "No!"

Edgar whirled. The turn was so fast that he almost overbalanced on his fettered ankles. Face wild, his upper body dipped and swayed. His glasses slipped off and fell to the floor. A hank of oily hair came loose to dangle across his brow.

Balance held finally, Edgar stood in a sag, staring. He looked pitiable. Mona's hatred of him swelled. She was able to regain comparative composure.

Averting her eyes from that sick, unrecognizable face, Mona said harshly, "Put your glasses on. Stand straight. Turn to face the wall."

Slowly, he obeyed all three orders, and then a fourth: "Keep your eyes to the front."

Mona went up close, within touching distance. She held her gun an inch from the soiled, creased blazer. But she knew it was no use. She knew she couldn't shoot. Even that extra burst of hate couldn't help.

Her arm sagged. She thought stonily that there would be relief for her if she could at least hit the man, punch him, crash the gun down on that bald spot. But no, she couldn't even do that. She had failed completely.

Mona's eyes filled with tears. She turned away. In doing so, she failed to see the coffee mug lying on its side. She stepped on it. It rolled. Her leg shot away and she pitched over sideways with a sharp cry.

Instinctively, her hands opened to break the fall. The gun went flying to a far corner of the room—though Mona had no immediate thought for this.

The next thing she knew, she was lying on her side, propped on an elbow, looking up into the face of Harold Devon Vale. The politician was on one knee close beside her.

He asked, "Are you all right?"

"What?" she said stupidly. She wiped tears from her cheeks.

"Did you hurt yourself?"

"I—I don't think so."

Vale adjusted his spectacles. He said, "Let me help you up."

"Yes. Thank you."

Then, at the same moment, they both turned to look at the corner, at the gun. There was a two-beat pause before they moved, again simultaneously.

The race was short: a scrambling, pushing, crawling rush. And Mona, unfettered, was the winner.

She grabbed up the automatic and swung it on the politician, who was right beside her. He steadied, and slowly sat back on his heels. Mona leaned against the wall. Panting, they stared at one another.

Her voice low and wondering, Mona asked, "Why did you do that?"

"Do what?"

"Come to me instead of getting the gun."

The man lifted up his palms to show emptiness. "I don't know."

"You came to help me," she said.

"Well...."

"You could have got the gun. You might have forced your way out. You might have got free."

Harold Vale hunched forward and lowered his head. There was a movement to his shoulders that suggested he was about to speak. But the seconds went by and he said nothing.

Mona got up. She circled Vale and went to the

door. Depleted, sad and thoughtful, she left the room.

Almost told her the truth then, Edgar thought. Came real close. But there was ample time for them to learn for themselves about the masquerade. The maid could still show up, delayed on the way. Perhaps Vale might already have been found but news of it was slow in reaching the media.

Edgar went back to the girl's question, the one she had asked after their race on hands and knees. Why, he thought, had he *not* leapt for the gun? Was it because he was so afraid of a weapon he couldn't even touch one? Or was it on account of that plaintive way the girl had cried out as she fell?

The questions vanished. All thoughts of Smith vanished. The memory of scrambling for the gun vanished.

The panic of the last few minutes had made Edgar forget. Now, flashingly, he remembered.

His face tight with excitement, he crawled over to the boarded-up window. He stood erect and pressed the side of his face to the wood. His fists clenched with hope. He listened.

Earlier, Edgar had heard a furtive tapping on the outer layer of planks. He had gotten up in order to be closer and to tap back. An answer had come, faintly. It was then that he had heard the girl shout, "No!"

That, he hoped, had warned the person outside to hold off for the time being.

Now Edgar got a coin from his pocket. He gave the wood three sharp raps. He winced—the sound seemed to echo with cruel loudness in the empty room.

He was torn by worry. Would the rapping be heard by the gang? Would it be loud enough to reach the someone outside, if he had moved away? Had the taps from out there been imagination in the first place?

Edgar heard nothing. Sighing, he gave one firm rap with the coin. It bounced around the room. And went on bouncing.

Edgar stiffened with a gasp. That wasn't the same rap in echo; it was an answer. He pressed his ear hard to the wood. When the rapping ended, he replied with the Morse signal for distress, the SOS.

Back came a rapid chatter of taps which, despite speed, had a rhythm and neatness. Edgar recognized it as expert Morse, though it was far too fast for him to get the gist, or even separate individual letters. It was more than twenty years since he had learned the code in the Boy Scouts.

He knocked steadily until the sender broke off; then, with care, fighting memory to produce each letter, he spelt out in Morse s-l-o-w d-o-w-n.

Back at a reasonable speed came the m-e-s-s-a-g-e u-n-d-e-r-s-t-o-o-d and r-e-a-d-y t-o r-e-c-e-i-v-e.

Edgar asked for identification. A pulse in his back made a mockery of his sluggish tapping. The coin was slippery in his fingers. Controlling his excitement was painful.

The answer came as f-r-i-e-n-d. Next the sender asked a-r-e y-o-u v-a-l-e?

Edgar sent the fast affirmative. The reply, again,

was so rapid that he gathered nothing—except its tone of ebullience and triumph. Then the hand became readably ponderous. It asked h-o-w m-a-n-y i-n g-a-n-g?

Edgar replied that there were four, that they were armed, that caution was necessary. His head was beginning to ache from the struggle for each letter combination of long and short taps.

The sender asked w-h-a-t k-i-n-d o-f w-e-a-p-o-n-s?

Edgar didn't know what arms might be in the back of the Jaguar or here at the farm. For all he knew, the gang could have machine guns, hand grenades, anything. He began on the laborious task of tapping out that he had seen only automatic pistols.

Halfway through, he froze. From the door behind him had come a sound. It was the handle being stealthily turned.

Edgar shot down to a crouch. He clutched the coin in his fist. He was sitting back on his rump when he heard the door being pushed open with a rush.

"What's going on here?"

Edgar glanced around. The Irishman stood on the threshold, hands on hips, frowning.

"Nothing," Edgar said. He swayed far back, went forward, touched the knuckles of both hands on the wall, started the backward movement again.

Steve said, "I heard noises. Knocks."

"I'm getting some exercise."

Suspiciously: "Oh, is that a fact?"

If the someone outside rapped now, Edgar thought nervously, there was a good chance of Steve hearing. But perhaps he was too far away.

As though in answer to that, the Irishman came stalking across the room. He stood looking down at Edgar. He said, "You're sweating."

"It's hard work." He tripled the tempo of his swaying. When going forward he tapped the wall with his knuckles, when going back he tapped with his shoes.

Loudly he began to talk, extolling the value of exercise. He spoke looking up, trying to gauge from the other man's expression if he was being successful. He jabbered.

"Shurrup," Steve said. "You'd talk a fella deaf. And for Jasus's sake keep still."

Edgar sighed into silence and stopped his rocking. He folded his arms, putting a fist tightly under each armpit. He prayed for exterior silence.

Steve turned to the window. He looked at the boards with a frown. He touched them, felt their edges, examined the nails.

Edgar held his breath. He was tortured by the thought of Steve tapping on the wood to test its firmness—and getting a reply.

The Irishman shrugged, grinned. "You wouldn't be trying to chew your way out, would you, laddie?"

"Wish I could," Edgar said with acted hopelessness.

"Cheer up. You're still alive. You've hours to go yet."

Edgar asked, "Who's going to do the job if they don't play?"

"Questions, questions. See you later. Back to your exercise."

Edgar closed his eyes with relief as the Irishman

moved away. A moment later came the sound of the door closing. For half a minute, in case Steve made a surprise return, he played at doing more exercises.

He got up quickly. Ear to the wood, he listened. There was silence. With his coin he tapped the SOS. No answer. He tapped again.

His knees sagged: from the outer boards had throbbed the fast signal I a-m r-e-c-e-i-v-i-n-g y-o-u. This was followed by the message that the break in communications was understood at last—c-o-n-t-i-n-u-e.

Slowly, using telegraphese phrasing, Edgar tapped out that he was unsure of the weaponry beyond the fact that each member of the gang had a pistol.

Acknowledging that, the outside hand asked if Edgar knew where he was, and, being given a negative, began on a detailing of location.

Edgar listened impatiently. This was irrelevant as far as he was concerned. He wanted to get the sender moving, acting. His concentration on receiving eased as he fell to considering the next steps.

He supposed the police would come in force—this, obviously, was one man, unarmed. They would come and there would be a shoot-out. Surrounded, the gang hadn't a hope. They would all be killed.

Edgar felt regret. It was for the girl. She really wasn't a part of this plot, he mused. She had her own motives. There ought to be some way for her to be treated differently from the others. Edgar mulled over how he should try to get this across to the person outside.

His attention returned to the code as the tapping ended. The pause was followed by more raps: a message assuring that help would soon be on its way. With only these few minutes of practice, Edgar was improving his ability to send and receive.

He decided to help the girl. To start with, he thought, before he began on the near-impossible job of explanation, he needed a closer relationship with the unknown person outside.

He tapped out w-h-o a-r-e y-o-u?

The hand answered y-o-u w-a-n-t m-y n-a-m-e?

Y-e-s.

Edgar listened carefully. He had only just got the finished reply clear in his mind when it was followed by a mad, loud, two-fisted battering on the wood that sounded like a drummer's version of derisive laughter. The sender had spelt out S-t-e-v-e.

Harold Vale slept through the first news telecast of the day. He came awake in time for the second. Slowly, bent to the shape of the chair he was tied to, he worked himself around until he could see the TV set. He lay there on his side and gazed with sleazy eyes at the screen.

The demands of the kidnapers left Vale unmoved. What did disturb and bring him to alertness was that no deals would be made and that the hostage would therefore be killed at twelve o'clock. Worst of all, he suddenly realized that Mrs. Neal was late, which had never happened before.

Maybe she wasn't going to come at all this morning, Vale thought. She couldn't be ill, because in that case her husband would have called, and the telephone hadn't rung. The Neals would have also called if there were another reason for her being detained. The reason she wasn't here was obvious. She saw no point in coming to what she assumed would be an empty flat.

Harold Vale carefully digested the fact that release was not imminent. He next thought that his continuing confinement must, of course, have occurred by now to the only other person who knew of his predicament—the mimic Edgar Carlton.

And Carlton was certainly not going to go to pretending to be someone else, not in the face of death.

Vale, however, went on lying there quietly. This time he didn't panic. He had no emotion to spare for that. The time had come for a different approach to the problem.

Vale put his mind to ways and means of getting free—ways apart from the tried and useless ones of screaming and struggling.

Presently, an idea came to him as his eyes roved the room—that of causing an electrical failure. If he could blow a fuse which would affect the whole building, there would be a flat by flat check to find the fault, and he would be found.

But there were difficulties. With only the use of his mouth, how was he to ram a metal object into an outlet? Also, the other tenants would be out at work by now. The porter could well have stayed away, like Mrs. Neal, believing the Vale flat to be empty. There could be no way of a failure being known about, until later, when it might be too late.

Still deadly calm, Harold Vale thought on. He considered every possible manner of breaking through the heavy, double layers of window glass; and gave them all up as useless, tied as he was.

Signalling through the window had possibilities, he mused. But only his head would show above the sill, invisible from the street because of the deep outside ledge. It was doubtful if tenants across the road would be idly gazing out. Something fast and sure was needed.

The squawk box occurred to him. He thought that if he could work his way to the apartment door, if he could figure out some system of raising himself to the box's shoulder-high level, if he could manage to press the button while. . . .

Vale gave up on that one. It would consume too much time and, if it worked, there might be no one downstairs to answer.

His next idea seemed foolish on first appearance. It would even have been funny had he been in that frame of mind. How could anyone dial a telelphone with his nose?

Then Vale tensed, blinking.

Could he do it with his tongue?

Excited, he began on the task of getting himself erect. It was much more difficult than when he had done it last night. His body was a collection of aches, with stabbing pains in neck, wrists and ankles. He had been in this one fixed position for more than twelve hours.

It took him ten minutes to get himself and chair upright, another five to work his way over to the telephone table, a last five to recover from all that physical labor.

He was ready finally, and even able to spare a

look of hate for the television set, which was yammering a pop tune in accompaniment to gyrating figures.

Carefully, Vale lifted up the receiver. It clattered to the table top and skittered toward its edge. With a snake-like dart of his head Vale prevented it from falling off. He gently maneuvered it so that mouthpiece and earpiece were in the right position.

Tongue out and pointed, he placed it in the hole of the nine. He began to circle the dial. Midway round, his moist tongue slipped out.

This caused him no dismay. The reverse. He was elated, for he could see how that the act was possible. It simply needed calmness and patience.

With an extra-painful twist of his neck, Vale managed to dry his tongue on the shoulder of his shirt. He tried again with the number nine. It went all the way around. When it had ticked back home again, he repeated the number, then did it a third time. He had succeeded. The 999 emergency call had been made.

He lowered his head to the receiver. A bright female voice asked, "Fire, police or ambulance?"

"Police, please," Vale said thickly. He sounded as though he had been talking for hours.

"Is it an emergency, sir, or would you like the number of your local police station?"

"Emergency. Hurry, please. It's important. Vital. A real emergency."

"One moment. I'll connect you."

Vale felt a passing annoyance that the girl still sounded bright and unimpressed. But he was more irked by the continuing pop blare behind him.

A male voice said, "Police. Good morning. Can I help you?"

Relief sent Vale's calm running off to the middle distance. He said rushingly, "Listen. Now listen. This is Harold Vale speaking. Harold Devon Vale. I'm tied up. I've been bound to a chair for hours. All night. I'm in pain. Come here quickly. Get here as fast as you can. You've got to—"

"Hold hard," the officer said, his tone brisk. "Take your time, please. Let's get it straight. First, your name."

At a slightly slower speed Vale said, "I'm the Member of Parliament for Caston North. *The* Harold D. Vale. Listen. That man who's been abducted, he's not me. He's an imposter. He's disguised himself as me. He tied me up. I'm helpless. I dialed the phone with my tongue. Come and release me. I'll explain everything then. Understand? D'you hear me?"

"Yes, sir. I understand perfectly."

"Thank you," Vale gasped. "Thank you."

The officer said, "Now I'll tell you what, sir. You give me a call about this time next week. And don't worry about a thing. We'll check it out."

"Eh?"

"Thank you for calling, sir. Good morning." There was a click.

"Hello?" Vale snapped. "Hello, hello, hello?" He got no answer. The officer had disconnected.

Harold Vale eased back and gaped at the receiver. Relief, confidence, excitement—they seeped away. In a hollow voice that broke on the last word, he asked the dead instrument, "Don't you believe me?"

Sadly, Vale realized that the officer had thought him a crank. The story must have sounded ridiculous, especially with pop music pounding in the background. And, of course, the police would have had hundreds of calls from fools and pranksters in connection with this big story. It was normal and expected.

So how about trying again?—Vale wondered. This time he would be cool and reasonable, and he would switch off the televistion first—if he could.

Or better still, there was Maxted.

The lift brought by that suggestion went as Vale recalled that he didn't know Maxted's number. Finding it in the directory or his own personal book would be impossible with only the use of his face.

Also, Vale thought, enjoying being defeatist, Maxted most likely would be out and about during this present crisis. Even if he were at home, would he believe the story any more than the police officer had? Hardly. He'd been taken in by Edgar Carlton at Wainford Hall.

Broodingly, face in a scowl, Vale played with the idea of a complex plot with himself as victim—a plot in which Carlton and Maxted were partners, as well as involving two pseudo-kidnapers, plus all the Whitecoats, and the police, and the media people. . . .

Vale gave up on the idea. For one thing it was getting out of hand. For another, he could find no motive in it.

He went back to considering other possibilities with the telephone. There was New Scotland Yard—he, like everyone else, knew that famous number.

There was the girl at the 999 switchboard. This time he could ask to be connected with the fire department, tell them he was trapped in a burning room, have them come and axe down the door. There was his cousin who lived in Highgate.

Vale ended the list because other thoughts kept on cutting in. They were disturbing. He had been returning in his mind to the kidnapers, to the demands, to the fatal deadline that would force the mimic to speak, to masked men coming here with machine guns.

Automatically, forgetting his bondage, Vale tried to get up quickly. He was snapped back. He nearly toppled over. The chair squealed a loud complaint as he swayed on it.

That gave Vale pause. He remembered that during the sturggle to get upright and over to the telephone, there had been a great deal of that same squealing. Last night, at least initially, the chair had been silent.

Therefore, all his struggles and falls had weakened the screws and joints.

Harold Vale sat up straight, his confidence returning. Right, he mused. It was impossible to break the tape bonds, but what if he would free them from the spindles they passed around?

Vale swayed his body to one side. The wood wailed like cats in the night. He pressed on in the same direction, forcing down with toes and buttocks, careless of whether or not he fell.

He did fall. He landed heavily on one shoulder. But he was indifferent to that, for, in the last second before he overbalanced, he had heard with delight two distinct cracking sounds.

Weakly but happily, Vale laughed. He knew now that freedom was simply a matter of time—short time.

There was a watery sun. It shone through a mistiness which intensified as it descended, so that at ground level it was like a light fog. Distant trees looked ghostly. Dew winked and glistened. It was not an unattractive scene.

All Mona saw was the ground. She gazed down at it from her sprawl on the back seat of the Jaguar, through the open door. Mona was thoughtful.

Kale sat on the car's front fender. He was chewing a piece of grass. He might have been on a picnic. Nearby stood Extra, feet spread, thumbs hooked in his belt on either side of the automatic. Steve was on his haunches in the open doorway of the farmhouse.

When Mona had come outside, the others had followed one at a time. It was warmer out than in. But that wasn't the reason for Mona's exit. She had wanted fresh air, wanted to get clear of her dizziness and nausea.

The feeling had come upon her when she had realized, earlier, how close she could have been to death. Vale had missed two chances to get the gun after she had dropped it. He could have grabbed it up and fired.

Recovered now, she was thinking it strange that she should have been sickened by what a few months ago she would probably have welcomed. She no longer wanted to die. That, oddly, made Mona experience a pale guilt.

She shuffled uncomfortably, sat up straight and got away from the emotion by returning to the why of Vale having missed that first chance at the gun. But playing with the question was useless. She had no answer. And, she thought, it could not possibly have been instinctive concern about her fall. Not with a man like Harold Vale. Surely.

Extra suddenly said, as if echoing Mona's thoughts, "He's cracked!"

"Who—Vale?"

"Yes. Cracked. Cuckoo. A nut."

"Look. I just been in there for half an hour. I tell you he's loopy. For one thing, he wanted to know what the next torture was."

Kale spat out his piece of grass. "Torture?" he asked, but without interest. He glanced at his watch. It was the third time he had done so since coming outside.

Extra nodded. "He says we keep telling him he's about to be shot, but then we don't do it."

Mona swallowed a sigh. She had been so concerned about her own feelings while trying to shoot Vale, it hadn't occurred to her what a shattering experience it must have been for him. But did he deserve any better?

Kale said, "Sounds like one of Steve's comic capers."

The Irishman grinned. "Not guilty, m'lord."

Extra went on, "Then he says something about tapping on the window. I didn't get it. Real cracked, I reckon."

While Steve, with a laugh, began to explain about the Morse joke he had played while Extra had been asleep, Mona turned her face away. It was showing the distaste she felt for the trick.

On turning back again a moment later, Mona looked from one to another of the smiling men. She realized how alien they were to her now, whereas scant hours ago they had been close associates, vital to her needs. They had become strangers because she had lost touch with the person she herself had been yesterday. Although she was not totally different, she was on her way. She no longer wanted death, for herself or anyone else. That had wrought the change.

Mona wondered who these strangers were. What made them tick? What was the fuel?

Extra, she thought, he needed no deep analyzing. He was an open book, a thriller with gunfire on every third page. He had joined in this affair for the romance. Alone, he was harmless. With an audience, he would kill out of bravado.

The Irishman was involved strictly on a cash basis. He was an outcast, a man without dreams or illusions, a man educated in violence on the streets of Belfast who would murder at the flap of a Union Jack or the passing of a wad of money.

Kale was something else. Not obvious. An enigma. He could be an idealist. He could be so fanatic a liberal that he had lost contact with the liberal ethos, would go to any lengths to destroy threats to democracy. He could be a paid political agent. Or he could be something that was beyond her understanding. One point was clear, he would kill without hesitation.

Mona wondered why, in her assessments, she had dwelled on lethal ability. Did she want one of the men to accomplish what she had failed at?

The answer to that was *no*. Perhaps it was the other way around. Worry.

The laughter following Steve's story fading, the youngest gang member put himself back in the limelight. With a smug twist to his mouth he said: "Hey, I bet I noticed something about ole Vale that none of you others did. Me, I got what they call powers of observation."

"You're a sharp lad, be Jasus. Go on, what didn't we notice?"

"I'll tell you. Vale, he wears special shoes, them kind that makes you taller. I call them a scream. A fucking riot."

Kale said, "Politicians are as vain as actors."

"You're right, Kale," Extra said. "Vale must be. Know what, when he'd done moaning about torture and tapping, he asked me what I thought of him, of his career like. He asked me what I remembered about his speeches."

Steve said laughingly, "Maybe the bastard *is* cracked."

"Yeah. Part of the time, when I told him, he looked as if he didn't believe me. A nut, that's what he is."

Kale glanced at his watch. He asked, "And what was that about a cigarette?"

Extra nodded. "He said he'd like to try one. Said he never had. But he smoked it like a champ. Nearly ate the damn thing."

Kale asked, "Didn't he cough?"

"Not a peep. I reckon that's real funny."

Kale was about to speak, but the Irishman got in first with, "I hope we're not forgetting the time."

Pushing himself off the fender, Kale said, "Not a chance. And the time is now." He looked around. "Smith?"

Mona got out of the car. "Yes?"

"The telephone call. Chief Inspector Raymond Atkinson, king of the pigs."

Steve rose stiffly from a squat. His face was alive with pleasure. "This is one I'd like to do meself. I'm a great horse trader."

Kale shook his head. "This is Smith's job. She can go out in public safely. No one knows a woman's involved. It's one of the cutest bits in the while deal. No one'll look at her twice."

"Sure, sure," Steve said. "But don't do too much haggling, Smith girl. Get the green stuff."

Mona moved away. She went around to the side of the house, Kale following. She lifted the motorbike away from the wall and wiped the damp from the saddle with her jacket sleeve.

Standing close, Kale said, "Got everything clear?" His voice was low, his manner tense. Both seemed out of keeping with the situation.

"I think so."

"Just ask if they're prepared to meet our terms. If they say no, put the phone down."

"If they make a counter offer?"

"The same. Say it's all or nothing. If it's nothing, ring off."

Mona looked up at him with a frown. "But Steve said—"

"Never mind Steve. I'm the boss. Do as I say."

She tilted her head and gave her attention to the machine. A minute later she was in the saddle and chugging off over the back field.

Mona was dazed. What Kale had just said had astounded her. She didn't understand. She felt more alien than ever to the three men, who, it now appeared, were equally as alien to each other. She was conniving at something that was beyond her comprehension. She was over her head in a swamp, an evil mess.

Mona looked back. The farm was out of sight, except for the tip of a chimney. Slowing, she got off the bike and flicked a switch to kill the motor.

Standing there alone and in the silence of the countryside, Mona soon recovered from her sensation of being dazed and entangled. She was even able to manage a faint smile on hearing a distant snatch of birdsong.

She thought about the hostage, Harold Devon Vale. She couldn't help feeling pity and a grudging respect for him. She mused that, after all, there did seem to be two Vales, the public personage and the private man—this from what Extra had said and what she had seen herself.

She felt closer to the private Vale than she did to her three partners in kidnap. He had a gentleness they lacked. She didn't want him killed or tortured or played with for amusement, not, at any rate, through any complicity of hers. If it weren't for that, for the fact that she was a quarter responsible for his predicament, she could simply ride off from here and never see any of them again.

Mona smiled. Her eyes grew wistful. It was a delightful notion, that of escape. It could all end right here. She could ride out of the swamp. Back home there would be a new life for a near-new person.

Mona looked at the distant chimney. She hated the thought of returning to the farmhouse. It was not only fresh air she had needed when she had gone outside. She had wanted to be away from the ugliness of it all.

Sighing, Mona shook her head. She said good-bye to the notion of immediate escape. It simply would not do. She had to help the prisoner. At the same time, she had a responsibility toward the gang. She couldn't turn them in. They hadn't done her any harm. So, how could she help Harold Vale without damaging the others?

For another five minutes Mona stood thinking. She found the answer. Getting back on the bicycle, she pedalled the motor to life and continued on her way.

It was going to be an interesting telephone call, she thought.

His shirt was grey with sweat. One sleeve had broken free of the stitching around the shoulder; it hung like a cod's mouth. There was an L-shaped tear on the right knee of his dirty, crumpled flannels. Rivulets of perspiration ran up or down or across his face, depending on the direction of his fight.

Harold Devon Vale hadn't been in such a filthy, stinking, battered, exhausted state since early childhood, since before he had started taking neat care of his person in order to please his mother.

But Vale was grimly pleased with himself. His lips, closed in determination and effort, had an upward curve. He didn't even mind the woman on television, who, giving a cookery demonstration, acted as though her audience was made up of the retarded. In fact, she had spurred him on to greater efforts.

Vale was sitting next to the front of the couch. He had worked his way here by rolling. It had been painful but swift.

Now, using the swaying weight of his trunk and the leverage of his feet, he flung himself sideways. The legs of the chair screamed and crackled. They were so loose that he expected victory at any moment.

He pushed back up from his safe landing on the couch seat. The chair wobbled clownishly as he wormed his way around until he had his back to the couch. He threw himself backwards—and gasped a smile at the resulting crack of wooden joints.

For some time Vale had been following this pattern, going in a circle, falling sideways, back, sideways again, forward. The chair legs had been strained in every direction.

The woman on television was saying that there was nothing traumatic about peeling potatoes so long as you went about it calmly.

Once more Vale worked himself back upright. And suddenly, with a crash, he found that he was lying on the floor. The chair legs had given way.

He was on his side. Firmly, he spread his feet. The

connecting spindle fell. His ankles were free.

Vale began a tentative straightening of his legs. Pain gushed through knees which had been bent for many hours. But, gritting his teeth, Vale went on straightening until the angle was gone. The pain eased. He looked down.

A front leg of the chair was dangling by each calf, held by the tape around the ankle. The wooden pieces looked like unfinished splints, looked ludicrous. Vale spent a minute in helpless laughter. His voice had a high pitch.

The chair now consisted of a seat and a backrest. Vale set about lifting his heels toward the front edge of the seat. It was an immense task for a man of his age and in his condition. It would have been impossible had he been paunchy. He whimpered at the returning agony in his knees.

Rolling onto his back he pressed his buttocks as far from the front as they would go. He slowly, grimly, forced his punished legs to fold.

At last he got the heels of his shoes into place. He swiveled them inward for the ultimate purchase. It was an unexpected gift that a slight ridge fronted the seat; he was able to click each heel behind it.

After a rest, he started to push, slow and with care to begin with but then using more vehemence when he saw that, thanks to the ridge, his shoes were going to hold there.

The chair seat eased away, sighing and crackling like a stick fire. Its defeat was abrupt. Though still only inches away from its true position, it broke free with a final yelping crack.

Vale himself yelped as his legs shot out straight.

Pain chased up from toes to groin, agony gave special attention to those knee joints. Yet Vale was smiling as he cried out.

Depleted but victorious, he got slowly to his feet. He felt as proud as if he had climbed a mountain. The way he gazed happily around the room made it appear that he had never seen the place before, and approved. He would have loved an audience.

His arms were still pinned behind to the remainder of the chair, but now he had all the rest of his body to work with. That and mobility.

He was looking about for a heavy piece of furniture onto which he could hook the chair back, and pull against, when he got a far better and simpler idea.

On unsteady legs he moved away. Before leaving the room he enjoyed the silliness of putting his tongue out at the woman on the TV screen.

He went through to the kitchen. A week seemed to have passed since he had last seen it. With his back to the cutlery drawer, he took hold of its knob and eased forward. The drawer came open.

Getting out a knife took much longer than he had expected. The frame to which his wrists were attached kept on interfering, the reach of his hands were limited, and he couldn't look around far enough to direct his aim properly.

He fumbled and struggled. Once he thought he had won when getting out an implement, but touch told him it was a fork. He dropped it and started again.

At length Vale pincered between two fingers a wooden roundness. He knew it to be the handle of a carving knife. Delicately, breath held, tongue protruding from a corner of his mouth, he lifted while simultaneously rising on his toes. He got the knife out.

Following a pause for recovery, Vale sank to a kneel. He put his feet together. Between them he placed the knife handle and held it tightly with his shoes. He began to slide the binding tape up and down against the edge of the blade.

His arms twitched as the tape gave way, cut through. The back of the chair fell with a lazy clatter. He let the knife follow. With a feeling of disbelief he gradually brought his arms around to the front. There was pain in his shoulders, but it was welcome.

Still slowly, Vale moved forward and down. He lay prone. He settled the side of his face on the wondrously cool linoleum. His arms he continued moving until they were stretched out ahead of him and spread in a V. He lay there quietly, smiling.

Lifting her motorbike over the padlocked gate, Mona turned to the right, whereas the night before she went to the left. She doubted if the authorities would have traced the call to the village telephone booth, but there was no sense in going there again, or even heading for that area.

Letting the small motor do the work, Mona went along the muddy lane. The sun was hidden now and the mistiness had intensified at ground level. Visibility ended gently at a hundred yards. It was like a dream landscape.

Mona wished she could wake up to find that

nothing was true of the past twenty-four hours, the past few weeks. But that wish was an old one. She had worn it out daily following her husband's death. She couldn't go back to that state of mind.

Nor, she mused, could she give in to another wish—that she had the toughness, callowness, to keep on driving and leave Vale and the others behind forever.

The lane joined a highway. Traffic moved along it in a steady stream. Mona turned with it and put up the hood of her jacket, holding it there with one hand.

Still in countryside, the highway met a junction formed by a traffic circle. Mona went around it twice before deciding on the narrowest of the intersecting roads—it was quiet.

Alone again, she let her hood fall back in the wind. She pondered on what she was going to say on the telephone to Chief Inspector Raymond Atkinson, selecting words with precision.

It was not Atkinson himself she was concerned about, but how the last part would sound to the three men back at the farm. They had to be convinced. But first, the policeman.

We have decided we cannot win, Mona thought. *You will not meet our terms, and we have no intentions of harming Mr. Vale. So we will leave him where he is, locked in, and later call you to tell you his whereabouts. By that time we can be far away.*

Yes, Mona mused, that seemed all right. Next would come: *Unfortunately, one of our members, the most radical and violent, would be opposed to this plan if he knew of it. He hasn't been told. He is prepared to go on, to fight to the death. But there is a way around this block if you and the media are willing to cooperate with the rest of us in releasing our hostage safely.*

Mona thought it sounded pompous, artificial, but when she actually spoke it she could tone that down. Atkinson, of course, must say he would give all the help he could. It was a present, as far as he was concerned.

She would ask if a message to the kidnapers could be broadcast on all television and radio stations during the next news feature. Again, the Chief Inspector would be sure to agree. She would ask him to write down, as she dictated it, the message he would give as his own:

I want you, the captors of Harold Devon Vale, to know that you are surrounded, though from a distance. We do not wish to endanger Mr. Vale's life by coming too close. We know you will get this message because we know you have a portable TV set. We also know about the sandwiches, the candles, and the Raleigh bicycle stolen yesterday. Your hideout was discovered early this morning by some hikers. If you want more proof that we have you surrounded, go and check the For Sale sign. We have taken it down.

That job, Mona thought, she could do on her way back to the farm, going the roundabout way. On the outside chance of Atkinson not agreeing to this scheme, mentioning the sign could do no harm. There were thousands of them in and around London. It could not possibly pinpoint the farm.

Mona went on with her mental construction of

Atkinson's message: *For the sake of Mr. Vale's safety, we are prepared to make a deal with you. We will give you an assurance, including my personal word, that from the end of this message you will have one hour of immunity. Leave Mr. Vale where he is and drive away in the Jaguar. We promise to let you through the ring. You won't even see us. This is your only chance. There will not be another. That is all. You have one hour.*

Mona nodded. She thought that unless they were obtuse, which she knew they were not, Kale and Steve would jump at the opportunity to escape—after the initial dismay and anger at believing themselves trapped. And believe they had to: the For Sale sign would settle that.

She decided, however, that to give the message more urgency and impact, more a feel of veracity, she would ask the Chief Inspector to have it broadcast as a flash, interrupting a scheduled programme. And she would ask that it not be done for twenty minutes or so, to give her time to get back. At the farm, she would make sure the others were watching.

Mona wondered if they would connect her with the message. She doubted it. In any case, she could act shocked—the supposed answer to her New Scotland Yard call was what they had heard already: no deals, no bargaining.

Houses began to appear. They were workers' row cottages that looked as old as gibbets and less attractive. Soon, above them through the mist, loomed a factory chimney. Mona could smell sulphur.

The houses came forward to line the road, like

squat grim sentries. Even so, there were few people about. A toddler sat tethered to a lamppost; on a corner leaned an old man, smiling as if he had invented patience; a woman with her hair in curling rags was sweeping her sidewalk territory.

There was a crossroads. Mona slowed. On each of the four corners stood a shop, a small and murky thing with windows purblinded by poster ads. One store was a combination post office and grocery. On the point of its curb was a telephone booth.

Mona stopped and dismounted. She leaned her bicycle on the shop wall. She raised her hood while looking around. In sight were only two women, gossiping together busily, and so far away they were grey in the mist.

Mona walked to the telephone box and went inside. She was calm. There was no hurry. This had to be done right. Leaning on the shelf while gazing around her, she went over again in her mind the wording of the message.

The British telephone booth, outdoors variety, is a clever piece of design. Its walls are made up of small panes of glass, easily and cheaply replaceable. Its door opens outward, rather than halving as it goes in, so that a collapsed person couldn't jam himself inside. The door is also heavy, unopenable by a child who might be intent on mischief.

But the touch of brilliance is the mirror over the shelf. The U.K. telephone box, as a rule, has little defacement in the way of graffiti. A caller finds doodling fun, but not half so much fun or as fascinating as looking at his own reflection.

It was this mirror that gave Mona the warning.

She was reaching into pockets for money and for the nylon to muffle the mouthpiece, when in the mirror she glimpsed a movement. She gave the glass her full attention, easing closer.

A man had come out of the shop on the opposite corner. He was staring at the telephone box. There was a hint of the predator in his stance—the rounded shoulders, arms held away from the body, slight sag of the legs.

More than that, however, what set Mona's heart tapping were the twin facts of his youthfulness and the wearing of a windcheater that had been bleached to paleness.

Bringing her hands from her pockets, Mona kept still and watched through the mirror. She saw the man move in a stealthy manner to the edge of the sidewalk. She saw his mouth flicker with eagerness as, in looking at her, he swept his eyes down and noted the black jeans.

The man was in his early twenties. He had long, greasy hair. His pants were stuffed into high boots. His face was lean and acne-scarred.

Lowering her head inside the hood, Mona watched and wondered. Could she bluff it out? Maybe. But the rest of her clothing under the jacket was black, and if she were searched, there was the gun, also the stocking.

The Whitecoat began to come across the street. He paused to bend down and take something from his boot. When he straightened, he was holding a knife.

Mona tensed to stiffness. There was nothing to wonder about now. She had only one idea: escape. The telephone call—that was forgotten.

The Whitecoat reached the curb. Through the mirror and from under the rim of her hood, Mona could see him behind her in sharp detail. She saw him come to the booth, saw him grasp the door handle.

At the same moment as the man pulled, Mona flung herself backwards. She used all her weight. The door crashed open, but, being heavy, with not enough speed to be effective.

Even so, the man was caught by surprise. He went staggering away. His face twisted both with anger and the knowledge that his suspicion had been right.

Mona slipped swiftly out of the booth. Her heart thumping and paining, she ran to the bicycle. She grabbed it and drew it from the wall.

From behind her came a clamor of footsepts. She still hadn't moved away when they stopped. A hand dropped on her shoulder. A voice grated, "Hold it, mate."

Resisting the hand's pull, Mona reached inside her jacket. She ripped up her sweater, grabbed the gun, pulled it free. Quickly she twisted around. At the same time she swung her arm high.

The Whitecoat saw the automatic. He glared at it as he ducked. But he moved in the wrong direction. Mona had been aiming to hit the hand that held the knife. Instead, the gun slammed against the man's temple.

He grunted and sagged, blood already spurting. He sagged toward Mona. He grabbed the front of her jacket. His weapon arm he drew back in an unsteady arc. His eyes were glazed.

Mona was terrified and sickened. She wanted to hit the man again but couldn't force herself to it. She gave him a mighty shove. His grip on her jacket broken, he went staggering away, reeling to keep a balance.

Mona turned. She fast-fumbled her gun into a pocket and gripped the handlebars. She ran to the bicycle to the road. Her legs were shaking.

There was a shout from a man who had appeared from one of the shops. The two gossiping women began to come forward. The Whitecoat called out urgently, "Stop him!"

Mona was still running with the bicycle. Now she leapt into the saddle. Head down, she pedalled madly to start the motor. The pedals seemed to weigh a ton.

The Whitecoat yelled, "Stop that man! Get him!"

The motor came to life. It put-putted with a gentleness that made Mona want to scream. Yet she was on her way.

The man from the shop came across the street at a run. It looked briefly as though he would be able to make an interception. But his reaching hand merely skimmed over the jacket's flying tails.

Mona zoomed on. She looked back. The last thing she saw, before the mist made a curtain, was the Whitecoat breaking away from the assisting hands of the two women, and running to the telephone booth.

Mona throttled for top speed. She bent low over the handlebars. Her nerves jangled when the motor coughed, stalled, coughed. But then it started to run smoothly again. She kept herself from wondering if she had enough gas.

The last of the houses flashed by. Ahead was a truck, moving slowly. Approaching was a car. Mona took a chance—had to, for she found it impossible to make herself reduce speed.

Cutting out into the other lane on the narrow road, she began to pass the truck. There was a squeal of brakes from the other vehicle. Cutting back, Mona avoided it with only feet to spare. Both drivers leaned out to screech obscenities.

Mona sped on. Oddly, she still seemed to be hearing the roar from the two vehicles. It rose above the sound of her own motor. There was nothing ahead to cause it. Fearful, she looked back.

The truck was lost in the mist. All she could see was the faint shape of a man on a motorcycle. She looked front, then behind again.

The shape had come fully clear from its misty cover. From the blood on his face, Mona recognized the motorcyclist as the Whitecoat.

Her pulses leapt like plucked flesh. She looked quickly ahead. She was almost at the traffic circle. Vehicles were moving around it in a steady stream. The roar from behind was louder.

Mona knew her motorized bicycle stood no chance at speed against a well-powered motorcycle. She debated stutteringly whether or not to ditch her machine and take to the fields. This she was still doing when she reached the circle.

She slipped into the turgid stream in front of a bus. From behind she heard a high wail of brakes. She prayed that they belonged to the motorcycle, that it had been forced to wait.

Keeping up her speed, Mona dodged in and out of the traffic. She was still crouched low, hood in position, jacket flapping out behind her. Her legs were still shaking. She thought repeatedly of that knife. Its blade had been long and evil.

Dodging, Mona moved to the inside, beside the island circle, which was covered with flowers. They mocked her with their placid beauty.

From her crouch Mona looked the other way. Beside her were two cars, moving parallel to each other. Through their windows she saw the Whitecoat. He was upright on his machine, head swiveling, face ugly in eagerness and worry. He didn't see her. He went on and out of sight.

Mona circled the island again. She saw no sign of the man who was chasing her. She hoped he had gone off searching along one of the intersecting roads.

"Stupid shit!"

The bellow at close range made every nerve in Mona's body leap. She swung her head. Coming level was the truck she had cut around minutes ago. The driver was leaning out, face livid. "Fucking moron!" he yelled.

Mona escaped by braking. The truck was forced to keep going by the press of cars behind. The driver threw back a final epithet.

Mona went on, dodging again. She finally reached her own road on the next circuit. The traffic here was still jammed, not yet drawn out from the island bottleneck. Mona positioned herself between a tall van and a car, the former at her back.

She felt so awful, so distraught, that she marveled at how she was able to go on functioning in a normal manner. She would have given anything to be able to sit in a corner and have a good cry.

She saw the mud lane. It was on the other side. Moving to the dividing line she forced herself to slow. Next she had to stop; the approaching traffic was too dense for a dash across.

She stood nervously astride the bicycle, stretching tiptoe to the ground. That reduced the shaking of her legs to a rigid trembling, as if she were lifting a great weight. Looking back, she saw two men on motorcycles. Neither was the Whitecoat. Her tension stayed strong.

A break came in the traffic. It was short but it would have to do. Mona pushed off and skimmed across the road. The first car beyond the break gave only a petulant horn-blast.

Mona entered the mud lane. Once off the road she looked back. What she saw made her gasp.

The man with the bloody face was coming.

He was speeding along the highway, straddling the white line. He had almost drawn level with the lane. He semi-stood like a jockey and stared straight ahead.

Sure that she hadn't yet been seen, Mona braked fast and let herself fall to the ground. She rolled, stopped, rolled back and grabbed the cycle.

She dragged it along with her as she crawled quickly to the hedge and into a shallow, dry ditch. There she crouched as the distinctive motorcycle growl swelled.

Then the growl faded.

Mona got up. The Whitecoat was passing all traffic, disappearing into the mist. Mona began to run. Pushing the bicycle, she held her upper body horizontal, bent to handlebar height. That kept her below the level of the hedge-tops.

A minute of this and she had climbed a rise. She started down the other side. The highway was out of sight. She jumped on her machine—its engine still running—and raced away down the incline.

Mona felt that she had made it. Her legs steadied and she allowed herself a watery smile at how good it was to have the wind through her hair.

The motorcycle growl came suddenly. It had been muffled while the machine was beyond the hill. The noise was like an attack.

After one frightened glance back to identify the Whitecoat, Mona leaned forward and speeded up. The padlocked gate was within sight. She yearned toward it. Fifty yards, thirty yards, twenty.

She reached the gate. Leaping to the ground, she hesitated for a split second before deciding not to abandon her machine. She heaved it up in the air by the handlebars and saddle, whining at the effort, and lifted it over to the gate's far side.

The Whitecoat was nearly here. His shouts could be heard above the engine.

Mona vaulted the gate. She grabbed the bicycle and ran. Jumping into the saddle she bumped on across the field. From behind came a down-throttle roar.

Mona looked back. The man with the bloody face was getting off his machine. He wasted five seconds by propping it on its leg instead of letting it drop. Springing to the gate he looked at the chain, shook it, slammed it down.

As the mist hid him from view he shouted, "I'll get you! I'll get you!"

Mona was gasping with fear and effort. But she knew she had a few minutes in hand. It would take some time for the Whitecoat to follow. He couldn't manhandle his heavy machine over the gate. He either had to break the lock or smash his way through the hedge—the last was doubtful, since he obviously loved his bike.

Mona thought that he might decide it would be quicker to work his way around by the lanes. A local man, he had to be familiar with the area.

Unconsciously urging the bicycle to extra speed by swaying her body up and down, Mona went over the next fallow field and then the next. The farm appeared.

Drawing closer, she pressed the horn and called out. She circled to the front without slowing. As she braked hard, the bicycle went into a skid. It flew away from under her and she was left miraculously on her feet facing the house door.

The three men came running out. Babbling, Mona told what had happened and what was about to happen at any minute.

Then all was panic. Shouts, questions, orders, curses, movement. Mona stood there and let the action swirl all around her.

Harold Devon Vale had wolfed the first sandwich and scalded his mouth with the first cup of tea. The second salami-on-rye that he made, he ate at a more leisurely pace, as well as spacing bites with sips from the refilled cup. His hunger ache was vanishing.

Vale stood by the kitchen table. His eyes were glistening with pleasure from the fast shot of whiskey he had taken before starting on food—no gourmet meal had ever tasted so exquisite.

The front legs of the demolished chair was still taped to his ankles, sticking up along his calves like external bones. Also, each of his wrists still had its half of the severed bondage. Nor had he washed. Nor had he changed his torn shirt and ripped trousers.

Humming, Vale made a third sandwich. He took it with him as he left the kitchen—stepping over the chair back and carving knife that were lying where they had fallen.

He went to the door of the apartment. Standing close, he listened. It was the second time he had done this. Outside in the hall all was still silent. Leaving the bolts and chain off, as before, Vale strolled away and went into the living room.

After turning down the sound on the television, he moved to the couch. He kicked aside the rear legs of the chair and its seat. While eating, he idly examined the possessions of the man who was being held hostage as himself, Edgar Carlton.

The gun, as the mimic had said, was useless, its barrel only an inch deep from the tip. Vale shifted aside the Maxted-type cap and the black slouch hat, lifted the topcoat.

Its pockets held only bus tickets, small change and a roll of surgical tape. The suit jacket was more fruitful. Vale found handout bills advertizing The Great Carlton, with blank spaces to be filled by club or theater name—an alien registration card and work permit—a card proving membership in the Variety

Artists Guild—a room key on a plastic tab that bore the name and address of a boardinghouse—cigarettes and matches.

At the last Harold Vale sneered. He had nothing but scorn for people who lacked the willpower to stop smoking. He himself had given it up years ago.

For the hell of it, and in celebration of his release, Vale got out one of the cigarettes and lit up. He thought what a ridiculous, messy and foul-smelling habit it was, to mention nothing of the dangers, ranging from simple burns to deathbed blazes, from coughs to cancer. Nodding at the ridiculousness, he went on smoking until the ash had reached the filter.

Cigarette stubbed, Vale looked around. He saw the telephone receiver lying where he had left it. He strode over and replaced it in its cradle.

Going back to the kitchen, he set about cleaning up all evidence of sandwiches and tea having been made.

The Jaguar, Steve driving, bucked and waddled as it sped along the track away from the farmhouse.

Edgar was mentally numb, still recovering from the swiftness of events. He sat in the back of the car between Kale and the girl. They were tense. They seemed not to notice when Edgar lurched against them with each sway of the car.

As had been the case for some time now, Edgar's features were relaxed, or at least, not pulled in the Harold Devon Vale mold. Had it not been for the tinted glasses, the slicked-down hair and the plastic rings in his nostrils, he would have had not the slightest resemblance to the politician.

The car slowed. Ahead was a gate set in a hedge. From one side rose a post topped by a For Sale sign. Even before the car had stopped, Extra was opening the door. He jumped out and ran to the gate.

Three minutes ago, Edgar had been sitting despondently in the back room. Time was getting on and there was no word of the real Vale having been found. The trouble was, Edgar didn't know if these people meant their threat or if they were simply playing with him cruelly.

From outside had come that gasoline-motor chugging, accompanied by shouts and beeps. Next, a babble of voices, sounds of frantic activity.

The door had burst open. Steve came in at a run. He grabbed Edgar and jerked him to his feet, snarling, "Let's go, let's go." Pulled forward, Edgar tripped over his handcuffed feet.

Cursing, Steve dragged him upright again and lifted him bodily, showing surprising strength in the act. Edgar flopped over the Irishman's shoulder like a half-full sack. He was carried through the main room, outside, dropped by the car and told to get in.

Kale had been at the back, trunk lid raised, filling his pockets with bullets and telling the others to come and get some. The youngest gang member was running in and out of the house, once with jackets, which he put in the car, once with the portable television set, which he was ordered to drop. Steve threw a motor-assisted bicycle clear of the track. Smith stood quietly through it all.

Then they had all bustled into the car—Steve grim, Kale keen, Extra grinning, Smith restrained.

Now, the gate opened, Extra was running back.

The Irishman gunned the motor viciously. He barely waited for the younger man to get in before slamming the Jaguar forward.

"Left," Kale commanded.

The car swung onto a narrow hard-top road and sped away.

Kale looked across Edgar at the girl. "Okay," he said tersely. "What happened?"

Coming back from her private distance, Smith talked, speaking in short, rapid sentences. She told of a telephone box, a man in a white jacket, a knife, a struggle, a motorcycle, being chased.

Extra glanced around at Edgar. "One of your snot-nosed Whitecoats," he jeered.

The leader asked, "But how did the bastard happen to be there?" There was a hint of suspicion in his tone, which Edgar thought odd.

Smith shook her head. "I don't know. No idea. It could only have been coincidence."

"What's it matter?" Steve snapped. "The damage is done. She should've led him away, not brought him to the bloody farm."

Extra sniggered. The girl said, "You can't do much leading on a puny little machine like I had."

"But there was no need to show him the way."

"All right," Smith said flatly. "I made a mistake."

Kale asked, "And he made a call before following you?"

"I saw him running to the box, yes."

The Irishman began cursing. He was inventive. He kept it up until ahead of them appeared a wider road. He said, "We go to the right here."

"Left," Kale said. He emphasized this by pointing.

Steve said, "I know left from right."

"Good. It comes in handy."

"But listen. Left takes us to the city, straight into trouble."

"And right gives us nothing but countryside."

"Isn't that what we want?"

"No," Kale said. "Don't be thick. They could catch us with a one-car roadblock. In the city we've got a thousand streets to choose from. Turn left."

"I dunno, be Jasus," Steve mumbled, bringing the Jaguar to a stop on the edge of the intersecting road.

Voice hard, Kale grated, "Left."

As the motor sank to idle, a yammering sound came from behind. They all turned, Edgar as well. Coming out of the mist was a man on a motorcycle. He wore a bleached windcheater. There was blood on his face.

"That's the one!" Smith gasped.

"Move!" Kale ordered. "And move left!"

The car jumped forward and went into a swinging curve. Kale grunted with satisfaction. He said, "Let's see you leave that thing behind. It's only a toy."

"I wouldn't bet on that," the Irishman said. He leaned on the wheel. "Depends on the traffic."

There was little of that around. The road was straight and with twin lanes on either side. Cottages and huge trees flashed by. Nervously watching the speedometer needle, Edgar saw it pass the hundred mark.

Everyone else except the driver was looking behind. Extra said, "I think the snot-nose is gaining."

Kale: "So do I." He sounded almost gratified.

Steve took the car at speed past a double-decker bus. The fast out and in swaying of the car made Edgar's stomach quail. He was hurting his fingers by gripping the top of the seat in front of him. He wished he were still in the farmhouse.

"Yeah, gaining," Extra said. "We're not gonna shake him off."

Coming rapidly into view were a set of traffic lights. They were on green. With fifty yards to go, they turned amber, then red. Edgar opened his mouth in fear and tightened his grip on the seat.

A truck came out from the right. Not slowing, Steve zoomed the other way. The truck driver saw him and braked, blanching as the Jaguar cut in front of his radiator with inches to spare.

Edgar closed his eyes.

When he opened them again he saw that the area had become suburban. Houses were spaced along either side. There were pedestrians. They stared at the speeding car. A dog ran out to wheel-yap but failed to reach its goal.

Extra said, "That slowed the Whitecoat a bit."

Another set of lights appeared. They were on green. The Jaguar went through safely. But traffic was thickening.

Smith exclaimed, "Look!"

Coming along on the other side, driving abreast, were three motorcyclists. They were young and wore bleached jackets.

Kale said, "The word's gone out all right. He made that phone call."

The Irishman said urgently, "Listen. I'm going to get off this road. Too many cars. I need some quiet streets."

Kale said casually, "You're the driver."

The Whitecoat cyclists came level with the Jaguar. Before it had whipped past they gave it a fast double take. Edgar looked back. The blood-streaked man signalled wildly to the others; but they were already slowing to make a turn.

Kale said, "The plot thickens."

The Jaguar came up behind two cars, one passing the other. The opposing lanes were equally crammed. Steve was forced to reduce speed. The needle sank rapidly below the fifty mark. Steve thudded his fist on the wheel and swore.

Edgar found, absurdly, that he was seized with the same sort of urgency, though he should have been hoping for the car to be stopped. Correcting this, he wondered about his chances if he were to push past the girl, open the door and throw himself out.

The overtaking car had gone on. Steve swept past it after first passing the other vehicle. He pressed one hand on the horn and kept it there.

"They're close," Extra said, his eyes bright as he stared back beyond Edgar. "All four of the snot-noses."

The Irishman had picked up speed, was overtaking car after car. Some swerved out of the way wildly, as if afraid of being hit. Passers-by stopped to stare. There were many more people about and the district was semi-commercial, stores mingled with houses.

With a final car passed, the way ahead was clear. Steve sent the Jaguar shooting forward. He released the horn. His grimness was an odd contrast to the near-gaiety of the other two men.

Edgar, tense again at the return to high speed, was thinking that this was getting more nightmarish by the second. He glanced at the girl. Also gripping the seat hard, she looked the way he was feeling—petrified. He resisted the foolish urge to give her arm a pat of reassurance.

On a corner ahead, a police constable leaned on a bike while talking to a girl. At the sound of the speeding car, he jerked his head around. He frowned in anger.

Reaching that point, Steve swung the wheel mightily. The car took the corner in a wide, tire-screaming arc. Staring, the constable saw Edgar. His mouth dropped.

Steve swiftly took several more corners. The Jaguar came onto a broad quiet street. There were no people in sight. The only cars were parked neatly at the curbs.

"Slow down," Kale said softly. "Slow down along here."

The driver turned his head to the side. "What?"

"Slow. Let the bastards get closer." He was rolling down the window.

Edgar's stomach lurched, as though he were in a dropping elevator, as the Jaguar suddenly reduced speed. He looked back when Extra said, "Here they are."

Closely behind were the four Whitecoats, side by

side across the road.

Kale tugged the gun from his belt. Turning, he knelt on the seat and put his head on one arm out of the window. Wind flung his hair into a panic. He aimed the gun.

The girl gasped, "No!"

Kale fired.

A Whitecoat arm shot up and back. The face sprang to a gape. The motorcycle swerved out of line. It swiped a parked car. The man fell off and went sprawling into the road. He bounced twice before settling.

Kale fired again. The noise was joined by shots from Extra, who was firing from the front at the other side.

One Whitecoat braked violently, went into a boot-scraping turn and headed back toward his fallen friend. They were both lost in the mist.

Kale and Extra kept shooting. Edgar felt pressure on his wrist; it was being gripped by the girl. He patted her arm.

One Whitecoat with blood on his temple had his whole face abruptly burst into redness. Streaks splashed out to form a star. That gone, his arms rose lazily as he drooped backwards. He fell to the road, landing in an ugly huddle. His machine careened on, leapt the curb, crashed into a garden wall.

"Got him!" Extra crowed. "I got the snot-nose!"

"Mine!" Kale shouted against the wind.

Letting go of Edgar's wrist, the girl turned away and sagged in her corner of the seat. Her face was sick-white.

Lowering his body to handlebar level, the remaining man behind reduced speed. He dropped back fast. As a final volley of shots rang out, he faded into the mist.

Extra and Kale brought their heads back inside the car. The latter said, "Get moving, Steve." The former turned with an anxious face: "I'm sure I got that second one. Honest."

The driver asked, "Fix 'em?"

"Three-quarters," Kale said. He was reloading his gun. "The last one might be crafty. He might stay there but out of sight. Fuck him."

"So what now?"

"Keep traveling. Get deeper into the city. We can hide among eight million people here."

"Sure and you're right about that," Steve said. He was pushing the car to its limits again.

Edgar felt too nauseated to be concerned as the Jaguar tore forward. The violence and blood had sickened him. Also, if he had harbored any doubts before about the gang's killer status, those doubts were gone now. The three men were not playing games.

Swallowing bile, Edgar leaned toward the open window near Extra, who had his head out to look back. Chill air buffeted in to perform a soothing massage on Edgar's hot skin. He was physically eased. He would have given two fingers for a cigarette.

Thoughts of past violence diminishing, Edgar was left with future violence, that which might be done to himself. There was one fast way out, he knew; the same escape he'd had all along. But he couldn't do it yet. He had to give Harold Vale a chance. Only at the last moment would he confess to being an imposter.

That the gang might then kill him out of rage, Edgar ignored. He had enough to fret about without introducing possibilities.

Extra called, "Yeah, snot-nose is still behind."

Kale: "Fine. Let him get bolder. We'll fix him."

"I'll blast him off the face of the earth."

The Irishman took a gloved hand off the wheel to wipe the windshield. He said, "This mist's getting worse. I won't complain about that. It can only help."

Houses on either side were barely visible. The mist was turning into a fog, which, as Edgar knew, would thicken the deeper they got into the sulphurous city and closer to the river.

Extra brought his head inside. He said, "Listen."

Faintly, drifting, came the wheezy hee-haw of a police siren. It seemed to be all around them, as if it were the voice of the fog, a keening lament.

The younger man said matter-of-factly, "That's for us."

Kale: "You might just have a point there."

Steve switched on his headlights. The beams bounced back from a smoke-like wall thirty feet away. He reduced speed, saying, "This is lovely. God bless it."

Kale said, "That sounds like two sirens to me, not one."

"Sure and they'll be all over the bloody shop."

The hee-haw had grown louder. Edgar willed it to greater strength while going back to the idea of making a swift exit from the car, should it be reduced to a placid speed.

He glanced aside at the girl. She seemed partway to recovery, her face less stark, less white. Sitting erect, she was looking around as though her surroundings were important.

Edgar and the girl locked eyes. He wasn't sure, but in the brief pause, before Smith turned away, he thought he saw her lips form a slight smile.

The car went along more residential streets. What traffic there was moved cautiously and with all lights ablaze. The fog became denser. Extra reported that the Whitecoat was still behind. The police siren or sirens continued at the same volume.

Abruptly, there was a child right in front.

The little girl was chasing a ball.

Smith screamed. Edgar felt as if he'd been punched over the heart. Kale swore. Steve threw his body back as he stood full-weight on the brake.

With a shriek of tortured rubber, the car shuddered to a halt. The child leapt away from the front fender. After looking back with wide eyes, she ran on into the fog.

"Holy Mother of Christ," Steve said in a hollow whisper. He blessed himself twice and kissed his thumb. The car was dawdling.

Edgar groaned as he breathed out his relief. Smith retreated to her corner again. Kale snarled that these young shits were a menace. Extra said sycophantically, "Too fucking right they are. A menace."

Kale ordered, "Drive on, drive on."

Only when the car was picking up speed did Edgar realize he had lost a good opportunity for a fast exit.

He shrugged it off. He'd had no energy to spare for that.

The occupants of the car were still recovering from the near-miss, the ambience tense, when Steve shouted, "Cops!"

Coming into view, pushing away coils of fog, was a car topped by a lighted police sign.

Kale snapped, "Down!"

Edgar found himself pushed onto the girl's lap. He also found that a hard object was being pressed into his spine. That gun stopped the ideas he was having when he saw the door handle a few inches from his face.

The gun left. Edgar sat up, as the others were doing. Kale asked, "Did they see us?"

Steve: "No idea. I was looking the other way. Casual like. I'm a great actor at the innocence."

Extra said petulantly, "The bastards had their siren off."

The Irishman laughed. "The English, they just don't know the meaning of fair play."

Kale ordered, "Change direction. Let's get away from here."

"Yes, sir. And you're right. They're bound to have seen us." He turned into a side street, followed it as it curved away, joined another street and went on. He drove in fast bursts, like drawn-out lurches, attacking the wall of fog between pauses of caution.

They came into a shopping district. All store windows were lit against the eveninglike gloom. Traffic was meager. The Jaguar passed within ten feet of two constables. Their backs turned, they were looking in the window of a bookstore. The siren hee-haw was still audible.

The shops began to thin out. Extra put his head outside and looked back. He said, "Would you believe it, snot-nose is still following."

Kale made a move toward his window. "I've had enough of him."

"Hold on," the Irishman said. "I'll handle this one. Leave him to me."

"How can you shoot and drive?"

"No shooting. Not in this fog. We might hit somebody else."

The girl spoke. She said, "A child."

Extra asked, "What you gonna do, Steve?" He sounded petulant again.

"Watch, lad," the Irishman said. He went ahead with one of his fast bursts. Slowing suddenly, he pounded the side of the steering wheel with both hands to get it at full lock, at the same time returning to speed.

Screeching, the car made the turn. It charged forward. On the other side of the street, a motorcyclist appeared through the fog curtain. He wore a bleached windcheater. He wasn't looking at the Jaguar.

Steve slammed his foot to the floor. The car shot across the road. Edgar heard Smith whisper, "Oh God." He stared in horror.

The Irishman was hunched forward. Through clenched teeth he said, "Kill or cripple. He's had his fun."

To Edgar's racing nerves it seemed to take forever

for the Whitecoat to see the hurtling car. Once he did, however, his response was fast.

The motorcycle began to rear, like a horse. The front wheel went up until the machine was almost vertical. Its owner leapt off backwards and kept his feet. He turned. He threw himself onto the hood of a parked car.

The Jaguar sideswiped the still-standing bike. "Missed the fucker," Steve snarled as he fought the steering wheel. The car swept away and careened across the road.

They were heading straight for a standing van. Edgar opened his mouth wide to let the air of fear gush out.

The brakes squealed and Steve battled the wheel. It seemed impossible for them to miss the van. But they did. They passed behind it and bounced over the curb and shot across the sidewalk.

With a horrendous crash, the Jaguar buried its nose into the window of a store.

In one hand Mona clutched the sleeve of Harold Vale's blazer, in the other she held her own throat. She was crouched low, knees jammed against the seat in front. She hoped she wasn't going to burst out crying.

The racket of the collision was over. The rending of metal, the crunch of shattered brickwork, the crash of breaking, falling glass—these were past. The car had become perfectly still. Its motor had died. There was silence, an awesome quiet.

Mona, like the others in the Jaguar, seemed

frozen. She stared ahead at a background display of sweaters, a collapsed pyramid of handbags, dresses glinting with shards of glass. In the middle, an unimpressed mannequin was rocking gently on its base.

The silence felt minutes long. It was probably five seconds. It ended when Mona let go of Vale's sleeve in order to cover her mouth, contain the threatening weep.

Noise began. Steam hissed from the radiator. The other gang members started calling out to each other. Masonry clattered down on the buckled hood. From inside the store, but weirdly seeming to come from the mannequin, sounded a female scream.

Kale's shout rose above the noise and the voices of the others: "Out! All out! Move!"

All the doors sprang open. Mona found herself standing on the sidewalk. With her were the four men. She was still more concerned with not crying than with anything else.

A woman came running from across the road. She panted, "Anyone hurt?"

Extra stepped forward. He met the woman and gave her a mighty shove. She staggered backwards, arms waving. She fell against the parked van and dropped to her hands and knees. Mona gazed at her without emotion, a detached interest.

Two voices were now screaming inside the store. There were shouts from the gang and elsewhere. The shrill hee-hawing was louder. It was the confusion at the farm all over again.

"Smith!"

Mona turned. Between them, Kale and Steve were

half-carrying, half-dragging the prisoner, hurrying him away. Extra was following, his gun out and nosing from side to side. Mechanically Mona tailed on behind.

Kale looked back, snapping, "The jackets. We'll need the jackets. You two get 'em."

Mona halted. Standing still as Extra dashed past her toward the car, she calmly congratulated herself for having her garment on. Unlike the others, her give-away black clothes were already mostly hidden.

It was the sobbing from the fallen woman that brought Mona alert. With quick looks around, she reassessed the situation.

Extra was pulling clothes from the car. The other two and Vale, were fading into the fog. She was alone and unnoticed.

There would be nothing to stop her slipping away, Mona thought. She could lose herself in the fog within seconds. Within an hour, she could have collected her things from the hotel and be at Kings Cross, waiting for the first train north. She would be out of this insane mess.

Extra ran by. He called, "Come on, come on."

Mona sighed. She was forced to let go of that lovely idea of freedom. At least for the moment. First, she felt honor-bound to help the prisoner escape. She couldn't desert him. She felt this more than before, now that she had seen what the man were capable of. Turning, Mona ran on, away from the people who were gathering around the car and the sobbing woman.

They were lost behind her in the fog by the time she caught up to the men. Steve had the hostage over his shoulder. Kale and Extra were struggling into their jackets as they went, the latter grumbling that he should have tried to find the Whitecoat to blast him.

"This is no good," Mona said. "We can't go on carrying Vale. We'll have to take those handcuffs off."

She was ignored. Kale, his jacket on, said briskly, "Here, this one'll do." He went into the recessed entrance of a small store. The window held shoes. The others followed.

Last in, Mona closed the door. Kale reached past her to shoot a bolt and pull down the shade. Steve let the prisoner drop onto a bench seat.

From the rear came a man, short and middle-aged, hairless except for a drooping walrus moustache. He was smiling until he saw the gun.

Extra jabbed it forward after tossing the Irishman his garment. Solemnly, not believing himself, the bald man said, "It's a joke."

"So laugh," Steve said.

Eyes round and sad, the owner put both hands behind his back. He said a gentle, "Excuse me, but there's nothing in the till. I haven't had a sale for two days."

"We don't want your fucking money, Dad," Extra said. "Get over there. Park your arse and shut up."

Meekly the man went to the bench and sat beside Vale, who was semi-lying in a sprawl.

Steve buttoned his jacket. "Listen. We've got to talk about this."

Kale said, "Not yet. We need to get away from

this area. Fast."

Extra: "That's for sure."

They spoke quickly, urgently, their voices rising against the continuing patter of running footsteps in the street outside.

Mona said, "We're not going to do anything fast as long as Vale's got those cuffs on."

Kale jerked his head. "Right. Take 'em off."

"Side pocket," Extra said. He wasn't about to do it himself, Mona knew, so long as he had a finer role to play, that of the gun-wielding tough.

Mona went to his side. While fishing out the key, she noted with relief that the store owner wasn't looking at her. His eyes were on the gun.

Mona turned her back to him when she crouched at Edgar's feet. Clumsily with gloved fingers, she set about unlocking the handcuffs. By the time she had finished, the owner, on Kale's orders, had been taken away and put in a storeroom.

"That's not going to last forever," Steve said.

Kale said, "It'll hold him long enough. Ten minutes is all we need, with this fog to help. Let's go."

They went through to the rear. There was a grimy backyard, a gate, a grimier alley. They moved along it. Kale led the way, with the Irishman next. Last was Mona. Extra was in charge of the prisoner; he held onto the blazer with one hand and kept his gun poked into Edgar's back.

The hee-hawing floated in the air above.

At the alley's mouth Kale looked out cautiously. He signalled the all clear. They crossed a street and went into another service lane. They continued this pattern until the police siren had grown faint. The fog was thicker, the air colder.

They stopped beside a row of plastic beer crates. As if out of habit, Steve lifted one of the bottles and looked at its bottom. It was empty. Letting the bottle fall back, he turned.

"So okay. What now? Do we split up?"

Kale shook his head. "Strength in numbers. And right now we're fine. We'll be even better once we get further away."

"So what we going to do?" the Irishman asked. "The Indian rope-trick?"

"Find somewhere to hole up, I suppose. I'm not sure. I have to do some thinking. I'll come up with something, don't worry."

Extra asked, "Where's my handcuffs?" He stared accusingly at Mona.

She said, "I left them on the floor in the shop."

The young man looked crestfallen. He cheered himself by jabbing Edgar in the back and saying, "What about this sod?"

Steve: "Sure. Do we take him, leave him, kill him—what?"

"We take him," Kale said. "He's our ace, our lever." He looked at the hostage. "You, take those specs off. Also the tie."

Edgar took off his necktie and glasses. He put them in his pockets. Mona was startled at how different he appeared. This was voiced by the Irishman, who said, "Christ in Egypt, son, you're not looking yourself at all these days."

Extra sniggered, "He's a bit upset about something. I can't think what."

Kale moved on. "Let's travel."

They went forward in the same positions as before. Mona was feeling calm and confident. The first hurdle was over—for the rest of Vale's escape, she would play it by contingency. The right moment was bound to come.

Mona didn't mind when the sound of police sirens died. She saw little help in that direction. The weather was going to be her best, hiding friend. And it was growing worse—meaning better. Visibility had shrunk to twenty feet.

The group paused at an alley's end. When the leaders moved on again, Mona touched Extra's arm and kept him standing there. She said, "I'll take over now."

"No. I'm okay."

"You might be needed as a rear guard. You're a better shot than me."

Extra said, "If there's any trouble behind, we can soon switch places."

"There might not be time for that."

"Course there will."

"Anyway, that Whitecoat might still be quietly trailing us. Shouldn't you hang back a bit and see?"

Extra said a scornful, "He couldn't trail us through that locked shop door."

Before Mona could press the argument, Kale called from the street ahead, "What's the hold up?"

They went on.

After a final stretch, there were no more service lanes. The group was forced to go along a residential street. But Mona had to admit that, strung out like this, they looked innocuous enough. In any case, there were few people about, and those who did pass by, did so hurriedly, scarves over their mouths.

Lights appeared through the yellowness. They belonged to a cluster of business places. First in line was a workers' cafe, a greasy spoon with a split handle. Tape covered the cracks in its steamed-up window. The menu was chalked on a board outside.

Kale stopped. The rest joining him, he said, "We'll go in here. A fast bite and hot tea, it'll work wonders."

"I think you're barmy," Steve said. "But the notion is dear to me heart."

Mona said, "And mine." This, she thought, had distinct possibilities.

Kale nodded. "Right. We'll keep in two groups. You three follow in a minute. Come on, Steve."

The Irishman said, "Maybe Smith should go with you."

Mona, quickly: "Don't bother about me. Go ahead."

The two men pushed open the door and went in. Extra mused aloud, "Looks nice and cozy in there."

Mona said, "Go in first, if you like."

"Oh well. I can bear it."

She held back from trying to persuade him, knowing it would not only fail but could have an adverse effect. She thought hard to come up with a better idea.

In a low voice Extra said, "That second Whitecoat. You know, when the four of 'em were behind us. Well, I'm sure it was my shot that got him. Were you watching? Did you see?"

"Yes," Mona said, forcing sincerity. "And I

agree with you. I think it was your bullet."

"Straight?" He produced an uncertain smile.

"Truly. I was listening to the shots as well as watching. I can show you what I mean, if you want."

The young man was blinking keenly. "How?"

"You go over there by that lamp," Mona said. "I'll guard Vale. Go over there and pretend you're on a motorcycle, holding the handles."

"Okay. Wait a minute." Extra began to put his gun in his belt.

Two women loomed out of the haze. One was telling the other in an offended-sounding voice that this was nothing, a bit of mist, not like the pea-soupers in the old days; you didn't get real fogs anymore.

She and her friend glanced idly at the trio, passed on, went from sight.

Mona said, "Let's get on with it. This is interesting."

Extra shrugged. "Never mind. We'll do it later. My feet're cold. We can go in now."

Mona gave up. For the present. She could try the same thing again, if nothing else came along. Her hopes were high.

The young man pushed Edgar Carlton forward, saying a growled, "I'll be right beside you, one hand on my gun. You get brave—I shoot."

They went into the cafe. Mona followed.

The place was small and had a bad smell, like old dishwater. A line of tables stood on either side of an aisle that led to the serving counter. The tables were bare wood, unpainted. One had an old man asleep.

One had four men in coveralls dipping into bowls of soup.

With tea and a thick sandwich each, Kale and Steve were sitting with their backs to the counter. Behind it, a woman looked at a newspaper with one eye; the other eye was screwed closed against the smoke trickling up from the cigarette in her lips.

Extra chose a table near the door. He guided Vale into a chair facing the window and sat on his right. He kept his own right hand inside his jacket.

He said, "We'll have tea and ham sandwiches, won't we, Fred old mate?"

Vale nodded. Mona went to the counter and repeated the order, for three. She glanced down at Steve and Kale. Chewing, they acted as though she weren't there.

The counterhand came close to that attitude. One-eyed, the cigarette dangling, she flopped ready-cut sandwiches onto plates, filled mugs from an urn and chanted the price, all the while throwing looks back at her newspaper. The page, Mona saw, was devoted to the kidnaping.

Returning to the table with the refreshments on a tray, Mona wasn't surprised that the woman and soup-eaters were showing no interest. The newcomers were not out of place here in their rough clothing; also, each of the men was in need of a shave.

Mona set out plates and mugs, put the tray aside and sat down facing the two men. She was thinking busily of ways and means.

Extra wolfed at his sandwich with his left hand.

Mona slid her own across to him. She was too tense to eat. She sipped her tea, which was good, and watched the prisoner, who had left his food after one bite. He looked up.

Their eyes holding, Mona tried to put into her expression what she couldn't say: *I want to help you. I'm through with all this. I'm no longer on the side of these men. I've been wrong. Whatever you are, I am going to try and get you away. Be ready to act.*

The captive frowned, his face puzzled. It was obvious that he read nothing of what was being conveyed—except, perhaps, the sympathy.

Mona stretched out her leg under the table. Her foot met another. She topped it, pressed down.

Extra looked up quickly. "What's wrong?"

She had made the wrong contact. Withdrawing her foot, she said, "Be careful."

"I am," he said grumpily. "Don't worry about me."

It was obvious that in leading the Whitecoat to the farm, Mona had lost the stature she had previously held in Extra's values. That was going to be a drawback.

"I don't worry about you," she said. "You're slick. I never saw anyone slicker."

The young man smirked in a way that at any other time would have caused Mona to laugh out loud.

Two men wearing bus-driver uniforms came in noisily. At the counter they joshed its keeper, who came alive with giggles. Two more drivers came in.

Mona noted a sign at the rear pointing the way to the lavatories. She wondered about that. If she could get Vale out there, if there was an exit from the back of the building, they could both make a run for it.

But then she saw that Kale and Steve were preparing to leave. And that gave her a different idea. Their way to the aisle was blocked by the four joking bus drivers.

Nerves taut, Mona got up quickly. She stepped around the table, took hold of Vale's arm, jerked upward. "Come on, you."

Through a mouthful of food, Extra said, "Hey, what the hell."

"I'll take over now," Mona said, one hand inside her jacket. "Let's go, Vale."

Extra: "There's no hurry."

"One of those drivers has been looking at us in a funny way."

Extra turned to face the counter. "Oh?"

"Come on, Vale," Mona said again.

He got up tiredly. Mona could have screamed at how sluggishly he moved. She hustled him toward the door. It was a yard away. From behind, Mona heard the squeak of chairs as Kale and Steve rose from the table.

She reached ahead, took hold of the handle, pulled the door open. Extra was getting up. He grumbled, "I don't see no driver looking at us."

Mona placed Vale ahead of her in the doorframe. She had hold of the outside handle now. Taking a deep breath, she put a hand in the small of the prisoner's back—and shoved. She shoved with all her strength.

As the man went away from her in a running

stagger, Mona gave a cry as if of surprise and fell to her knees in the doorway, though keeping a grip on the door handle.

With a rush, Extra came up. He tried to pass swiftly through the space. He couldn't stop himself in time. He tripped and fell on top of Mona. Her grip on the handle was broken. She was forced flat to the ground.

She looked up. Harold Vale was a dozen feet away. He had recovered his balance, was leaning on the side of a car. He was faced in the opposite direction.

Mona thought urgently: *Run, you fool.*

There was a crash as someone leapt over the two on the ground. It was the Irishman. He went racing across the sidewalk. His gun was in his hand.

He reached the prisoner just as he was turning. Steve raised the gun high. He bought it down smartly on the politician's head. Harold Vale fell.

The real Harold Vale yawned. It was a comfortable, even luxurious yawn. He gave himself over to it with a will—vocalizing, craning his neck, and ending with a shudder in shoulders and feet.

Vale was stretched out supine on the thick carpeting of his hallway. His head was near the apartment door. Close to his right hand lay a gun in a shoulder holster.

Vale had been here since cleaning up crumbs in the kitchen. He was content. The chair legs taped to his ankles were no trouble, nor were the strips of tape still attached to each wrist.

He felt quite safe, although the door was held only by its one lock—the bolts and chain were still off. Through the wood he would not only be able to hear any approach, but also to judge whether it bode for ill or good.

If an enemy came, Vale would shoot bolts and fix the safety chain into place; also he had the gun. If rescuers came, he would swiftly replace the holster in his bedroom, go to the kitchen, and from there shout for the people to break in; when they had done so, they would find him on his knees in the supposed final moments of freeing himself with the carving knife.

Vale was taking no chances. He would stay where he was still after zero hour, after Edgar Carlton had been killed—the man was a criminal and deserved nothing better. That killing over, the gang would surely be caught. If they were told now that they had the wrong man, they would let him go, and try for the real target some other time.

Harold Vale yawned again.

First Edgar was aware of pain. Next he found that he was in a sitting position, and low, on a floor. Third he realized he was slowly moving both hands over his face and head. He told himself that he was, of course, waking up in the back room of the farmhouse.

His hands went on roving. They found stubble on his chin, cold sweat on his brow, and near the crown of his head's shaven patch a lump, source of the pain.

A voice said, "He's coming to."

Another said, "About time, be Jesus. Must have a skull as thin as tissue paper."

As he seeped to full consciousness Edgar remembered. He recalled everything up to seeing the gun in Steve's hand as it came toward him. For the rest, he listened to the others' continuing talk as he recovered.

He had been unconscious for ten minutes. The patrons who came out of the cafe had been told that he had fainted; it had been a close thing, with more than a little suspicion on the part of one of the soup-eaters. The gang had carried him away and brought him to this place, a church porch, where they had dumped him on the step. They thought he had been trying to run away when leaving the cafe.

Which, Edgar thought, was not true. It simply hadn't occurred to him, not at that moment. Before, yes, several times he had thought of escape, and twice had actually been on the point of making a run for it. Unfortunately, the girl, as well as Extra, had been nearby both times.

Now, Edgar felt he could accomplish nothing strenuous. His head ached—a throb spreading out from that lump. His stomach quavered. His legs were trembling and feeble. And the cold was making him want to curl into a ball. He sighed drearily on hearing Kale say, "Up you get, Vale."

"Let me sit a little longer."

"No dice. Time we moved on."

"Yeah," Extra said. "Who knows, them cafe people might've taken seconds once we'd gone.

Inside, one of the drivers was looking at us, Smith said."

Steve: "Is that a fact now?"

The girl: "I could've been mistaken."

Kale said again, "Time we moved on."

The Irishman grabbed Edgar by the arm and pulled him upright. Ramming a gun in his back he urged him off of the porch. They went along a fog-vague street. The others were behind, Kale first.

Steve said, "Talking of time, I think we've forgotten something."

Kale asked, "What?"

"The deadline. That witching hour of twelve."

"It did sort of slip my mind. I haven't been thinking straight since you smashed up the Jag."

"Is that meant to be the needle?" Steve asked, lightly but with an underlying hint of displeasure.

"Meant to be nothing," Kale said. "How far off is the deadline?"

"An hour and a half."

"Okay. And another little matter's been neglected, if not forgotten. The call to Atkinson. It hasn't been made yet."

"Sure. Our girl Smith made a fuck-up of that one too."

Extra called, "Do we contact Atkinson now?"

"Of course," Kale said. "Let's find a box."

They went on. The far side of the street was hidden by fog. On this side, there were railings to guard a spread of gravestones that were crowding each other as if eager to get out.

Edgar moved awkwardly, chilled and stiff. But he

was feeling better—the pain less—by the time the group came to a red telephone booth, its light gleaming eerily through the yellowness.

The five people clustered together. Kale pulled the door open, saying, "Okay, Smith. This is your scene. He knows your voice."

He ushered the girl inside, followed her and kept the door open wide with his foot. The space was filled by Extra and Steve next to Edgar.

Stone-faced, Smith lifted the receiver, put a coin in the slot, dialed a number. From her pocket she took what looked like a black stocking. She used it to cover the mouthpiece.

A distant call signal sounded. It was followed by a voice that came faintly but clearly to all present. The girl said, "Put me through to Chief Inspector Raymond Atkinson. The code word is K.E.S.S." She spoke gruffly.

After a pause, a different voice came on the line with a crisp, "Atkinson here."

Smith said, "You know who I am."

"I do. And you're in trouble."

"Why's that?"

"You're on the run and you have nowhere to hide. You'd be wise to give yourselves up. All of you."

"Never mind that," the girl said. "What about our demands?"

"No deals. That's final. We wouldn't give you a phony quid or spring a pickpocket. No deals."

"I see."

"And," the policeman said, "in case you don't know it, you're wanted for murder."

The girl looked at Kale, at Steve, at Extra. Into the receiver she asked, "You mean the motorcyclist?" Her voice was less gruff. Her hand seemed to be trembling.

Atkinson said, "Right. He died with not much of a face left. And the other one's on the danger list. So if—"

Kale broke the connection by putting his hand on the cradle. He said, "That's all we need to know."

"No deals," the Irishman said bleakly. "No fucking deals."

"Don't worry," the leader told him. "They'll change their minds when it gets closer to the deadline."

It occurred to Edgar that Kale, curiously enough, looked pleased.

Extra startled them all. He burst out with a loud, "Hey!"

Edgar swung around with the others. Fading away into the fog with a backward glance was a man. Young, he wore a bleached windcheater.

The girl gasped, "Just like before."

Extra went running off after the Whitecoat, his gun held high. He was back almost at once. "Not a sodding hope."

Kale said a curt, "Right. Let's move. We've got to get away from here. They'll have us pinpointed within minutes."

They left the telephone booth and went on, Edgar and Steve in the lead. Edgar still felt too wretched to care about the outcome of this strange situation. It didn't make him feel better to know that the

Whitecoat motorcyclist had been killed—though that should have come as no surprise, the way the man's face had burst into blood.

"We need a car," Kale said, coming up from behind. "We must have wheels." He went ahead, and began trying the door handles of vehicles lining the curb.

They covered two blocks. People walked by and showed no interest. Visibility was down to a swirling fifteen feet. Passing cars had their lights on.

Kale came back, stopped and pointed over the road. "That'll do. It's quicker."

Glowing dimly was a circle of light. Though indistinct, it was recognized by Edgar as the sign of the Underground, London's subway system.

Steve said, "You're losing your grey cells."

"I've been right before," Kale said. "Come on."

"Sit in a train? We'll be seen as clear as clear."

"We were seen in the cafe too. Come on."

The Irishman laughed. "Why not?"

The group moved across the road. Still strung out single file, except for prisoner and guard, they entered the station. It was busy, a bustle of people and talk and clicking ticket machines. Even in here the fog had penetrated, making for a soft misty light.

Kale led the way past an unmanned entry barrier and to the top of the escalator. He, like the girl, had the hood of his jacket lifted. As they would onto the escalator, he bumped against a stout woman who was loaded with shopping. He said a polite, "Excuse me."

Edgar thought how weird it all was. He went on thinking it as they descended to the bottom, walked along a passage, chose a platform and stood there quietly waiting, separated one from another by other commuters.

The gun in his back felt different and Edgar knew it was now in Steve's pocket. He obeyed its nudge, moved over to where Kale was looking at a poster advertising female underwear.

In a tone of light conversation, the Irishman said, "Got news for you, friend."

"Nice crotch on this one. What news?"

"We were naughty. We neglected to buy tickets."

Kale deadpanned, "I can't begin to tell you how worried that information makes me."

"What about the other end?"

"We'll manage."

"We could've bought tickets easy enough."

Irritably, Kale said, "I can't think of everything."

"Sure and it's nothing too terrible," Steve grinned. "And you're right about that crotch."

A train came rumbling in. It dropped speed rapidly and squealed to a halt. The middle doors of a carriage appeared directly in front of where Edgar and the other two stood. People pushed toward them as the door hissed open. Kale went on, heading for an end access that was not being used.

Following with Steve, Edgar became suddenly alert.

Surely, he thought, here among all these people, the gang wouldn't dare to go in for gunplay. Certainly Steve, if not the other man, would be concerned about hitting bystanders—the way he had when he tried to get the Whitecoat with the car instead of shooting him.

It was a chance to make a break.

His face nervously rigid, Edgar followed Kale into the end of the carriage. The leader stood beside the closed door at the other side.

What happened next was, for Edgar, like performing an act in slow motion.

He turned into the body of the coach. There were one or two people standing, some sitting on either side. The strides that Edgar suddenly started taking seemed as fast as a wade in thigh-deep water. But they took him away from Steve.

Edgar circled a standing man. From behind he heard sounds of hurried chase. He next approached a woman who had just entered. He recognized the laden shopper to whom Kale had been polite.

Edgar slipped around the stout woman like someone doing the hesitation waltz. But he knew he was actually going quickly because the woman looked startled and turned with him. He went on.

At a crash he looked back.

Parcels were falling with balloon speed from the woman's arms. Steve was trying to get by her, his face twisted with rage. Farther back, Kale was coming forward at what to Edgar looked like a stroll.

The shopper began to stoop to the side, blocking that way. The Irishman went in the other direction. He kicked a parcel.

Edgar turned and strolled on. He counted each step he took. There were six and then he was at the center door.

In through it crowded schoolgirls. Edgar knew there could only be ten or a dozen of them even though it appeared as if there were fifty, just as he knew they were giggling and not screaming with laughter.

His heart pounded. He pushed into the wriggle of girls. They were in the mid-teens, hefty in their uniforms. Some were almost as tall as he was.

He forged ahead against the stream. But he didn't know if he was moving or being held in one place. Again he looked back. Steve was just leaving the woman shopper behind. Kale was still far to her rear. Neither man had produced his gun.

Edgar forged on. He went past the last of the girls, snailing free of encumbrance. Passing through the doorway he reached the platform. He was free to run. There was not a person in sight.

The slow motion impression ended.

With a gasp Edgar flung himself forward. He wheeled his arms and legs with all the force and desperation the moment called for.

Extra appeared.

One second the platform was clear, the next it seemed entirely occupied by the young man. He had stepped out of the carriage's far end door.

Extra held forward the side of his jacket that was toward the train windows. It hid from view the fact that he had his gun out. He was aiming it and grinning.

Edgar clattered to a halt. Not even briefly did he doubt that Extra would shoot. He halted. Turning around without waiting for an order, he went back to the middle door. He entered the carriage, brushing by Steve and then Kale.

The escape attempt was over.

Edgar took a seat, folded his arms, sank chin to

chest. He was breathing heavily and his legs had tremblelike twinges. But he realized with some surprise that throughout it all he had not been as terrified as he would have expected.

The train moved off.

Edgar soon recovered. He was, in fact, vaguely elated. Whether this was euphoria at still being alive, or pride in having responded well, he didn't know.

The journey went on, the train speeding between station stops. Passengers left, others boarded.

Beside Edgar sat Steve, his attitudes full of menace. The youngest gang member stood in a lazy, hoodlum slouch by one door, Kale strap-hung near another. Directly opposite sat the girl, face shrouded by the hood of her jacket.

Edgar wished he could figure her out. At times she was as belligerent as the three men, at others she seemed full of compassion. And occasionally, looking at him, it appeared as if she were trying to get a message across with her eyes. But then perhaps the message was only, I hate you, you killed my husband, I'm happy to have you in my power.

As the train slammed into another station, Kale gave a signal. The group left by the three doors and went along the platform.

The Irishman put his pocketed gun in Edgar's back. He said in a chatty manner, "That was a nice try, son. But if it happens again I'll destroy your spine. I'd hate to be embarrassed in front of the others."

They went up an escalator. Kale was leading, next came Edgar and his guard, with the girl behind and then Extra. There were other commuters in between, breaking up the group.

At the top they moved toward the barrier, where a porter was collecting tickets. When Kale strode straight past him he called, "Ticket, please, sir!" It had the clack of repetition; he met forgetful people a hundred times a day.

Two women pushed him their tickets and went on. Next were Edgar and Steve. They went straight through. This time there was less monotone in the porter's complaint. And his next call was a strident: "Hey, hold on! What is this?"

That was followed by a vicious, "Stop, you! Come back here!"

Then came other shouts and a woman's scream.

The Irishman grabbed Edgar's arm and whirled him around. The girl had also stopped to look back. What they saw was a confrontation between Extra and the porter, who had left his post in pursuit of the younger man.

Extra had his gun out. With it he was threatening the porter and a half-circle of people. All of them were retreating. One, a woman, gave a prolonged scream.

Steve turned to Edgar again. He snapped, "Run."

With one arm held by the other man, Edgar ran. They went out of the station. Ahead in the fog was Kale, also running, though his gait was more jaunty than hectic. From behind came a stammer of footfalls.

They ran to a corner, rounded it and went along another street. The old passerby fell back in alarm.

They took two more fog-shrouded streets before joining Kale, where he had stopped by a lamppost. The other two gang members arrived together. All were panting. There were no sounds of chase.

Steve turned on Extra, snarling, "Fool. Frigging idiot. Maniac. You're right round the bend."

"What's wrong?" the young man asked with a face of blank surprise.

"You didn't need do that. He wouldn't've chased you far. He couldn't leave his post for long."

"So what's it matter?"

"What's it matter?" the Irishman spat. "Christ! We take a big risk to put distance between ourselves and the last sighting, and then you pull a stroke like that. Now we're pinpointed again."

The young man blinked uncomfortably. But he said in sulky defence, "It wasn't my fault we didn't buy tickets."

Kale said a placating, "Okay, okay, the damage is done."

"Damage is right," Steve said. "I wish this silly shit'd stop playing gangster."

Kale: "Okay okay."

Seeming to take strength from the leader's attitude, Extra drew himself up and sneered at the Irishman, "Who was it who let Vale nearly break away, eh? Who was that then?"

Steve leaned forward pugnaciously, although his voice was honeyed as he said, "Another twitter from you, ducky, and I'll kick your arse up around your neck."

Extra flinched, lost his sneer. He flinched again as Steve eased back with a chuckle.

"All right," Kale said. "Steam's over. Now let's get on. We have to move. And the answer is wheels. Let's go."

They went on at a smart stride. There was no sound of pursuit. Kale was ahead, checking the door handles of likely prospects. Edgar could hear Extra grumbling to the girl about tickets.

In a moment Steve called, "Never mind the parked jobs. There's plenty already on the move."

Kale looked back. "Meaning?"

"Let's commandeer a car."

The other man smiled. "Neat idea. Keep moving, keep abreast." He stepped through parked vehicles to the roadway and continued walking there.

A car came along, seen mainly as a smudged glare of headlights. Kale waved urgently. The car went by. It was followed at once by another. This time Kale held a hand to his face as if hurt. It made no difference. Nor did it work with the next half-dozen cars that swept indifferently past.

"Listen," Kale called. "This is no good. Hotwiring's best. I'll take the other side, you take this. We'll soon find one." He turned away, fading from view as he crossed to the other side of the street.

Steve glanced back. "George Raft, come and be guard. Try not to flip a coin at the same time."

Extra came up. "You're not so funny."

"Balls, laddie."

"And why don't we just break into a car?"

"See, there's these silly little details like time and noise."

"You're real funny."

"Make up your mind," Steve said. "Either I'm a

riot or I'm not." He strode in front and began trying door handles.

"Okay, Vale," Extra said. "You stay nice and quiet and you'll be fine. Boy, I nearly blasted you at that station."

Edgar nodded. "I believe you. I won't try anything." He meant the first statement but not the second. Every minute that passed took him closer to that uncertain deadline.

Beside them as they walked were mean, flat-faced houses. That he was in a slum area was all that Edgar knew. He had been too preoccupied to get the name of the subway station they had run from.

The Irishman, who had been in a semi-crouch, moving from car to car, abruptly changed his attitude. He walked erect, hands clasped behind, and began to whistle.

Edgar stopped wondering about the oddity of this when into sight came a policeman. He was standing on a corner. Sitting neatly beside him was an Alsatian dog.

An idea came to Edgar. The tinted spectacles were in his breast pocket. What if he were to bring them out, let them be seen by the policeman while looking at him in a meaningful way? And, at the same time, perform the face of the man he had been impersonating?

The idea was excellent. Those glasses were practically the trademark of Harold Devon Vale. They and the features, together with the curious scrutiny of the guard, would surely get the message across.

Edgar's right hand was already on his chest,

holding together his blazer lapels against the cold. He would only need to shift the hand slightly. The movement wouldn't be seen by Extra or the girl, both behind.

Steve went by the constable, who glanced at him casually and then looked down at the dog.

Edgar coughed to gain attention. He moved his hand to his pocket. He coughed again, louder. He felt a hard, warning nudge in the small of his back.

The policeman looked around.

Between finger and thumb, Edgar took hold of the spectacles. He looked at the officer, who was idly watching the trio's approach.

It occurred to Edgar that if the message got across, the young constable, keen, mindful of promotion, might try to take charge of matters himself, rather than the sanely preferable hurrying for reinforcements. If he tried to take over single-handed he would be shot, Edgar knew. The dog was useless against a bullet, despite what usually happened in movies.

The spectacles were halfway out. Edgar pushed them back in again and turned the other way as he went by the policeman. He felt dreary. He doubted if there would be another chance as good as that.

"Smart old you," Extra said softly. "I thought for a minute that you was gonna yell for help."

"Know what you need?" Edgar asked.

"Sure. Hung, drawn and quartered."

"No, son. Put to bed without any supper."

Extra drew his breath in hissingly.

They walked on. They covered block after block. The two car hunters were having no success. The only unlocked vehicle the Irishman found was propped on a jack, a wheel missing. The fog continued dense and the air grew colder.

Passing a side street where a car stood, Extra said, "Steve missed that one." He glanced back. "Smith. Here a sec."

The girl appeared at Edgar's other side as he drew to a stop. Extra told her, "Watch this slug. And try not to fall down this time."

He walked off, toward the car.

With an abruptness that startled Edgar, the girl was speaking. Quickly, breathlessly, she said, "Vale. Listen. Now's your chance."

"What?"

She was looking up at him earnestly. "Make a break for it. Now. Run."

He stared at her. "Run?"

"Yes," she whispered, now angrily. "Don't be stupid. Get moving. Run for it. He'll be back in a minute."

Edgar hesitated. This could be genuine. Also, it could be what the girl had been looking for all along. She couldn't kill him in cold blood, even to revenge the dead, but she might find she could do it if she created the excuse of stopping him from escaping. Edgar just didn't know.

Slowly, he shook his head.

Mona was stupefied. She stared up at the man beside her and felt her anger seep away, her nerves slowly steady. The man was not being obtuse. He understood what she was saying. He really didn't want to make the break. It was insane.

She asked, "Why?"

He said, "I don't want to get shot."

"There's no one to see you go but me."

He nodded. "That's what I mean. I can't be sure about you."

It was Mona's turn to shake her head.

And then it was too late anyway; Extra was on his way back from the parked car. He said, "Locked tight. Let's go." He returned his gun to the prisoner's spine. "Move."

Mona stood and watched them walk on. She felt tired, defeated. She felt hurt, as if an offer of friendship had been rejected. Which was ridiculous, she knew.

As the two men disappeared into the fog, Mona grew angry again. This despite her grudging admission that Vale had every right to put no trust in her. She had, after all, tried twice to kill him.

That reminder made her prickly-hot and uncomfortable. She got away from it by wondering if she should leave, alone, simply turn and walk off. There was no sight or sound of the others.

It was a sweet thought. But again there was that matter of responsibility. She couldn't leave Vale. She had to stay, and somehow convince him of her wish to help.

Walking on quickly, Mona remembered the gun. Her own. She knew now that she wasn't capable of using it herself; but what if she should slip it to Vale?

When Mona caught up with the prisoner and his guard, they were standing with Steve by a car. Its window was open two inches and the Irishman was trying to get his arm inside.

Beyond the sedan, in the roadway, Kale swiftly materialized. "Okay," he said. "I've found one. Come on."

Mona followed the others to the road and across the street. On the sidewalk they halted as Kale said, "Hang on here till I get her working."

He went ahead alone, going to a gleaming Rover. He took hold of the handle, opened the door—and froze as a voice said loudly, "Hey there!"

Mona instinctively took a step backwards. She had to fight hard to disobey her body's order to run. She locked her knees, clenched her fists.

A man came from a doorway right opposite the Rover. He was tall, heavy and well dressed. His face had a grim frown. He strode to where Kale was standing with the door open, stopped and leaned forward with attack in every angle of his pose.

Kale turned to face him. In a calm voice he asked, "Were you talking to me?" His face bore a mild expression.

"Yes, I bloody was. What the hell d'you think you're doing with my car?"

Kale smiled. "*Your* car?" He looked away, then back again.

The man said, "Right. My bloody car."

"I think you've made a mistake, old man."

"What d'you mean?"

Kale said easily, "This is my car. Look here at my things on the—" He broke off on glancing inside, and ended, "Well, for God's sake, it *isn't* my car at that."

"Damn right it isn't," the tall man said curtly, though his pose was losing its look of attack.

Kale closed the door. "Sorry about that. I've got the same year and model. Same color, too."

The man said a doubting, faintly sarcastic, "Really?"

"I left it here somewhere. Got confused in this rotten fog. Tell me, how do you like the new transmission?"

"What? Oh. Well, I—"

"Frankly, I don't think it's a patch on the old one. I gave her a trial at Silverstone a month ago. The new box lacks something."

The man looked bemused. He said, "Oh, I don't know."

"Well, give her a good run and you might agree with me. But I must be off. Got to find that car. Good-bye, old man."

Kale walked on. The man stared after him. He didn't look aside as the others went by, Steve talking about a movie they were supposedly on their way to see.

Kale waited for them at the end of the block. He was grinning like a schoolboy. Mona thought he was one of the strangest people she had ever met. And she hoped she never met another like him.

Steve said, "That was cool. Like a piece of cake. I give you nine out of ten for it."

"Thanks. It wasn't bad."

Extra said, "You shoulda blasted the sod."

Kale and the Irishman gave him a look of derision. He winced.

Mona said, "Listen. Maybe we should have another think about what was mentioned before. You know, splitting up."

"No way," Kale said. "We're a team. We stay together."

"And the team still needs wheels," Steve said.

"So we go on looking."

"Why bother," replied Steve. "Why, for Christ's sake, don't we just grab a cab? If we can risk the Underground, we can risk a taxi."

Kale nodded. "Mate, you're full of neat ideas."

Extra grumbled, "Trouble is, they don't work."

"You're a broth of a boy," Steve said. "And piss on you."

With a wave of his arm, Kale stepped into the roadway. Followed by the others he walked along beside the parked cars. Vehicles went by, their lights blazing. One driver snarled at the walkers to get off the road. Extra called, "Fuck off."

Two taxis passed, both occupied.

Mona began to like the idea of a cab. If she could arrange to get Vale in first, with herself immediately behind, she might be able to push him out of the other door before the others realized what was happening. And if she closed the door on him, Vale would have to see that she wasn't going to shoot. He would run.

If that didn't work, Mona thought, it might be possible to do it when they got out. It had a chance, was worth a try. If not that, she would have to get the gun to him. The deadline was getting closer.

More traffic passed, coming at the group from behind. They all swiveled their heads back constantly. Mona grew nervous as she heard Kale begin to talk again of commandeering a car.

Then she saw the light. Being last in the line, she

saw it first, glowing squarely on top of an approaching vehicle. "Here's one," she called to the others.

Stopping, she stepped further into the roadway, waved her arms and shouted, "Taxi!"

The sign became fully clear before the vehicle itself. It didn't say For Hire, it said Police.

Next, all was panic.

Startled, Mona fell back. She bumped against Extra.

The prisoner lurched away and moved toward the front of the police car. Brakes shrieked.

Kale and Steve went running by in the same direction, their guns in their hands.

The car stopped. It held two plainclothesmen and a uniformed driver.

The prisoner halted his rush against the hood. Extra ran up behind him, automatic held high.

The detectives sprang from the car, one on either side. One of them nearly got hit by a passing truck.

At almost the same second, Kale and Steve arrived at different sides of the car, beside the detectives, who, with almost the same movements, showed signs of fight until the guns were put in front of their faces.

Extra had charge of the prisoner again.

Mona was slowly backing away.

The driver was halfway out of the car. He got back in when so ordered by Kale. From behind the police car came impatient horn-blasts.

Steve snapped, "Get Vale in the car."

While Extra moved to comply, Kale pushed his detective around to the other side. He took charge of the other man as well, saying, "Search 'em."

The Irishman patted coats, delved inside, came out with two handguns. He shoved them in his pockets. From behind came shouts mingled with the horns. The patrol car's radio squawked.

"Everybody in!" Kale called. "Smith!"

Mona went forward. She climbed into the back of the car with Extra and the prisoner. Steve squeezed in after her. She heard Kale order the detectives to run; they went. The next moment he was in the front passenger seat.

He raised his gun level with the driver's head. "Move, boy, and move fast."

The uniformed man set the car in motion. His face was expressionless. He was young and had a blond beard.

The radio squawked, "Come in, Z37."

"Don't answer," Kale said. "In fact, switch it off."

"Can't be switched off," the driver said. His voice was steady.

"Then ignore it."

They moved along the street, most of which was invisible. The uniformed man went as fast as he dared. Mona hoped he wasn't going to try anything clever. She wished he weren't so young and didn't appear so calm.

The radio went on giving its ugly, nasal request for contact, the speaker's tone growing sharp.

Steve leaned forward. "Excuse me, gents," he said, pointing his gun at the radio. He fired twice. The sound was deafening, making Mona go into a fast huddle. The radio died.

"Fine," the driver said. "But do you mind if I tell you something?"

Kale: "Go ahead."

"You haven't got a hope. You might as well give in."

"So why haven't we got a hope?"

"There's a roadblock ahead. And behind. There's a roadblock in every direction. The whole area's sealed off. There's no way you can take that'll get you out."

"Very interesting," Kale said. "Thanks for the info. But you forget one little thing, boy."

"What's that?"

"We're in a police car."

The driver turned to look at Kale. In doing so, he saw Mona. He blinked, looked back at the road.

Steve said, "Yes, a lady. Now ain't that something? You piggies didn't know that, I'll bet."

"I don't know anything," the uniformed man said. "I'm just a driver."

Kale: "Keep doing that and you'll be all right."

They had come up behind a van. It was moving cautiously. The driver pulled out to pass. There were other vehicles ahead of the van. The driver drew back in the side again.

"Would this be where your roadblock is?" Kale asked.

"No idea. I only know there is one."

"Slow down. Keep well back."

The driver reduced speed until the van's taillights were mere specks of red. The atmosphere in the car grew tense. Extra muttered about blasting the hell out of any lousy coppers at a roadblock.

The car was now moving at a walking pace. Steve said, "Fuck this for a lark, we'd be better on a bike."

The van stopped. Following orders, the driver brought the police car to a halt. There was no sound other than the throb of the engine. It could also be felt; it pulsed through Mona's taut body and limbs.

Steve broke the silence. "They'll know by now we're in a cop car. Word must have been passed."

Kale said, "Maybe not. We'll see."

The van disappeared into the fog. The driver moved on. At once two police constables came into view. They were signalling for a stop with flashlights.

Kale rolled down his window and stuck his head out, Steve meanwhile putting his gun to the side of the driver's neck. Kale called out in a friendly tone:

"Stand aside, lads. We're after that van."

The policemen moved back and waved the police car through. And then, when it came abreast, they both shouted as they looked inside.

"Move!" Steve snapped at the driver. "Pass that traffic!"

The car sped forward. It reached the van and swung out. Mona held her breath, closed her eyes. Nothing happened—except that from behind came the yip of a police siren.

Eyes open, she saw that the car was on a clear stretch of road. As if he had x-ray vision the driver was attacking the wall of fog. Mona was still stopping her breath from time to time.

The siren climbed and twisted and zagged. As before, it seemed to be coming from all directions as it grew louder. But soon, distinguishing different tones, Mona realized that more than one siren was being sounded.

Steve and Kale obviously realized the same. They exchanged a look. The latter told the driver, "Take a side turning. Take the first one you come to."

"If you say so."

"Do you know this area?"

"No," the policeman said, still calm. "We're out of my district now."

"Steve? Extra? Smith? Anyone know where we are?"

No one knew. Kale said, "Doesn't matter. We're out of the roadblocked area. We'll be golden when we lose those cars."

Extra said quickly, "There's a street."

The uniformed man braked and began to make the turn. He put his foot back on the power. Tires squealed a complaint until the car straightened out.

There was nothing to see other than ghostly parked cars on either side and the yellow boundary ahead. The car shot forward. The sirens seemed farther away.

A wall was right in front.

Mona choked on a scream. The wall was real, made of bricks. The street was a dead end. They had come to a railroad embankment.

Now the rubber sounded like dying animals. The car was shuddering. The driver was pressed back in his seat as he braked. Kale had one foot up on the dashboard.

And the wall was still flying at them.

The uniformed man spun the steering wheel. The car, tires still screaming, went into a skid. Mona and the others in the back were thrown together, heads knocking.

The car made one complete turn. It was slowing as its front came around again to face the wall. The rubber-squeals died, the bodywork stopped shuddering—and the bumper met the wall with a gentle, whispering thud.

Into the new silence came the loud yammer of sirens.

"Out!" Kale shouted.

They all hustled out of the car. Mona stumbled along with the others as Steve led the way, calling, "Through this door!" They went to the sidewalk and toward steps leading to a house.

The sirens were yipping close.

"We'll go through to the next street," Steve said.

He was up the steps first, with Extra and his prisoner right behind. They had passed through the open doorway when Mona heard the gasps. She swung around.

The bearded young policeman had thrown himself at Kale's back. He held on although he was flung from side to side. Sirens filled the street. Headlights appeared in the fog.

Kale doubled over. The driver shot forward over his head and landed on the ground. Still on his knees, he quickly turned. His hands were raised. He looked like he was putting them together in the act of praying.

Kale stood a yard away. He pointed his gun down straight-armed. Mona shook her head. She jerked back as a shot sounded and Kale's hand jerked.

Arms drooping, the young policeman began to

fall over sideways. The headlights glowed on Kale. He turned to them and fired off four rapid shots. There was a sound of breaking glass.

Mona moved back and up toward the doorway. She was stunned. She acted numbly malleable as Kale reached her, twisted her around and pushed her into a gloomy hallway.

The other three men were coming toward them, beside a flight of stairs. Extra said, "Back way's blocked. Prams and all kinds of crap. We can't get through. Not fast like."

Steve tried a nearby door. "Locked."

"Upstairs," Kale snapped. "Hustle."

Extra, plaintively: "What were those shots?"

"Our driver. Got clever. I rubbed him out."

They were now all clattering up the linoleum-covered staircase. Mona, one hand on her gun, was telling herself dully that it was now or never. She felt sick. She knew she couldn't take much more of this.

The house, a Victorian relic, had obviously been divided into flats, one to each floor. Near the top of the stairs was a door, open. Framed in it was a youngish woman holding a baby.

Wide-eyed, she asked, "What's going on?" She held the child close.

Steve: "Who's in there with you?"

The woman shook her head before saying, "No one."

"Where's your man?"

"Out at work. What's going on?"

The Irishman grabbed the woman's arm. He pulled her forward roughly. "Piss off, darling. We need your flat."

Holding her baby up beside her face, the woman circled the group to the stairs. She began to go down. When out of sight she started to shriek.

As the others went on into the apartment, Kale stopped beside Mona. He reached inside her coat, and tugged out her gun.

He said, "You're in no shape to use this at the moment."

Harold Devon Vale was sitting on a chair. He had grown tired of the floor. And he had changed locations. He had moved to a spot midway between that dangerous main door and the open doorway of his living room. From here he could give an ear to both.

He had again turned up the sound of the living room TV set. His new moves were triggered some time ago when he had heard about a startling new development in the Vale Affair. Details, said the announcer, would be broadcast as soon as they became available.

Vale felt cheery and tranquil. He was still getting enjoyment from his freedom. Occasionally he put his hands behind the chair's back, and then casually brought them around to the front again. That was lovely.

He hummed. He thought of all the press space this kidnaping was winning for him. He scoffed at the foolishness he heard from the television. He wondered if he should treat himself to another of the mimic's cigarettes.

"Thank you, Jenny," an announcer said. "That's

one of the sweetest voices around. We'll be back with you in a moment for the song that's held the number three spot for a month. But first, here's a flash on the big story of the day."

Harold Vale perked up. He sat straight and eager. Even though he could hear perfectly well, he leaned his head toward the doorway.

"It's not the development we're waiting for," the announcer said. "At least, not so far as I know. It could be that, but unofficially. Scotland Yard is keeping a tight cap on this case. No doubt they have their reasons. They're not giving anything away until they're good and ready."

Come on, come on, you blithereing idiot, Vale thought, though with amusement rather than pique.

"There is an unconfirmed story that the hostage, Harold Devon Vale, has escaped. That he has got free of the gang. It *is* known that he had been held by handcuffs, and that these chains are now off. Which has given rise to the rumor, reasonably enough. And I'm afraid that's all there is in this flash. Repeat: Harold Devon Vale is said to have escaped from his kidnapers.

"Now, Jenny, let's get back to you and . . . ."

Vale shot up from the chair. He ran to the door of the apartment. Rapidly he shot bolts and put the safety chain in place. He turned, leaned back on the door and pressed it with his hands.

His amusement had gone. He was no longer tranquil.

He believed the rumor.

Not necessarily did he accept that the prisoner had escaped, only that he was free. It was more likely that the gang had discovered their mistake, or had been convinced of it by Edgar Carlton, and had let him go.

That meant they would be now looking for the real Harold Devon Vale. Coming here.

Even if the straight escape story were true, Vale thought, he still needed to contact the police.

Disjointedly, body awkward, he moved back down the hall. His hands were shaking. He glanced in the living room, thinking, telephone? No, the response might be the same as before, disbelief, and there was no time to waste on persuasion.

Movements quicker now, Vale picked up his gun from beside the chair and put the shoulder holster on. He went into his bedroom, found and donned a raincoat.

Almost as soon as he had started to wonder where his spare eyeglasses were, he dismissed the idea of searching. They were too much a Vale symbol anyway. He wanted the reverse.

This thought sent him at a run into the living room, where he lifted the phony Maxted cap, fitted it to his head and drew the peak down to his eyebrows. That, he thought, would serve two purposes, disguise, and shading the harsh light of outdoors from his delicate eyes.

He hustled into the kitchen, got out the carving knife and cut through the tape still on his ankles. The chair legs fell free. He flung the knife aside as he rose.

Quickly, nervously, he plucked at the tape on one wrist. It began to come free of the flesh—but took hairs along with it. Yelping, Vale removed the tape with one fast yank, then did the same to the other wrist.

Running, he went to the front door. He listened. All was quiet outside. But he was silently stealthy as he unfastened the chain, slid bolts, turned the lock, opened the door.

The hall was deserted. Vale slipped out and headed away from the elevator. He reached the service door, at which point it occurred to him that the gang would be more liable to use the back way than the front.

But he felt safer here himself. One hand inside his coat, touching the gun, he went through the door and started down the stairs softly. There was no sound from below.

Vale came to the ground floor. Letting himself out into the backyard, he found that he was in heavy fog. He hadn't noticed it from upstairs.

All the better, Vale thought, his confidence growing. He crossed the yard and entered a brick tunnel. This brought him out onto a street.

He saw safety. A car was passing slowly, its lights on. A woman was hurrying along with a handkerchief held to her nose and mouth. A youthful voice was laughing.

Vale felt like laughing himself. It was partly nerves. Although his tranquility hadn't returned, he felt better for being out of the apartment.

A chuckle that was humorless seeped from him as he set off along the street. He kept one hand inside his coat, his head lowered. He twitched every time a figure took shape out of the fog, chuckled when the figure proved harmless.

He began to hurry. He crossed to the opposite side of the road, but then changed his mind and went back again. He had a sensation of eeriness—the fog, and the fact of being outdoors after so long.

Traffic was increasing. It crawled along beside him. In a moment he saw the reason for the backup. He had reached a crossroads, a danger spot because of the poor visibility.

He also saw, as he stopped at the edge of the curb, something that made his heart pound. In the center of the junction stood a tall bulky shape with a pointed top. It was a helmeted policeman directing the traffic.

Lifting his head grandly, Harold Devon Vale, Member of Parliament, stepped off the curb. He ignored the car he was cutting in front of and which gave him a horn-blast. He strode to the middle of the crossing.

The policeman was a giant, a sergeant in his late fifties. He had a fierce moustache and a harried expression. When Vale stopped at his side he gave him a look of disapproval.

"Pardon me, my good man," Vale said.

The sergeant waved vehemently at the passing traffic to speed it up, keep it moving. "I'm busy, sir."

"You are indeed. And doing a fine job."

"Thanks. Now if you'll kindly return to the side."

Vale smiled. "I believe, officer, that you'd be interested in hearing my name."

"I doubt it," the policeman said. He held up a large white-gloved hand to stop the flow of vehicles.

"Don't bother me, please."

"I beg your pardon?" Vale said, not believing what he had heard.

"If it's information you want, just step along to the station. You'll find someone there."

Believing, and annoyed at having his moment sullied, Vale said, "I'm offering information to *you*, my good man."

The sergeant waved on the traffic. "Mind yourself, mate. You're going to get your arse knocked off."

Vale gasped, even though he moved away from a passing truck. He said, "Officer, I am Harold Devon Vale." He looked sternly at the policeman and removed his cap, believing along with every other politician that his face was as well known as the beholder's own.

The sergeant glanced, gave his attention back to the traffic. "You're who?" he asked absently.

"Harold Devon Vale, M. P. The man everyone believes has been kidnaped, the man all—"

He broke off because the large hand had come down heavily on his shoulder. Still with his gaze on the traffic the policeman said a gruff, "Mate, if you don't move your bloody arse back over to the side, I'm going to kick it over. Shove off."

He himself did the shoving. Vale teetered back, kept his balance, opened his mouth for a snapped retort—and changed his mind. Swinging around he stalked off.

He got grim satisfaction out of the knowledge that the policeman would be paid back doubly. First, because he, Vale, would make a point of telling the media about the incident, so that the man would be the laughing stock of everybody. Second, because the sergeant had missed the greatest opportunity of his blighted career. The stupid bastard.

Vale strode along the sidewalk. He watched approaching cars for a taxi. He was going to do what he should have done in the first place, instead of wasting time with underlings. You should always go to the top. It was the only way if you wanted results.

A minute later, on Charing Cross Road, Vale saw and stopped a vacant cab. He got in and said, "New Scotland Yard, please."

Everything in the room was pink. The wallpaper, the woodwork, the wall-to-wall carpeting, the child-sized furniture—pink. There were frills and fluffy toys everywhere, and they were pink as well.

The peaceful room, home of innocence, only served to increase Edgar's sense of unreality. He felt more weird than at any time during the past hours of fantasy. If a trap door had opened in the floor, he would not have been at all surprised, just grateful.

Leaning tiredly against the cot's high rails, Edgar looked at the room's only window. He had done this several times. It was as if he were unable to accept that the space, though open, was too small for escape.

The pink frame would not have allowed passage to an adult head, never mind a body. It was a token window, leading to an airshaft in the center of the building.

Through it Edgar had peered upward and down;

there was nothing to be seen but ancient brickwork. He had called out; the only answer had been echo.

Edgar looked the other way, at the pink door, as from beyond it came sounds of gunfire. That, sporadically, was all he had heard since being pushed into the room—after its lack of other exit had been checked. All, that is, except for the voice of Extra at an early stage.

Exultingly the younger man had called out to the other gang members, "We're home and dry! We got it made! This is the stuff!" There was food, he said, laughing. There was drink. There was TV and radio and hi-fi. It was perfect. They could stay here for weeks. Months. They had the front and rear approaches covered. They would blast anyone who tried to get near.

Now another shot rang out. Edgar shivered. He had been reminded of the other killing, that of the police driver. The bearded man had been so young and vital, calm and brave. His life had been given for nothing, thrown away.

Edgar tried not to feel guilty. It wasn't easy. There had been two deaths and possibly a third. They might not have happened if there had been no impersonation, if Vale himself had gone to Wainford Hall.

That, of course, would not have made any difference to the gang, Edgar thought. But the politician may not have allowed himself to be abducted, may have fought or made a run for it. Or, if taken, he might have had the acumen to talk his way out of the situation, or worked harder at escape, or made some clever deal with the gang. Or he might have been able to understand the girl, Smith, who could be an ally.

Edgar sighed. He began to look at his wristwatch, but stopped himself. He didn't want to know how much time there was left until the deadline. He didn't....

Edgar turned quickly to look at the door. The idea had come to him of locking himself in. This hope fizzled like a damp firework. There were no bolts, no locking devices.

Also, he thought dismally, the furniture was too small and frail to be used as a barricade. The men would soon be able to force it out of the way.

His gaze still on the door, Edgar noticed something that kindled hope again. True, there was no bolt; also, there was no keyhole. Could it be that he wasn't locked in?

Edgar went to the pink door in three long strides. Softly he turned the knob and softly pulled. The door opened.

Sound grew. There were two cracks of gunfire, and, from Extra, a high-pitched laugh. A radio or television announcer was talking about a cricket match in Australia.

Drawing the door wide open, Edgar stepped out cautiously into a passage. He saw it ran between a main bedroom at the back of the house and a lounge at the front. Earlier, he had been too preoccupied to notice layout.

On his own side of the passage were the pink bedroom, bath and kitchen. Opposite, in a long wall, was the door of the flat.

Edgar took another step out. Turning, he was looking directly into the lounge. Its one window had been broken. Kneeling at the sill, gun in hand, was Steve. He peered out at the yellowness of the fog.

Beside the windowframe stood Extra. His back was to the wall, his head was turned sharply for an outside view, his gun hand was up by his shoulder. He was smiling. He appeared to be posing for a movie still.

A large TV set was playing. Over a picture of Wainford Hall an announcer was saying, "There are worries in the Vale camp about the M.P. having enough stamina to . . . ."

As Edgar watched the men at the window, thinking he was about to be seen at any moment, the Irishman bobbed up above the sill and fired off a quick shot. From outside came a volley of return fire. Holes appeared in the ceiling and plaster snowed down.

Steve sank down again for cover. He said cheerfully, "They will go on chancing their arms, these thick cops."

"Dumb bastards," Extra agreed.

"They're outclassed, that's what it is. They're playing in the wrong league."

Edgar was afraid to leave. He felt that the slightest movement he made would draw attention, especially from Extra, who only needed to shift his eyes this way.

"And their guns," the Irishman said. "Joseph and all the other cuckolds, them guns is a million years old."

The younger man jerked his upper body forward. His stabbed his arm down and out twice, squeezing off shots. Snapping back into place, he crowed, "Got the fucker! See that? See it? I got the one with the riot helmet."

"Sure, I saw."

"Got him in the shoulder, I did. Spun the crap out of him. You saw that, didn't you, Steve?" Extra sounded as if he had just won at pinning the tail on the donkey.

A stammer of gunfire came from the fog. The ceiling thudded, a lamp shattered, the two men laughed.

Edgar told himself that the longer he delayed, the more difficult it would be. He backed off. The men continued to give their attention to the outdoors. And with two more steps Edgar put them out of his sight.

At a tinkling sound he stopped and turned. He was right beside the doorway of the master bedroom. The passage was shorter than he had realized.

The room's single window had also been broken. Kale, his back to Edgar, was using his gun to tap remaining pieces of glass from the frame, though keeping his body out of the way.

On the floor, between doorway and window, lay the girl. She was prone, and with her head resting on folded arms, her face to the side. Her eyes were closed. She was pale. Her brow was creased in a frown, not one of anger or discontent but as if to counter a pain.

Edgar felt there was less risk here of being seen. He took a quiet step to the rear. But apparently it had not been quiet enough.

The girl opened her eyes. She saw him. Her frown went and she raised her head.

They looked at each other. After a solemn moment, the girl turned the opposite way to glance at Kale, turned back, closed her eyes, returned her head to the pillow of arms.

Edgar blinked. The action had appeared deliberate. It was a message, it seemed, one telling him that as far as she was concerned he was free to do as he liked.

Edgar took another step backwards, and another. Kale, finished with the bits of glass, was peering around the edge of the window. Smith's eyes were still closed. From the other room came the announcer's voice:

". . . recap, while waiting for that official statement. It is still not sure how many gang members there are, beyond the certain three, which we knew after. . . ."

Edgar's nerves jumped as Kale called, "Smith!"

The girl answered, "What is it?"

"If you've got over the zombie bit, you can do something for me." He was still looking out of the window.

"Do what?"

"Hand me some of your bullets."

"All right. Wait a minute. I'll have to get up." She opened her eyes and glared at Edgar. *Leave,* the eyes seemed to say.

He took another step backwards, aiming for the front door of the apartment. The TV announcer was listing all the countries which had sent messages of congratulation for the no-deal stand against the gang.

Kale said, "Come on, come on."

Smith: "Okay. Stay there."

"What's the matter with you?" Kale asked. He turned.

Edgar stopped moving as he was seen by Kale, who, surprisingly, gave a wry smile. He left the window to come forward. Passing the girl's feet, he said in a conversational tone:

"Thinking of going for a stroll, Vale?"

"No—I—no."

"Put your specs on. You're just not the same man without 'em."

While getting out and putting on the glasses, Edgar mused that at least he had drawn Kale away from the window. Perhaps now the police could rush in downstairs.

The other man halted nearby. He held his gun casually, as if it were a pamphlet he would like to give away. Edgar looked at it. He licked his lips.

Kale asked, "Wondering if you should jump me, Vale old man?"

Edgar shook his head. "No."

"Too bad. And no strolls either?"

"No."

"Well, in case you did have the great outdoors in mind, you ought to know that the door's locked."

"Oh," Edgar said.

Kale patted a pocket. "I have the key."

The television announcer was reading a statement made by the Home Secretary, defending his no-deal stand against the pro-Vale outcry it had provoked.

Edgar asked, "What happened outside? The policeman with the beard." He was thinking that the longer he kept the other man standing here the better.

Kale shrugged. "He attacked me."

"Without a weapon, though."

"He was a strong boy."

Edgar said, "You didn't have to kill him."

"I do what I have to do."

"Is he still lying there?"

"No," Kale said. His handling of the gun seemed more relaxed than ever. "They took him away while we were getting in here."

"Poor kid."

Kale glanced behind. "Which reminds me. I better get back to that window."

Edgar sighed at himself for having mentioned the policeman, instead of choosing another topic. But he hadn't been able to help it. He couldn't stop feeling that he was partly to blame.

Kale raised his gun. "Go back in the room. Close the door. Stay there."

"All right."

"If this happens again, I won't be so lenient. But you won't have long to wait. Time's nearly up."

Edgar shook his head. "You won't go through with it."

Kale smiled. "I do what I have to do. Move."

Edgar went toward the pink room.

The taxi moved slowly through the fog. The driver was leaning forward over his steering wheel in order to be closer to the windshield. The wipers were working at top speed, but they didn't increase visibility, they only served, by comparison, to make the cab's pace seem slower—at least, as far as the passenger was concerned.

Harold Devon Vale sat impatiently on the edge of the seat. One foot was tapping. He had both hands pressed hard on his thighs in an unconscious attempt at pushing.

Not helping his aggravation was the fact that the driver had a transistor radio playing, this in addition to the crackling whines that came from the control radio. The dispatcher tolled out names and addresses nonstop.

Vale had already asked for the repetitious pop music to be switched off. The cabbie had replied that anyone who didn't like it could pay up and get out, it was a free country.

Now, changing his hands to fists, Vale said, "Can't you go any faster? Cars keep passing you."

"Let 'em," the driver said. "I'm not taking chances." He was an older man, thin and warty. He wore an old-fashioned bowler hat. His coat had a greasy velvet collar.

"The fog's thinning out," Harold Vale told him.

"It is, a bit, in patches. I'm still not taking chances. There's not a mark on me licence in forty years' driving."

Vale was forming a caustic remark when the music ended abruptly in the middle of what had been passing for a tune. Vale hoped gleefully that the radio was broken. But the chirpy disc jockey said, "Sorry to cut in there, friends and neighbors, and all you girls at Hartford Packaging. There's something in the wind and I'm switching you over to the newsroom. See you."

Vale leaned forward expectantly. He unclenched his hands, gripped his thighs.

A different male voice, one with weight, said, "Newsroom. Ladies and gentlemen, here is that development in the kidnaping that we have been waiting for. It is official, a police bulletin issued minutes ago to the media."

Harold Vale nodded, smiling.

"A little over an hour ago," the newsreader said, "the gang was flushed from the farm where they had been holding Mr. Vale prisoner. No details as to location are given. The gang left in their stolen Jaguar. The discovery of the hideout was made by supporters of Mr. Vale, the so-called Whitecoats."

Vale's smile became broader. He reached out and pulled down the folding seat behind the driver. He moved onto it to be closer to the radio.

The announcer was saying that presently he would read a statement by Clifford Maxted relating to the hideout's discovery. "First, here are more details on the escape. The gang, probably three in number, came toward the center of London. They were followed by several Whitecoats on motorcycles. There was a shooting incident. The shots were alleged to have come from the Jaguar. One of the Whitecoats was severely injured, another was killed instantly. He has been identified as. . . ."

The rest faded in Vale's ears. His smile drained. Draining with it was what little color his face contained. The phrases "severely injured" and "killed instantly" smacked repeatedly through his head. He would not have been able to say which terrified him most. He clasped his hands together with as much fervor as if one of them had belonged to someone else.

When he again became conscious of the newsreader's words, he was talking about a crashed car, an escape on foot, a shop. "The handcuffs which had been on Mr. Vale's ankles were taken off there. That, of course, is what led to the rumor that the M.P. had gotten away from the gang. As far as we know at this point, there is no truth in the story.

"The gang have been spotted several times. But they could not possibly have been in all those places in one evening. They were said to have been spotted getting into a boat near Waterloo Bridge. They were said to have traveled on the Underground. They were thought. . . ."

Vale said, harshly, "Turn around."

The cabbie started. "Eh?"

"Go back. I've changed my mind. Get me back to Bloomsbury."

"Now look. I thought you wanted to go to the Yard."

"Not any more," Vale said. "Turn back. And as quick as you can."

The cabbie sighed. Peering ahead, he looked for a side street.

The radio announcer interrupted himself. He had been talking about how much help the fog was giving the gang. He said, "Another bulletin has just been handed to me. They're coming fast now. Not very long ago, the gang disarmed two plainclothes officers and took their car. They kept the driver with them. They drove to a cul-de-sac, Gormon Place, EC2. They are three at this moment, in the second floor flat of number eighteen. The police have the building and the area surrounded. Mr. Vale is still being held hostage."

The cab turned off the main road. Vale said, "Hurry up, for Christ's sake." He drummed his fists on his knees.

The cabbie said, "Keep your shirt on, mate. And keep quiet so's I can listen to this."

Announcer: "We are sending an outside team to the siege area. We will be reporting to you very soon right from the action spot. Meanwhile, here is that statement by Mr. Maxted. We will not, after all, read it to you in full. It has been decided that some of Mr. Maxted's remarks regarding the police are libelous. He is not happy with the lack of cooperation he and his associates received from New Scotland Yard."

"Bloody coppers," the cabbie snorted.

Newsreader: "It seems that Mr. Vale's followers were organized into some three thousand single units. Mr. Maxted, aware that the gang was going to make contact with the authorities, arranged to have every telephone box in Greater London kept under observation. These were street call boxes, since it was assumed that the gang would consider these the safest. The idea paid off and—"

Again the newsreader interrupted himself. He said, "Back to that in a moment, ladies and gentlemen. I've been handed another flash. Sadly, the driver of the commandeered police car is dead. He is thought to have been shot by one of the gang. His name is being witheld until next of kin. . . ."

"Stop!" Vale shouted. "Stop the cab!" He flopped back onto the full seat in order to get away from the radio.

"I wish you'd make up your bloody mind," the cabbie growled. He brought the taxi to a fast stop.

Vale got out quickly. He thrust an excess of money into the cabbie's hand, turned and began to run madly through the fog.

"We've got to give in," Mona said. She was sitting by the wall in the main bedroom, leaning on it dispiritedly. Her legs were tucked underneath, her hands lay languidly in her lap.

She asked, "Did you hear me?"

Kale, at the window, give as brief a nod as it was possible to make, a downtwitch of the head. He was standing boldly in the center of the glassless frame, silhouetted against the yellow light. His shoulders swung constantly as he scanned the area below.

Mona said tonelessly, "We have to give ourselves up."

Moving aside, into cover, Kale turned to look at her. "You're in a state of shock, Smith. You don't know what you're saying."

"Yes, I do. And I know we're trapped."

"Rubbish," he said, glancing outside. "We hold all the cards. I've told you that before."

Abruptly he leaned out of the window and pointed

his gun down. But he didn't fire. He leaned away again with a laugh, "I scared the balls off him."

Mona said, "It's all over for us, Kale. Can't you see that?"

"I can only see the state you're in, dearie. It's made you defeatist. Go to sleep. Keep out of my hair."

"I'm being sensible."

"A nuisance. Either shut up, or go to sleep, or make yourself useful. Fix us warriors some coffee. Find some whiskey. You could do with a shot yourself."

As Kale finished speaking, a weird nasal sound came from the other end of the apartment—echoing in from outdoors. It sounded like a ship's siren.

"Christ!" Mona gasped, clutching the front of her coat. "What's that?"

"A hailer."

"What's a hailer?"

"A bullhorn," Kale said. "An electric loudspeaker."

"What're they doing with it?"

"They want to talk to us. I guess they went to make a deal."

"Good," Mona said. "Thank God." She still spoke lifelessly. She wondered if maybe it was true what Kale had said; she was in a state of shock. It wouldn't be surprising. She had gone through a long nightmare. And it wasn't over yet.

Kale called out, "Steve!"

Back through the apartment came, "Hello?"

"Slip over here and watch this end. I'll talk to them."

In a moment the Irishman appeared. He looked at Mona while crossing the room and asked, "She get hit?"

"Only on her maidenly emotions," Kale said.

Steve snorted, "Bloody women."

"True. How's your ammo supply?"

"Pretty good. I'm not wasting any. That shit-head Extra, he's using bullets like they grow on trees."

"I'll speak to him."

The two men exchanged positions by the window. Steve said, "Money and a car, that's what we need. Never mind anything else."

"Leave it to me," Kale said. He left the room.

Mona got up and followed. She went tiredly along the passage to the doorway of the lounge, where she stopped, leaning there and touching her head on the wood.

Indifferently she glanced at the television set. For a second or two she thought there was something wrong with it. The screen was misty. It showed dim figures, little more than shapes.

Then, from the accompanying voice, she realized that a camera unit was here, filming the scene in the street outside. She remained indifferent.

Mona looked toward the window, where Kale and Extra crouched, as from the fog came that nasal booming. The voice it was wrapped around said, "Attention. Attention. You people there in the flat. Can you hear me?"

Kale cupped one hand to his mouth, shouting, "I hear you loud and clear. But I'm not talking to anyone except Atkinson."

"This is Chief Inspector Atkinson speaking."

"Okay. So you want to make a deal now."

"No," the voice boomed. "No deals. Nothing has changed."

Kale shouted, "Then what the hell you making all this racket for?"

"I have an offer for you. Not a deal, an offer."

Extra nudged the leader and said, speaking low as if he could be heard from outside, "They're trying to pull a fast one."

"They can't pull anything."

"Tell 'em to fuck off."

Kale called, "What's the offer?"

The bullhorn brayed, "If you all come out, one at a time, with your hands on top of your heads, we will not shoot. That is the only concession we are prepared to make."

"Generous bastard, aren't you?"

"Under the circumstances, yes. Very."

"You forget something, copper," Kale shouted. "You and your offers. We have a hostage."

"We are not forgetting that."

"Do you want to save his life or don't you?"

After a pause the voice belled, "You are forgetting something as well. You are surrounded. There is no possible way you can get free. We either shoot you out or starve you out."

"Is that your final word?"

"It is. Be sensible and give yourself up. You have no chance otherwise."

Kale shouted, "Okay, copper. That's it. There's twenty minutes to the deadline. So long."

Extra chuckled, "That's the way. Show the bastards they're not dealing with a bunch of kids or amateurs."

Kale got up directly into the shattered window. He fired off three fast shots, each making his arm jerk up as if tugged by string.

As he dodged out of sight again, laughing, shooting cracked from various points outside. The ceiling sent down flakes of plaster. A deflected bullet smacked into the wall a yard from where Mona was standing.

With an odd lack of concern, she moved aside and squatted by a breakfront. She felt a continual need to sit or lie or lean. Her body seemed to have little strength.

Kale was loading his guns—his own and the one he had taken from Mona. He wore a smile. With a mentor's interest in his eyes, he looked up as Extra rose into the window space.

The youngest gang member darted his head searchingly. He stopped this on seeing a target. He jabbed out his gun and fired. His arm leapt, his features flinched.

"Take that, pig!" he shouted.

He squatted quickly beside Kale. They both laughed, then turned to look at the television set. Mona did the same.

The mistiness had gone. The camera was indoors, Mona saw, focused on a man holding a microphone. Mona knew him as Arthur Price, a political commentator. There was a loud hubbub of background noise. Behind Price could be seen large cameras and other men with microphones.

Without interest, Mona gathered that the scene was taking place in a nearby hotel. It was being used as headquarters for press, radio and TV.

Arthur Price was talking excitedly about the gang's position. "Impossible," he said. "These men haven't a hope. And in less than twenty minutes they'll have to make a decision. Let's hope for Mr. Vale's sake that it's the right one."

Extra jeered, Kale laughed.

Price said, "But now let's switch back to our street unit, see what's happening at this siege in the fog."

Mona pushed herself up. She left the room, went along the passage and into the main bedroom. Steve was standing beside the window. He glanced around with, "Fog's thinning out. That's bad."

"It is?"

"The way it is now, the houses across the yards are hidden. When the fog lifts, they'll put marksmen in the windows there."

"Steve," Mona said. "Listen."

"What's up? You still crushed like a flower?"

"No. Listen. We should give up."

He looked interested. "You think so?"

"Yes. And so do you. We should give ourselves up. We can't go on this way indefinitely. We've got to give in."

She knew she was talking tiredly, that she lacked conviction. But she couldn't rouse herself to greater effort, the needed vehemence. She was too tired. Sick and tired.

"Don't fret," the Irishman said. "They'll make a deal at the last minute."

Mona let herself sink down to the floor. She listened dully to the television voice saying that thousands of people were pouring into the area to watch the siege. It sounded as if he were referring to a circus.

Mona wondered about the two dead men. She hoped they were not married. But she knew that somebody must have loved them. She lay down.

The man snapped, "Watch where you're going!" He pushed Harold Devon Vale off from their collision-meeting on a corner. "Bloody fool."

"Sorry," Vale gasped, though the response was automatic. He had hardly been aware of the man. He was too distressed in mind and body.

He blundered on along the foggy street. He was going almost too fast for safety in such reduced visibility. His feet pounded, his arms wheeled. He knew he would have to stop, now, now this very second, yet he kept on running.

Not since he was a child had Vale moved at such a headlong, reckless speed. But it was worth it, he thought. Also he couldn't have endured any more of that taxi's cautious crawling.

Home was near. One block to go. Vale swayed his body, wagged his head, ran on with the found strength of panic. The cap bounced and twisted.

He turned the final corner, chased the final yards. Panting, his lungs in pain, he reached the brick tunnel that formed the house's rear entrance. He staggered along it and went across the yard.

Letting himself into the building, quietly except

for his gasps, he was then forced to stop at last. He sank down onto the bottom step of the service stairs. He felt destroyed by his run.

You're safe here, he assured himself. Everything's all right. There's no one coming along behind. No one sneaking in the front entrance.

Vale got up. Semi-recovered, lungs still hard at work but not giving pain, he trudged up the stairs. He saw and heard no one. On his hallway he went quickly along to his apartment and inside. He fixed all locking devices into place.

Removing the phony Maxted cap, Vale threw it into the living room enroute to the bedroom. He took off his raincoat and put it back in the closet. His movements were fast and sure despite the fact that he was in a lather of fear. He twitched when he heard a TV voice mention the Gormon Place seige.

When he moved a painting on the wall, the face of a safe was revealed. He dialed the combination—his birthdate in reverse, plus his age. Opening the safe door he took out a wad of banknotes, two diamond rings and a checkbook. These he stuffed into his trouser pockets. He closed the safe again, swung the painting back into place.

Going to the living room, to the couch, Vale lifted and donned the suit jacket belonging to Edgar Carlton. It was a reasonable fit—not, he thought, that it mattered. His shoulder holster didn't make too much of a bulge.

Next he put on the mimic's topcoat, last the black slouch hat.

Vale turned to look at himself in a mirror. That he appeared sinister and vaguely absurd faded into insignificance beside the fact that he did not look like Harold Devon Vale.

He swung around with a gasp on hearing, from the TV, the voice of Arthur Price saying, ". . . latest on that second Whitecoat, which is that he has died in the hospital without regaining consciousness. He has been named as. . . ."

Vale didn't wait for the rest. Terror chased him to the front door, back down through the building, to the rear entrance, across the yard and along the tunnel to the street. There, collar turned up, he began to hurry through the fog.

Three deaths so far, Vale fretted. Well, he wasn't going to be the fourth. Obviously the enemy would stop at nothing. They would kill a hundred times if necessary, to get the right man. They, the enemy, could number in the thousands, just like his own followers.

Vale's thoughts jittered away. They went to the solace of his plan. Or rather, to the man who had given him the idea. John Stonehouse was a Member of Parliament who, a few years before, had been presumed drowned when he disappeared in Florida, his clothes folded neatly on a beach. He had left behind him in England a tangle of dubious financial affairs. That Stonehouse had later been discovered living in Australia, had been extradited, tried and jailed, was, to Vale, beside the point. The man had botched it. Vale would not.

He knew that his only hope of permanent safety was to get right away, vanish. He could no longer pretend to get free of his bonds once the mimic had been killed in his place. He had to let everyone go on believing that the dead hostage was himself.

He, the real Harold Devon Vale, was from now on an American entertainer called Edgar Carlton. He had that man's identification, he had the key to his lodgings. He could not, of course, hope to pass himself off as the mimic to anyone who knew him. That was unimportant. With luck he wouldn't meet anyone who knew Carlton. He would contrive to sneak in the boardinghouse and get the one remaining item he needed, though he might not necessarily use it—Edgar Carlton's passport. Abroad, there would be real safety. Freedom from death.

Again, Vale started to run.

The deadline had arrived.

Edgar, standing with his back to the pink wallpaper, knew that time was up without needing to look at his watch. His last look had showed him he had two minutes left. Those one hundred and twenty seconds he had counted off in his head.

Edgar was afraid. Concurrently, he could not really believe that he was about to be killed. Also, he still had a possible escape route via the truth about his identity—barely possible because the gang might then kill him out of rage and frustration.

Edgar stared at the pink door. It was all the more horrific on account of its sweet coloring. It was the hangman's politeness, the eager granting of a last request, the respectful look in the eyes of the firing squad.

Edgar tensed still further. From the other side of the door had come a slight bumping sound. He stared at the pink handle.

It began to turn.

Straining tautly forward on the balls of his feet, Edgar cursed himself despairingly for not trying what he had thought of before, blocking the door with furniture. It would have given him another ten, perhaps fifteen minutes.

The slab of pink wood moved inwards. Around its edge came the gang leader. Kale's face was solemn. His eyes had an odd expression, almost a dreaminess. He came into the room and stopped.

"Mr. Harold Devon Vale," he said softly. "Your time is up."

"Listen," Edgar began.

"You want to plead?" Kale asked. "Go ahead. I'll give you thirty seconds."

"No no, it's nothing like that."

"If you think I should ask the cops if they've changed their minds, forget it. There'll be no deals if we wait a year."

Unsteadily, Edgar said, "I don't want to plead and I don't care about deals. I want you to listen to me with great care. Listen to the truth about this man you think is Vale. If you don't, you'll make a terrible mistake."

"Please don't confess your sins to me," Kale said, his voice still low. He was holding his arms loosely at his sides. The gun pointed toward the floor. That casual stance held a world of menace.

Edgar said, "I am not Harold Devon Vale."

Kale nodded. "Of course you're not."

"Eh?"

"You're Chief Inspector Raymond Atkinson of Scotland Yard."

"Listen to me, please."

"You're the Pope, the King of Siam and Napoleon."

Forcefully, spacing the words, Edgar said, "I am not Harold Devon Vale."

Kale glanced around as the girl came through the open door. She entered slowly, halted. In total contrast to the other gang member, she was tense, taut, like an athlete waiting to erupt into action. She reached behind her and pushed the door closed.

Kale was still looking at her, his face averted from Edgar.

Jump at him, Edgar ordered himself. Do it now.

Kale said, "Well, Smith, you've come back to life, I see." He changed position so that he would have both the prisoner and the girl in view.

Edgar trembled down from his leaping point.

Smith's eyes were hard, unblinking. "I've been thinking about you," she said. "I believe I understand now."

The man slanted his head. "You understand what?"

"Everything. Right from the beginning."

"You better leave. Don't get in my way."

The girl said, "There's going to be no more murder."

A spasm moved across Kale's face. In a voice that had less caress he said, "This is a political assassination."

"Listen," Edgar put in. "Both of you listen to me."

But they seemed hardly aware of his existence. Standing four feet apart, they were staring at each other intently. Kale had become more alert.

He asked, "What's your problem, Smith?"

She said, "I, at least, had a true reason for getting involved in this."

"I'm in no mood to hear about your ideals. We're wasting time."

"I understand now why you didn't ask for proof that I represented the Anti-Vale League. You wanted to believe it. You needed the League as an excuse for yourself, to hide the truth from yourself."

Kale's eyes lost their dreaminess. "What truth?"

The girl said, "That you like to kill."

That spasm moved over his face again. "You better shut up."

"It's the reason for everything. You didn't want a deal. You don't care about money or the release of terrorists from prison. That's why you made the demands so insane, so impossible. You didn't want the demands met."

A casual, "No?"

"No. You just wanted power. And a reason to kill."

"You're talking like a fool."

"No I'm not," Smith said. "You wanted power, violence and death. Maybe you don't know that yourself, but everything points to it. Everything."

Kale said, voice louder, "Get out of this room."

"Let me tell you. Let me try and make you understand."

"Get out," Kale said, one arm describing an unfinished gesture toward the door.

"You deliberately left the For Sale sign up at the farm," the girl said. "You were hoping someone might come, that there'd be a shooting match."

As though to himself, Kale said, "I've never killed a woman."

Smith went on, "The reason you didn't disable the cars behind Wainford Hall was because you secretly wanted a chase, action, all the rest of it."

"Are you getting out of here or not?"

"It was for the same reason that you headed for the city, instead of the country, when we left the farm. And do you know why you didn't keep Vale tied up properly, only that chain on his feet?"

"Tell me on your way out," Kale said.

"You were hoping he'd make a break for it."

Sarcastically: "Sure."

"And the masks," Smith said. "Finally the masks. I understand now why you didn't care about Vale seeing your face. It's obvious. You knew he wouldn't be able to give evidence against you, because you knew he wasn't going to live through this. If you didn't get a chance to kill anyone else, you were surely going to kill him."

"Smith," Kale said, tone low again. "You've said enough."

She stared on at him. "The trouble is," she said, "I don't know if you're mad or evil."

After that, what happened was for Edgar a repeat

of his try for freedom in the subway station. It was like watching a film being run at a greatly reduced speed.

Slowly, Kale cut the space between himself and the girl by half. At the same time, his left arm rose up in front of him. As he stopped, the arm was going down.

The intended slap never landed. In a fluid crouch Smith sank gracefully beneath the slow motion hand, which floated harmlessly off into space.

Kale's other arm had risen in a natural balance of sympathy. Almost of its own accord it came into the girl's forward-moving hands. She took hold of Kale's wrist.

Her head and shoulders were moving. Her face was closing with the hand that held the gun. Her mouth was open in an animal snarl.

Kale's free hand had started on its way back. His features were twisting weirdly, as if made of wax that was melting. His hand crept toward the girl's hair.

Edgar told himself to move. This was the only chance. And move he did.

At a lifeless pace Edgar oozed forward from the wall. He was afraid of arriving at the struggle, afraid of not arriving.

Smith's mouth met the hand that held the gun. Languidly her teeth sank into the flesh. A single bubble of blood rose in the middle of her top lip.

Kale's other hand reached her hair. It took hold, the fingers gripping. It began to pull back. Smith's eyes swelled to a wide stare. More blood was bubbling leisurely by her lip.

In a simultaneous movement, the gun crept free of

Kale's suffering hand and the girl's mouth was eased from its bite.

Edgar was still moving forward.

The gun floated across the room. Gently it hit the wall and gently fell. It bounced once, lay still.

Edgar had changed direction. He sent himself forward into a slow motion dive. His feet left the pink carpet. He went over it at the speed of a blown feather. Behind him he could hear sounds of struggle, a tired sound.

He landed. Like a dragged weight he slid across the carpet. Both hands were reaching. His fingers met the gun. They fumbled for possession.

The sounds of struggle had ended.

Edgar, with great effort, managed to get the gun's grip into his right hand. Slowly he rolled over. Ponderously he raised his head and arm.

The girl was falling back from a push. Kale, eyes on Edgar, was in the act of drawing his hand from a pocket. In the hand was a gun.

Edgar aimed his automatic. He pulled the trigger.

The resulting crash of an explosion ended the period of languid action. Edgar's hand jerked. The girl slammed against the wall and steadied herself.

Kale froze for the space of two beats. He had a fixed smile. Next, he neatly put his hand back in the pocket, nodded, and began to fall backwards.

He landed on the floor with a thud. His arms settled and then he was motionless.

Edgar sat up. He could hardly believe that it was all over, that he was alive and unharmed. Stupidly he stared down at the gun in his hand—next, sensing movement, up at the girl.

She was bending over Kale, touching him here and there. She said quietly, "He's dead." She began to go through his pockets. Once she paused to wipe her mouth and then wipe the bloodstreaked hand on her jeans.

Edgar asked dully, "What're you looking for?"

"The key to the flat door. We can get out."

Edgar came out of his daze. He got up swiftly. "No," he said. "There's still the other two. They'll see us and shoot."

"We have to take that risk," the girl said. She produced a key and stood erect.

They looked at one another. Their breathing was uneven. Edgar said, "Thank you."

She blinked slowly. "I—I didn't exactly do it for you."

"I know," he said, tone gentle.

"I owe you nothing."

"I know that too. But thank you anyway."

She said, "I'm through with hate."

"I'm glad."

She took her head. "You're a strange man. I just don't understand you at all."

"Some other time," Edgar said. He gave and released a smile. "At the moment we have something else to think about."

"If not sneaking out with the key—what?"

"I'm thinking."

"Not of swapping shots with the other two, I hope."

Edgar shook his head. He had found an idea and he felt sure it would work. Its very obviousness was what had made it come to him so swiftly.

He went to the door, drew it open two inches from the jamb. He whispered, "Come here. Put your weight on the wood, like me. When I give you the nod to let go, move back quickly. Understand?"

"No," she said. "I mean, I don't know what you're doing, but I can manage that simply enough."

"Come on."

Beside him, she leaned on the pink wood. Edgar put his mouth to the space between door and jamb. After clearing his throat he called out. The voice he used was a duplicate of Kale's. He said, "Extra! Extra! Come here a minute!"

The young man answered, "What's up?"

"Just get here on the double. Never mind the questions."

There was the sound of approach. Next, close at hand, Extra asked, "What's the strife?"

Edgar said in Kale's voice, "I just blasted this guy. He's lying against the door and I can't move him."

"You can't?" the young man said, as if with surprise.

"I hurt my hand. Push the door hard."

"Did you get shot?"

Edgar snapped, "He bit me, for Christ's sake. Now do what I ask."

Weight came on the door. Edgar and the girl had no trouble resisting it. Edgar, as Kale, said, "Harder. Don't you have any strength?"

The door pressure became heavy. Edgar hissed to the girl, "Now!" He stepped quickly back. Smith did the same. The door shot open.

Extra came careening into the room. He crossed it

obliquely, staggering off balance. He hit the high-sided cot with his midriff and sagged over.

Edgar was beside him at once. He put the dead man's gun against Extra's cheek. In a non-Kale voice, but one that also was neither his own nor that of the politician, he said, "Keep perfectly still or I'll blow your head off."

The young man became like a statue, all except his eyes, which he shot to their corners. In a thin tone he said, "You?"

"Yes, me. Drop your gun."

Extra obeyed, letting the weapon fall onto the pink blankets. The girl came over and picked it up. Edgar grabbed the young man's collar and pulled him upright, saying, "Get over here."

Mona went back and closed the door. She turned to watch the former prisoner moving Extra to sit by the wall with his hands on his head. Extra was gaping at the body of Kale.

Mona felt bemused. What she had just heard from Vale's mouth was amazing. She would never have believed such a thing possible. The voice had been a perfect copy of the original. Again Mona thought what a strange person this Vale was.

He came over to her. "Keep our young friend covered. If he tries anything, or shouts a warning—shoot him."

Although knowing she couldn't shoot, whatever Extra did, and knowing the politician realized this, Mona said a hard, "That's for sure."

Vale opened the door an inch. "Now for Steve," he said softly.

Mona whispered, "He's no fool. Please remember that."

"I know."

"He might not fall for that same trick."

"I don't think he would. I'm going to try something else."

Extra spoke. In a quavering voice he asked, "Is Kale dead?"

Mona nodded. "As dead as the others who've been killed today." She wondered at herself. Why hadn't this death sickened her the way the others had? Either she was hardening, or in this death she could read justice.

Vale said, "Lean back against the door. Don't take your eyes off Extra."

She obeyed. Vale also used his weight, closing the door until it was open a mere crack, held there by his fingers around its edge.

Mouth to the space, he again used Kale's voice to call, "Steve? Can you hear me?"

The likeness was uncanny. Mona shivered. She saw Extra's expression of stupefaction increase. He looked from Vale to the dead body and back again.

Steve's voice came to them faintly. "I hear you. What's the problem?"

"Come here. Quick. I've found something good."

There was no answer. Mona, tensing, strained to listen. Next, her nerves leapt as from close beyond the door came the voice of the Irishman. He asked, "What's all this about?"

"Listen," said the ex-prisoner, as Kale. "There's a trapdoor here in the ceiling. It's a way out." He was making his tone excited.

"Naw. It'll only be into an attic."

"No, I know these houses. I lived in one like this. I know the layout. It's a single terrace, and we can go through one attic to another. No dividing walls. We can go right along the row."

"Is that a fact?" Steve asked. He sounded intrigued.

"It is, and we're going to do it. It's a gift."

"Let's see. Let me in."

"Can't. I've got a table here. The trap's right above the door."

Mona was disturbed to see that Extra was looking less dazed. He licked his lips. Mona sent the gun out to arm's length and pointed it at his face. He winced, but came still more alert.

Steve asked, "Where's Smith?"

Vale said, "Here, lying on the floor."

"I knew she'd turn out to be useless. I don't know why we had a woman in this deal in the first place."

"I was wrong about that."

"You sure were, Kale."

"If she doesn't shape up, we'll leave her."

"Fair enough," the Irishman said. "So where's Extra?"

"He's here too."

After a slight pause, Steve asked, "You all right, Extra?"

The young man's lips moved. No sound came. Yet Mona was startled to hear his voice. It was produced by the politician. Turning his head away from the door he said in Extra's youthful whine, "Sure I'm all right, mate. We're golden. We can break out of this joint and blast the bastards from behind."

There was another pause from outside. Extra was staring at Vale with an expression of disbelief that matched Mona's feelings. She had never heard anything so perfect in voice copying.

Steve asked, "Sure you're okay, Extra?"

In the young man's voice, and making it sound offended, Vale said, "What d'you mean? Think I'm gonna fall apart like this stupid bitch here?"

"Not exactly."

The prisoner still as Extra, switched tones to one of eagerness, saying, "Hey, Steve, tell Kale how I got that cop in the shoulder. You remember, the pig with the riot helmet. Tell him, Steve. Go ahead."

"Later," the Irishman said.

"Okay. Let's get out of here and blast the sods."

Steve laughed. "Never mind the blasting. Let's just do the breaking out."

Back in the Kale persona, the mimic said, "Right, Steve. Now listen. We need something more to stand on. Something heavy and strong."

"I'll get a chair."

"No. It could topple over. The perfect thing's that television set. Bring it, eh? And quick. Let's get moving."

"Right," Steve said. "Hold on."

When the sound of his retreat had faded, Mona whispered, "Why the TV set?"

"It's big and bulky. He'll need both hands to carry it. He might not be holding his gun."

"That would be a relief."

"It would," the prisoner whispered. "I'd be no match for that one."

"What's the next move?"

"Same as before. When I give you the word, get back fast."

"Got it," Mona said.

Footsteps sounded in the passage. They were heavy and slow. Mona saw that Extra had lowered his hands to the nape of his neck. She gestured warningly with her gun, but couldn't risk speaking.

The footsteps halted on the other side of the door. Steve said, "Here it is."

The Vale persona snapped, "Now!"

Mona moved away quickly as the prisoner drew in the door and threw it wide.

Standing in the passage was Steve. He held the large TV set in front of and against himself. He was leaning backwards to counterbalance the weight. His hands were free of weapons.

The prisoner faced him, his gun held forward. "All right," he said with an accent that sounded to Mona oddly American. "This is the end, Steve. It's all over. Kale's dead and I'm in charge."

The Irishman had been blinking in surprise. "Jasus and Mary," he said softly.

Vale nodded. "And all the saints. Back off and put the set down." He sounded more like himself now.

Steve: "What?"

"I said back off and put the TV on the floor."

What followed was fast, a blur of action. Steve lunged forward and tossed the television set. Vale began to dodge out of the way. Extra, unseen by

Mona, had gotten his feet under him; now he leapt up and threw himself at the prisoner's back.

Mona swung around into the doorframe. Steve was jamming both hands into his pockets. He froze that way and in a stoop when Mona jabbed her gun into his chest and gabbled, "I'll kill you, I'll kill you."

The television set had missed Vale. It fell to the floor just as Extra reached that spot. He fell over the set and landed in a sprawl.

The action was over.

A few seconds later, the Irishman and Extra were standing against the bedroom wall, their hands atop their heads. The younger man looked stricken. There were tears in his eyes. Steve was surly. He asked Mona, "What the fuck you playing at?"

"Just what you see."

"You're on *his* side? That turd?"

"I'm on the side of law."

Vale, his blazer pockets bulging with guns, said, "Now listen, all of you. It's over, finished, done. We're going out to the street nice and quietly. I'll shoot if there's trouble. Understand?"

Reluctantly the two men nodded. Mona nodded.

"Good. What we'll do is this. Steve takes Kale's shoulders, Extra takes his feet. We go out like that, me in the rear. We leave together, the three of us and the body."

Steve asked, "What about the darling girl?"

Vale said, "She stays here."

Mona looked at him. "What do you mean?"

He answered without taking his eyes off the two men. "Listen, Smith. You have a chance. You made a mistake, getting into this. You've done no harm. You have a chance to go free."

She shook her head slowly. "I don't get it."

"The point is, nobody outside this room knows for sure how many there are in the gang. Right?"

"That's true."

"And," Vale said, "nobody knows that one of the gang is a female. No one saw you, as far as I can remember."

She nodded. "One did. The driver of the police car."

"He, sad to say, is dead."

"Yes."

Vale asked, "On the telephone, did Atkinson guess he was talking to a woman? Or that it was a possibility?"

"No, I'm sure he didn't."

"So you're in the clear," said their ex-prisoner. "When we've gone out, wait for a while and then sneak away. Maybe you could change clothes. It's up to you. That's all I can do to help—give you this chance."

The Irishman sneered, "Now I call that real sweet."

Vale told him, "And you, I want you to keep your mouth shut about Smith."

"Why should I?"

"For the simple reason that if you don't, I'll do my best to get you the longest prison sentence in British criminal history, at the same time making it easier for Smith by telling how she helped me. Does that make sense?"

Slowly, the Irishman nodded. "It does. You shit."

"And is that clear to you, Extra?"

The young man also nodded. One tear had leaked from an eye and was on its way down his cheek. He looked as forlorn as a schoolboy whose comic book had been ripped up.

Mona asked, "Can I get away with it?" Her heart was beating quickly with excitement, hope and worry. "And if I can, do I deserve to?"

"You made a mistake," Vale said. "Grief makes people do strange things. You'll be all right now."

Steve said, "Send me some cigarettes, Smith darling, and I'll send you a piece of the hemp from my gallows rope. You can hang your rotten fucking self with it."

The politician said, "That's all. Now we move."

Edgar, Vale no longer, said, "That's all. Now we move."

He pointed. "You first, Steve. Go over there nice and slowly. Lift Kale off the floor by his shoulders."

The Irishman said, "I'd be interested in knowing what'd happen if I gracefully declined."

Edgar put on a vicious smile and eased the gun forward. In his best Vale voice he said, "Don't tempt me, you foreign bastard."

Steve shrugged and moved to obey the order.

Edgar said, "You, Extra, stay exactly as you are." But Edgar wasn't concerned about the younger man. Obviously he was finished. He was about as dangerous as a rabbit. For him the game had ended, finally, after it had been brutally crippled with the death of his hero.

That hero was now partly off the pink carpet, being held under the armpits by Steve. Kale's head lolled to one side, his eyes were slightly open, there was a wet patch on the front of his sweater.

Edgar was glad of the sweater's blackness. He would not have liked to see the blood's color. But otherwise he felt nothing. He was surprised to find that he had no remorse over having kileld the man.

This, Edgar mused, had nothing to do with the excuse of self-defence, which was legitimate—another two seconds and Kale would have had his gun out and been shooting. Edgar supposed that remorse had no chance against his vast relief in being alive.

He said, "All right, Extra. Get the legs."

The young man, robot-like, went across and did as ordered. The body was raised from the floor between the two men.

Edgar said, "Main door, Smith."

The girl swiftly left the bedroom, producing the key with her gun-free hand as she went. The two men followed, Steve first and moving backwards. He showed no strain at bearing the major part of the load. Extra was already sagging.

Smith unlocked the door of the apartment. She swung it wide open and stood aside. The body-carriers went through into the hallway. Edgar and the girl went out after them.

"Start down," Edgar said. "Keep the way you are."

The men moved to the head of the stairs. Awkwardly, Steve began to go down in reverse. He snarled up at his helper, "Take it slow, God blind you."

"I am," Extra mumbled tonelessly.

"Kids and fucking women. No wonder the deal went sour."

They descended at a suitably funereal pace. Extra had his knees bent. Kale's shoes and dangled hands clumped a mournful tattoo on every step.

Edgar went to the stairhead. The girl joined him and stood close. She put her gun in his pocket, squeezing it in beside the other weapons. Facing him she held out her hand. Edgar took it with his left.

They looked at each other unsmilingly, like strangers forced into unwanted intimacy on public transport. The girl said a simple, "Good-bye." Her voice was husky.

"Good-bye," Edgar said. "Thank you for saving my life."

"He might not have gone through with it. But I think he would."

"I do too. So thank you."

"And my thanks to you," Smith said. "For giving me this chance."

"I'm happy to."

They went on looking at each other. Edgar thought how pretty she was. Her hand, small, felt soft through the black glove.

After a glance aside and down, checking on the body-bearers, Edgar said, "I didn't mean it, calling Steve a foreign bastard."

"I understand," the girl said. She added, "No, I

don't really. I don't understand anything about you."

"I said it to make him believe I'd shoot."

Dismissing that with a movement of her head, Smith said, "I wonder if we'll ever meet again."

Edgar nodded slowly. "Somehow," he said. "I think we will."

The girl also nodded. Moving even closer she raised herself on tiptoe, face uptilted. She kissed Edgar on the cheek. Away again, she said, "Good luck."

He felt as awkward as a teenager on his first date, very touched and moved by her. He said, "Good luck to you as well, Smith."

She smiled faintly. "My name's Mona. Mona Dubois."

On the stairs, the Irishman was cursing Extra again. The voice brought Edgar alert. He had been lulled into peacefulness by the girl's presence and her murmuring voice. He squeezed her hand, let it go and went down after the others.

They were nearly at the bottom. Along the hall, three yards from the foot of the stairs, gaped the open doorway of the house. Beyond that hovered the yellowness, but thinner and paler now. Also there was a mumble of talk.

Steve, after a nervous glance behind, looked up at Edgar. He called out, "Hey, someone's liable to take a potshot at me."

Edgar said, "Get off the staircase and hold it there."

The body-bearers moved off the last step. The Irishman edged close to the wall and stopped. He repeatedly looked behind him at the doorway. Out in the fog, a dim shape formed and faded.

Edgar went off the staircase. He stood with his back to its bannister post. When Extra, stooping, began to lower his load, Edgar snapped, "Keep holding him up." The young man obeyed dully.

Edgar looked toward the door. He lifted his head and called, "Hello, you people outside!"

The voice he used was that of the politician. At the same time, almost unconsciously, he assumed Vale's features. They were, in fact, an aid in perfecting the verbal mimicry.

From outside came, "What is it?"

"Is Atkinson there?" Vale would never have given the policeman his title.

"Hold on," the voice answered. There were mumbles, footsteps, a shout. Edgar waited placidly. He was watched grim-eyed by the Irishman. Extra stood in a sag with his eyes closed.

From the fog a deep voice called, "I'm Atkinson. What is it?"

Edgar shouted, "This is Harold Devon Vale speaking."

That was followed by a silence which signified surprise. It was broken by, "Say that again."

"I believe you heard me perfectly well," Edgar said. "Now pay attention, please. I have disarmed the gang, one of whom is dead. I am bringing them all out. Therefore hold your fire. Is that clear?"

The silence that came here spoke of disbelief. The Chief Inspector called, "I recognize your voice, but how do I know you're not being forced to say that? This could be a trick."

"It hardly matters, as far as I can see. Just hold your fire."

"All right. Come on out."

With his gun, Edgar gestured to the two men with the body. They moved on, heading toward the doorway. Steve was leading as before, walking in reverse.

Edgar looked back and up. Mona Dubois was leaning over the landing rail. Unsmiling, she nodded. He smiled, turned, and went after Steve and Extra.

The next moment they were outside. Edgar strode tall behind them, his gun held prominently, his Vale manner in full flow.

From out of the fog came men, cautiously at first, but then at a run. Shouts were thrown back. More men appeared, some in plainclothes, some in uniform; some with handguns, some with rifles.

All the policemen bore expressions of excitement and awe. Calls of triumph rang back and forth along the street. Edgar and his prisoners were surrounded. Everyone talked at once.

Edgar, as Harold Devon Vale, took it all with a noble calm.

Mona trembled and gasped. Her face was alive with moving nerves. She berated herself for having delayed, for staying out on the landing to watch Vale go instead of coming straight in here.

She was in the kitchen of the apartment. Without trouble she had found a string shopping bag, and had next taken off her jacket. Feverishly, her hands shaking, she was stuffing the balled-up garment into the bag.

It's not going to fit, she thought, panicking. And they'll be here any second. Get another bag. No, there's no time.

While struggling, Mona was listening acutely for sounds of approach, even though it would have been difficult to hear anything with all the noise that was coming in from the street.

She pushed hard. The bundle slipped from her grasp, fell, skittered across the waxed linoleum, hit a cupboard. Jacket and bag separated.

Mona darted to the closet where she had found the bag. There were others. She chose a large one in plastic that bore the name of a laundromat.

Going over to the garment she got to her knees and rolled it tightly. It went into the bag with ease. She ripped off her gloves and shoved them in as well. Grabbing up the bag she went out to the passage.

The flat door was still open, a threat. Mona passed it at a run, doubled back, pushed it closed and went on again. She felt no better.

In the master bedroom she swung open the doors of the wardrobe. It was jammed with clothes, both male and female. Some garments protruded from the squeezed mass, like cards from an untidy pack. One of these was a green dress.

Mona pulled it out and off its hanger. It was suitably ordinary, a chain-store product. The owner wouldn't complain if it disappeared, and might not even notice that it had gone. Mona dropped the dress to the floor and began to roll up the legs of her jeans.

It occurred to her that she was wasting her time, that all this was unnecessary. There was nothing odd about jeans and a sweater. Except that they were black, she reminded herself, and black was suspect.

From outside, at the rear of the house, voices were shouting. Unlike at the front, these were more in the form of question and answer. The latter were confirming that the seige was over, the gang had gone out the front way, captured by Harold Vale, who had shot and killed the ringleader.

Mona had gotten one jeans leg rolled up to the knee. Swiftly but shakily she started on the other.

She shuddered as she heard a male voice below the shattered window. It said, "They've blocked the door up with all this junk."

"No, sergeant," another voice said. "That's been there for ages, seems to me."

"Anyway, let's clear it out and go through."

"Right you are."

There came dragging and crashing sounds.

Mona worked on, twisting up the heavy denim. Sweat fell from her chin to her hands. She felt she would never get the job done; but she did.

With both jeans legs rolled up to her knees, Mona lifted the green dress. She dropped it again. She had realized that by itself the flimsy dress would look curious in such cold weather—and she didn't want to risk taking anything else, a topcoat or jacket.

Panting, she ripped her sweater off. She picked up the dress, slipped it on, fumbled two large buttons closed at the neck. The garment felt a reasonable fit. More out of habit than anything else, Mona turned to look in the wardrobe's full-length mirror.

The dress was short. For two inches below its hem, her jeans were showing. Holding back a sob she bent to do more rolling.

From beneath the window outside rose loud noises. "Nearly there," a voice said.

Two vicious twists on either side got the legs turned up and out of sight. Mona put her sweater back on as she moved to a vanity table. She pulled out a drawer.

It was full of underwear. She dragged out another. It held a smelly mess of cosmetics. Reaching for another drawer, she remembered that she no longer wore her gloves—she was leaving fingerprints. She felt, however, that this was not important, not now with the others caught.

She found what she wanted—a collection of scarves. She pulled a bright red one out. Mouth open, face glistening with sweat, she put on the scarf peasant-style over her hair and tied a hurried knot.

She picked up the plastic bag, left the bedroom, went along the passage. Fearfully she drew open the door. The hallway was deserted. The only sound was the thump and clatter of junk removal at the lower rear.

Mona stepped out. She went to the head of the stairs.

There she jerked back with a gasp. Men were coming in below. A group of them were entering through the front door.

Mona looked around wildly. She knew she couldn't go back into the apartment. The only hope seemed to be the stairs which rose to another floor from the end of the landing.

She ran there on tiptoe. The men were clumping up, laughing and talking. One said that if old Atkinson had disliked Vale before, he would hate his guts now.

Mona got onto the stairs and raced silently up. The way ended against a door. She tried the handle. The door was locked.

Footsteps thumped on the landing as the men arrived. A voice asked, "Up again, eh?" One pair of footsteps came closer.

Another voice said, "No, this is it here. This door."

The lone footsteps went back to join the others.

Mona was trembling. Sweat stood out on her face in globules like overgrown gooseflesh. She had the terrifying urge to end the tension, to run down and give herself up.

The voices and footfalls lessened; the men had gone into the apartment. One hand on the wall, Mona started back down the stairs. Her legs ached with weakness.

Bending, she looked cautiously over the sloping rail. The apartment door was still open. There was no one to be seen. She could hear the men inside, moving around and talking.

Mona, hurrying now, reached the foot of the stairs. Breath held, she started along the landing. From inside the flat, the sound of talk and movement grew louder. Also louder were the crashes from below.

Mona came to the end of the rails. The open door seemed to be glaring at her. She kept her body turned toward it as she rounded the post to get to the stairhead.

Inside the flat, a man appeared. He glanced out, saw Mona, snapped to a halt.

Mona released her breath with a noisy gush.

The man came closer to the door. He asked, "Who the hell are you?"

She grabbed the plastic bag to her chest, stammering, "I—I—"

"Couldn't you give us five minutes, lady, before barging in?"

Unable to speak, Mona made a helpless gesture. The man asked, "Is this your place?"

Working by touch, Mona moved down one step. She swallowed and said, "I'll come back later."

"A lot later, lady," the man said, nodding. "A lot later, if you don't mind."

She turned and hurried on down. Her heart was thudding painfully. She wore a smile that had nothing to do with joy or wit.

There was no one below. The crashes from the rear were echoing loudly. Mona hustled to the front door and went outside. The street was deserted.

Mona was alone. She was free. As she walked off through the lifting, drifting fog, she began to weep quietly.

Harold Devon Vale had gotten halfway to his goal before stopping. For one thing, he thought it might be better to wait for nightfall for his foray into Edgar Carlton's boardinghouse; that needed careful consideration, the weighing of risks. For another thing, he had been seduced by what was being called the Siege of Gormon Place.

Vale had seen the coverage on television sets in appliance store windows, and had been as fascinated as the other people who clustered there.

Now, huddled in the mimic's coat and hat, Vale sat in a coffee shop. Before him on the table lay an untouched cup of tea. With a dozen customers and two waitresses, he was staring at a television set.

When it had been announced, some minutes ago, that the siege was over and the politician was free, unharmed, the real Harold Devon Vale had felt annoyance that his impersonator had gotten off so lightly. But, he had thought, there might be shooting in the streets. The gang could of course be vast, as he had reasoned before, not the mere handful that had been trapped in the house.

Annoyance had been forgotten when the commentator had said that the siege had been ended by the Member of Parliament himself. Vale had wondered: What was going to happen next? When would Edgar Carlton identify himself as an imposter?

Vale had begun to feel peculiar.

He was staring at the set transfixed.

The screen showed, mistily, a man with earphones and a hand-held microphone. Behind him people were crowded thickly. There were background noises of applause and cheering.

"Any minute now," the commentator said excitedly. "Any minute now, ladies and gentlemen, Mr. Harold Devon Vale will appear. He will walk past this spot on his way to the hotel, where our other unit and Arthur Price is waiting."

Vale wrinkled his nose at the grammar. He was not aware of having done so. He was taken out of himself. He had never felt so strange.

"At this moment, Mr. Vale is talking to the police. It has already been arranged that he will give a press conference at the hotel. The place is jammed with media people.

"Meanwhile, here in the streets, there are thousands of local folk and others from every corner of the city. It's a crowd in holiday mood. They have seen a victory for law and order. They have also, more pertinently, seen a personal victory for the M.P. for Caston North."

Vale blinked rapidly as a spasm moved across his face.

The commentator said, "Yes, it's official. It has been confirmed. Harold D. Vale actually had a gun duel with the leader of the gang, and killed him. Next, he disarmed the remaining two members and brought them out of the house. And this man, ladies and gentlemen, is the one who has been called a coward."

Vale stared on, his mouth partly open. He was sitting tensely on the edge of his chair. With wondering eyes he watched as the camera panned across the crowd. The commentator, meanwhile, went over details of the chase that had ended in Gormon Place.

A customer said, "Takes a bit of guts, that."

A waitress said, "Never woulda thought it, meself."

"I bloody would. Vale's all right."

"He's a big pain in the arse."

The other waitress shushed the speakers as the commentator broke off his recital and said, "Here he comes!"

The camera made a fast swing, then zoomed to a close focus on one section of the street. Into view through the mist came several police constables. They were pushing back the people who crowded thickly forward on either side down the center of the road.

Next along the lane of people came three men. The middle one, Vale saw with an odd sensation in his stomach, was Edgar Carlton in the role of Harold Devon Vale. He was smiling and waving.

Beside him walked Maxted, also smiling. The man at the other side was big and middle-aged. He had no smile. He was identified by the commentator as Chief Inspector Raymond Atkinson.

People cheered and clapped. They reached forward to touch the man they thought was the Member of Parliament. Some managed to get to shake his hand.

Behind came more policemen and a group of Whitecoats. The latter were grinning.

It was a triumphal parade. The crowd might have been greeting a monarch or a war hero or a spiritual leader. They laughed as they jostled for position. The mimic raised his arms in a V for victory sign.

The real Harold Devon Vale stumbled to his feet. He hit the table and slopped his tea. It went unnoticed by himself and by the others present. Like a sleepwalker he went to the door and outside.

He moved to the edge of the curb, where he leaned

weakly against a lamppost. All that glory, he thought. All that beautiful glory. It was genuine, and not just from his own fans and followers, but from everyone, people who before might have sneered. The glory belonged to him, and it was being stolen by that imposter.

The lure, for Vale, was irresistible.

He pushed off from the post. He began to walk. After a dozen steps he was striding. Another dozen, and he broke into a run.

The crowd pressed forward. There were smiles and waves and clapping hands on every side. Some called his name, some took pictures, some shouted praise. Spotted about were children perched on adult shoulders.

Edgar felt as light as air. He was walking on feathers. Never had he had such an experience. It was a greatly magnified version of that which he had earned on most evenings of his professional life, that which all artists crave and need—applause.

This was adulation. It was what his subconscious had given him in dreams. And there was, true enough, something strongly dreamlike about the present scene—the mistiness, the laughter and reaching hands, the faces of strangers.

Yet Edgar knew he was awake. The sole connection with dreams was of the day variety—his reveries had been made of this, when he had played with ideas of impersonating a famous person and winning fame.

The fantastic thing, Edgar mused, was that reality

had started outstripping daydream. Wainford Hall would have been fine; and he would have played to a portion of the country's television watchers. In a few minutes, at the press conference, he would be playing to the whole word, via TV, newsreel, radio and press.

As Edgar thought of the coming moment, that old tingle ran up his body—groin, belly, chest, throat. He saw himself taking off the tinted glasses, drawing out the rings in his nostrils, letting his features relax, mussing his hair, and announcing his true identity.

That reminded Edgar of the real Vale. He realized he had not thought of the politician for some hours. The man was still tied to the chair. He would be in a wretched state by now.

So, Edgar thought, the unmasking would have to be brought off as swiftly as possible. Then someone could go and release the prisoner.

The crowd was still pushing forward. Those at the back waved handkerchiefs. Some people were standing on top of cars. The fog had thinned sufficiently to show the houses on either side; their upper windows were full of cheering people. The noise was tremendous.

Edgar only barely heard when Maxted shouted, "This is the best thing that ever happened to us, Harold."

"Yes, I believe you're right."

"You did a marvelous job, simply marvelous."

"Ah, well."

The bearded man said, "Nothing can stop us now."

"I agree," Edgar answered. He looked away to raise both arms in the V sign for a nearby minicam unit. There were three other similar units from different networks.

A man burst past the police. He managed to get through to Chief Inspector Atkinson, who thrust him back, but not before the man grabbed Edgar's hand and said, "You're what this country needs."

The noise was growing in volume—the crowd was denser—the procession was nearing the hotel. It was a gaunt Victorian edifice. Staff hung out of windows waving linen.

Lining the way on the last stretch were dozens of young men in bleached windcheaters. With linked arms they formed a barrier against the pushing crowd.

The Whitecoats were flushed and smiling. Their eyes had a glow as they looked at the man they thought was their leader. Edgar felt a momentary queasiness.

Accompanied by a final burst of cheering and clapping, the group went into the hotel entrance. There was a vestibule before the lobby proper. Edgar was brought to a stop there by a hand on his arm.

Chief Inspector Raymond Atkinson, expression solemn, said, "I'll leave you here, Mr. Vale. But I'll be in the area for a while yet, should you need me."

"Ah, very well."

"If you can call in at the Yard tomorrow morning at eleven, as agreed, we'll take that formal statement from you."

Edgar nodded. He felt that he should say something of consequence. The senior police officer had more than just a kind face, it was a tired face. Probably he had spent all night on the Vale Affair.

Also, he had kept his questions to a reasonable minimum earlier, when they had met outside the house.

Edgar recalled further that at that same time, the Chief Inspector had spoken sharply to one of his men, who was being rough in taking Extra and Steve away.

Maxted said impatiently, "Come on, Harold. Everyone's waiting."

"Until tomorrow, Inspector," Edgar said. He put out his hand.

Atkinson's hesitation was brief, but noticeable. He shook hands quickly and turned away. With him went the constables.

"Come on, Harold."

Backed by a covey of Whitecoats, semi-led by Maxted, Edgar went on into a packed lobby. More of the young men in pale jackets were waiting to form an advance guard.

Applause spattered into being as Edgar entered. It moved around the people in waves, growing to concert pitch. There were no shouts, no gestures, only smiles of satisfaction. The crowd, obviously, was formed of serious Vale-watchers.

As Edgar was ushered across to an archway, certain people were allowed to briefly penetrate the phalanx. Edgar assumed that these were known personally to the politician, were perhaps part of his machine. He greeted them in typical Vale fashion. One woman had tears in her eyes.

Through the arch the group came into a large room. It was crowded. Most of the media representatives were under forty. Ninety per cent were male.

There were scores of flash cameras, a dozen of the movie and TV type. One of the latter, Edgar was gratified to see, bore the name of a United States television network. There were other foreign units, so labeled.

A good section of the people present needed no labels to state their national origins. Trained in facial characteristics, Edgar could pick out reporters from many countries. He was happily alert to all this.

At his entry, and during his slow passage over to a podium on which shone strong lights, there were no cheers and only a polite stammer of applause.

Here was no partisanship. These were hardened, cosmopolitan journalists. Years of sitting in on history-in-the-making had rendered them blase and objective. They were exactly what Edgar wanted.

Despite growls from the bodyguards, flashbulbs popped in Edgar's face and reporters tried for an individual word by calling questions at him. He stayed smilingly aloof.

Leaning close, Maxted said, "The speech. The one you were going to make last night. Give it to 'em. This is too good a chance to miss. This is fantastic."

Edgar nodded, though he had no intention of making speeches. He was going to end the impersonation as soon as he had let the people and the cameras have a good look at him in his role.

He reached the podium which was a bandstand, with a piano backed against the wall. It was raised two feet above the floor and covered in red fabric.

The glare of lights made it appear to be smouldering like a bed of charcoal.

Edgar stepped up. Maxted followed. Three of the Whitecoats did the same. The rest clustered at the front, though they began to squat, reluctantly, when yelled at by the cameramen and reporters.

There was a yammer of talk. Those close by were still calling out questions. Some were shouting for silence. There were arguments as positions were jokeyed for. It was like a thousand other press conferences, which meant it was like a party for spoiled children.

With Maxted and the Whitecoats ranged behind him, Edgar faced the lights and microphones, cameras and faces. He raised his right hand. The noise slackened, seeped away, died. Edgar became the center of keen attention.

He let his hand fall slowly. He looked around. He said, "I am, ah, sure that many of you here today have seen me before in person."

There were nods, gestures of agreement; and more of the same when Edgar, still gazing around, added, "In fact, I see quite a few familiar faces."

He saw, in truth, only one person who was known to him—a political commentator he had sometimes glimpsed on television and whose name was, he thought, Arthur Price. Standing beside a large camera, which two other men were operating, Price was watching carefully.

Edgar said, "I have a statement to make, ladies and gentlemen. It has nothing to do with the past few hours."

Among the crowd were some blinks of surprise,

some exchanged looks of enquiry, some bored frowns from the politically wise, who knew that no public man could resist this opportunity to press his brief.

Edgar took off his glasses. Into his mind came the girl, Mona Dubois. He saw her face, thought of her story. He found himself putting the tinted spectacles on again.

"Yes," he said. "I, Harold Devon Vale, have a statement to make. When I said it had nothing to do with the past hours, I meant directly. I am not going to talk of my experience with the kidnapers. But that experience has wrought a change."

The audience was silent and still. Edgar was wondering what he thought he was playing at, even as he went on: "The past hours have taught me only one very important thing. That is, that I have been wrong. Yes, I have been totally in error in my social views."

Through the crowd moved a ripple of awareness. This sounded like a real piece of news. People leaned forward.

Conscious of tension from those behind him, Edgar moved a step closer to the array of microphones.

"I have changed," he said, gravely and quietly, using the Vale voice but not the Vale manner of light arrogance. "I know now that I have been mistaken in my opinions. Particularly so in my attacks on the foreign workers in this country. They are not to blame for the ills of Britain. In fact, we would be worse off if we did not have these people, who are diligent workers, who help in every field. It is an absurdity to try to make scapegoats of those whose only desire is to do a day's labor for a day's pay. We can learn from their industry."

From behind him and from the Whitecoats crouching at his feet came a hiss and shuffle of disbelief.

Edgar pointed down. "These young men, who number in the thousands. They can be cured of their addiction. They have followed me faithfully, but only because they yearn for power and a uniform. They can be weaned to another cause, one not based on hate. They can be shifted from the juvenile to the mature."

One Whitecoat got up and began to push his way roughly through the crowd. The others sat still, staring up, looking stunned.

At Edgar's side, Maxted appeared as a furtive shape. "What's wrong with you?" he whispered. "Harold, what on earth's wrong with you?"

Edgar said a curt, "Get back. Go on."

The shape retreated.

The audience had stilled again from the waves caused by the Whitecoat's exit. Edgar looked around. He was no longer wondering about what he was doing.

He realized he had started to let the Vale features slacken. Firming them he said, "Ladies and gentlemen, I want you all to know that I now believe in brotherhood. Forgive me if I begin to sound trite. These things have been said before by better, nobler men. And I am not noble."

He paused, continued, "While I do not believe in

God, though I may previously have claimed the reverse, I do believe in the Christian ethic."

Another Whitecoat got to his feet. He glared, turned and went off through the crowd, some of whom were looking sceptical.

Edgar said, "I have been through a fifteen-hour ordeal. I was awake all night. Awake and thinking. I had a great deal to think about. It takes a situation like that to make a man see into himself."

Noting the fading of scepticism, he pressed home, "I am lucky to be alive. Three times I was close to being killed. That gave me further food for thought."

Edgar smiled in a quiet and friendly way. "All politicians are liars," he said. "If only by implication. For instance, one may make a controversial act or statement. His opponent might agree one hundred per cent, privately, but because he is a politician, he must make capital out of it, must decry and deplore that statement or act. It is a professional lie.

"I have done it often. So have most of my colleagues.

"Now, thankful to be among the living, I want to state that my campaign against the foreign workers was a professional lie. It was a gambit, a gimmick, an angle. It was a flag for the discontented to follow.

"I reject that campaign, as I reject all the other hard-line pronouncements I have made—made to further my career. I reject xenophobia. I reject isolationism. I am opposed to clubs, groups, organizations and sects as barriers. I am opposed to some people being *in,* while others are out. I am opposed to boundaries. In the long-term, foolishly idealistic though it may seem, I believe in one world, one federation of peoples, a global government."

Again Edgar paused. There was total silence. He raised his hands to an offering position, wanting to end with a powerful line, an absolute. But all he could think of, letting his hands fall, was, "I believe in peace."

The silence went on. There was not a movement in the room.

With no urgency, Edgar told himself that now was the time to do it. Now he should remove the Vale image and identify himself. The moment was truly ripe. He would be made forever.

Instead, he said, "And that is all I have to say." He stepped back from the microphones.

The room slowly came alive, creeping into sound and movement. The people acted as if coming out of a doze. Reporters went toward the exit arch. Radio announcers talked into tape recorders and live microphones. Television cameras swung focused on their own accompanying commentators, who had a lot to say.

Sound grew to noise. There was congestion at the exit. One reporter began to climb out of a window. There were shouts for silence. Smiling, Arthur Price was talking to his camera quickly and excitedly.

The crouching Whitecoats got up and moved off, some backing away and still looking stunned or surly.

A radio man came to the cleared space. He asked

for a personal statement. Edgar shook his head. When that wasn't enough he turned away. He found himself face to face with Maxted. The three Whitecoats strode past, pushing the radio man and sending him sprawling.

Maxted's face was pale and slack. He was talking to Edgar, apparently asking questions. The noise had grown too great for his words to be heard, realizing this, he switched to shouts. The only clear word was *sick*.

Edgar turned. The crowd had been reduced by two-thirds. The congestion at the exit arch had finished. Men were still talking into microphones and at cameras. Maxted stepped down from the podium and walked away. Three times he shook off importuning hands.

Edgar stood on under the lights. He felt tired, peaceful. He felt that he could go happily to sleep.

Harold Devon Vale stopped running. He walked slowly while getting his breathing under control. He would have preferred to stand or sit, but nerves kept him moving.

He was near the hotel; he could see it a block away. However, there were no signs of the crowds he had seen on television, only stragglers and isolated knots of people—these talking together quietly. But Vale realized that, once the mimic had gone into the hotel, everyone had hurried off to watch the proceedings on the small screen.

Drawing closer to the hotel Vale saw a larger

group. It was composed of Whitecoats. They looked curiously dejected, without swagger. One was disconsolately kicking the wheel of a motorcycle.

People were straggling from the hotel entrance. They too had the spiritless appearance of the young men. Vale recognized many of the people. They were the staunchest of allies, proud bearers of his standard.

Could it be, Vale thought, that the mimic had spoiled the hero image? It would be just like that idiot to go and botch everything.

Vale quickened his pace. He reached the hotel, went inside. He lifted up his coat collar and kept the brim of the slouch hat turned well down.

In the lobby were groups of two and three. Also, there was Maxted. He stood dismally, talking to a couple. He was pale. He shook his head, wiped a hand over his face.

Vale sidled unnoticed over to an archway, where he had to move aside as men came out wheeling a camera. They were smiling. He went on through.

In a large room were thirty-odd media people. Most of these too were smiling. Arthur Price was talking expansively into a television camera.

Up on the stage, alone, stood the impersonator, Edgar Carlton. He was bathed in brightness.

In the limelight, Vale mused grimly. The bastard.

He went forward. He was seen by no one—except the mimic. Edgar Carlton watched the approach with interest. He smiled. The smile didn't falter as Vale slipped his gun from the holster and transferred it to a pocket of the topcoat.

He reached the podium, lifted one foot onto it and

looked up. He scowled when the other man said, "This is convenient. I was just wondering what to do about you."

"Altruistic of you, I'm sure."

The mimic eased his smile. "Look. I'm sorry for what I did to you. You've had a rough time."

"You're going to be more than sorry, Carlton. You are going to be deeply regretful."

Folding his arms, the impersonator asked, "Going to tell the police? Think they'll believe you? Think I didn't give a great, convincing performance?"

"Never mind what I'm going to do," Vale snapped. He was angered by the man's easy manner. He should have been quaking, whereas he looked like he didn't have a care in the world.

Vale stepped up to the stage. He poked the gun forward in his pocket. "There," he said, tilting his head toward a door at the side of the podium. "Get through there."

"Why?"

"You'll see. Move."

Carlton went to the door, pushed it open. Vale followed into a short passage. There was a washroom on either side. They went into the men's room.

Closing the door behind him, Harold Vale said, "Obviously you haven't yet declared your true identity."

"Right."

"You never will. For one thing, you would be wasting your time."

"Is that so?"

Vale smiled. "Think anyone would believe you?

Think you didn't give a great, convincing performance?"

The mimic shrugged. "You said, for one thing. Tell me the other."

Vale stopped smiling. "I would have you taken care of."

"Somehow," Edgar Carlton said, "I accept that as gospel."

Vale brought the gun out. "This shoots bullets, not blanks. Give me those glasses and my blazer."

Still casual, the mimic took off the tinted spectacles and passed them over. Vale slipped them on. Next Carlton took off the jacket and draped it on a washbasin.

He said, "Your tie's in a pocket. I didn't care for the color."

Vale took off the hat, threw it to the floor. Switching the gun from hand to hand, he removed the topcoat and then the suit jacket, letting both drop.

He said, "Now take your grubby things and get the hell away from here."

At an infuriatingly slow pace, Carlton donned his clothing. From his nose he plucked two plastic rings, which he tossed into a wastebasket. He looked like no one at all. With a mocking salute, he turned and left the room.

Vale, after holstering the gun, put on his blazer, and his tie, and combed his hair. Leaving the washroom he returned to the podium. There was no sign of Edgar Carlton.

As Vale stepped down to floor level, a man intercepted him, asking, "Sure you wouldn't care to add to your statement, sir? A special word for the B.B.C.?"

"Nothing," Vale said. "Not at this present time." He thought he had better find out how much of a botch Carlton had made of things before saying anything to anyone.

He crossed the room. Accompanying him was a chorus of, "Well done, Mr. Vale," and, "Good day, sir," and, "That was fine, sir, very fine," and, oddly, "Thank you, Mr. Vale."

Harold Vale was boosted. Perhaps after all, he mused, the mimic had not made such a mess of the hero image.

Vale passed through the arch. There were fewer people than before. Maxted was on his way out. Vale called to him. Clifford Maxted turned, stared, swung away and went on.

Vale stood there in bewilderment. He looked at the others still present. They averted their eyes. One couple linked arms with a curious firmness and strode out.

Vale followed to the street. Maxted was driving off in a car. Across the way, a dozen Whitecoats were sitting astride motorcycles. Vale called out to the young men. They looked at him coldly while kicking their machines to life.

Vale went over, arms spread to express his need for an explanation. He asked what was wrong, but couldn't even hear what he was saying himself under the roar and snarl of the engines.

He shouted. He was still unheard. The young men

drove off in a body. They went in the direction taken by Maxted's car.

Harold Devon Vale was left alone in the center of the road.

EPILOGUE

Some hours later, Mona Dubois was at Kings Cross station, sitting in a train. It was pulling out on the start of its journey north. Mona had checked out of her hotel after bathing and changing. She had heard all about Vale's press conference, even before reading of it in the evening newspaper that lay on her lap.

Mona wondered what he was doing now, that strange man whose photograph looked up at her from the front page.

He was on his way to work. He had an engagement to fulfill at the Dockers Social Club.

Edgar Carlton walked briskly along the street in Limehouse. The lighting, faint and ochre, was losing a fight with the darkness. Hidden were dangers such as uneven curbstones and sidewalk cracks. But also hidden were the signs of decay, the gutter litter and the hopeless air of the stores.

Good-bye, Edgar Carlton said mentally to everything he passed, for he knew there would be another time, another celebrity to mimic. Good-bye, good-bye.